THE BEST OF EVERYTHING

Sherrie rushed past Byron and Jasmine, went into her suite and slammed the door, locking it.

In a few minutes, she heard Byron's soft knock.

"Sherrie, let me in!"

She didn't answer, but stood with narrowed eyes, hot tears dammed behind her eyelids. The tomcat! How dare he?

"Sherrie!" This was a command. "Open the door. I can explain."

Oh, I'll bet you can explain, she thought. River's unkind comment had been right, but what about him? He hadn't seemed to exactly fight Jasmine off.

"Sherrie," Byron said in a low lion's roar, "don't let me have to break this damned door down!"

She opened the door. He came in and gripped her shoulders. His eyes were sad. "Honey, don't walk away from me like that. I love you, and it kills me."

"You were otherwise engaged."

"She said it was a last kiss, that she wouldn't bother me again. She kissed *me*. I didn't kiss her. Sherrie, I love you. I've always played fair and square with you and I always will."

"People change," she said stubbornly. "Mike—"

"Don't go there," he said sharply. "I'm not Mike. Stop comparing me with Mike. You're going to have to stop that."

His sharp words cut through the fog that had enshrouded her—jealous and raging—from a past she wanted and needed to forget. This man loved her in ways she had never been loved before and she didn't want to lose him. "I'm sorry," she said softly. "Will you let me show you I'm sorry?"

Humbled, she moved closer to him, opening to him completely. He caught her to him fiercely and, relenting, said huskily, "Try me."

The Best of Everything

FRANCINE CRAFT

BET Publications, LLC
http://www.bet.com
http://www.arabesquebooks.com

ARABESQUE BOOKS are published by

BET Publications, LLC
c/o BET Books
One BET Plaza
1900 W Place NE
Washington, DC 20018-1211

All Kensington Titles, Imprints, and Distributed Lines are available at special quantity discounts for bulk purchases for sales promotions, premiums, fund-raising, and educational or institutional use. For details, write or phone the office of the Kensington special sales manager: Kensington Publishing Corp., 850 Third Avenue, New York, NY 10022, attn: Special Sales Department, Phone: 1-800-221-2647.

First Printing: March 2004
10 9 8 7 6 5 4 3 2 1

Printed in the United States of America

This book is dedicated to my readers, with deep appreciation and heartfelt thanks. Many of you have been with me since the beginning, starting with Devoted *and* The Black Pearl. *You all have my love and devotion, and I wish you always the best of everything.*

ACKNOWLEDGEMENTS

To Charlie K., June Marie and Bruce Bennett, my fervent appreciation for your continued help. I write this so often to you, but how can I stop? You're just the greatest.

I really appreciate the expert and warm help two chemists and two administrative people at two well-known cosmetics manufacturing companies gave me. They thought it best that their names and the names of their companies not be published, and I respect their wishes. I would have been lost without them.

Beginning with Bitterness

Mid-March 2002

Chapter 1

Sherrie Pinson stood in front of her husband Mike's expensive, pale gray tombstone and stared at the inscription:

Michael Pinson
Beloved and loving
Husband, father, friend

Tears filled her eyes. This was the first anniversary of his death, a murder. When would the pain begin to ease? She walked to the head of the tombstone, bent and touched the big vase of lilies of the valley she had brought.

In her mind's eyes she could see him as plainly as if he stood in front of her. Tall, handsome, caring, so vividly alive. To deflect her thoughts she looked around her at the beautifully landscaped cemetery, Minden, Maryland's finest. Weeping willows flourished, and a large fountain threw its waters into the spring air. A warm mid-March let yellow daffodils, white narcissi and early clusters of violets blossom in all their glory. Evergreens were massed around the borders.

Hearing a slight cough she turned and nearly fainted. Her vision blurred. A tall man with a short black beard, a big, virile body and a craggily attractive face stood before her as she whispered, "Mike?"

She swallowed hard and whimpered inside, facing Byron Tate who with his beard so eerily resembled his close friend, Mike.

"Hello, Sherrie. How are you?" His voice was tender, concerned.

Hot tears seeped behind her eyelids. "Hello, Byron. You've grown a beard," she said, as if in accusation, her voice flat. "You look so much like Mike."

This man had been clean shaven before he left Minden. He carried two vases of multicolored flowers to place on the graves of his wife and young daughter.

Her whole body felt weak, shaken, and he moved forward to steady her, but she stiffened. "I'll be shaving it, maybe today," he told her. "How have you been, Sherrie? And how's Tressa?"

Anger at him filled every pore of her. The core of her was hot with rage. She didn't answer his questions. Instead she said, "You're back earlier than you expected to be."

She was determined not to hate him. She couldn't help being angry; she had just cause, but she refused to let herself mire in hatred. He had been away for four months traveling the world, assuaging his grief over three deaths he could not exorcise.

Byron Tate was six feet, two inches tall, olive skinned, with soot-black, rough, curly hair and a long, handsome face with startling pale blue-gray eyes. He had heavy, smooth black eyebrows. His big body was well exercised, and he had a pensive, warm, humorous expression.

Why was she studying him? She should be running away. But she knew it was because he was so much like Mike, the husband, the lover for whom she ached.

"You didn't answer my questions," he said gently, and repeated them. "How are you? And how is Tressa?"

She drew a harsh breath. It was eight o'clock in the morning and the air was crisp, clear. She pulled her wool spring reefer tighter about her. "How am I, Byron? You tell me. I never stop hurting. That's how I am. As for Tressa, she adored her father. She was nearly five when he died. Now she's nearly six. . . ."

"Saturday," he said softly.

"Yes." Her eyes filled with hot tears again. "She can't seem to get over losing him. She doesn't sleep well. She wonders if I'm going to die, if she's going to die. She doesn't eat well, doesn't want to go anywhere, do anything."

"God, I'm so sorry."

"So am I." She looked at him then. "But you're hurting, too, with your loss."

"Yes," he said. Alicia and Ronnie had died in an accident a year and a half ago, then Michael a year ago. "I had to get away." His voice got husky then. "We were close friends once, Sherrie. Closer than close. Our families were so close. Michael and I were like blood. He saved my life. I can't ever forget that."

His saying it tore her up, and she couldn't stop the bitterness. "He saved your life," she said, "and you indirectly took his."

"Sherrie, don't." His voice went ragged.

She continued, "I don't know the whole story, but when you drove him out of Tate Manufacturing, it broke his heart, and it destroyed him."

"He hurt you a lot," he stubbornly reminded her.

"Because he changed." Her voice rose. "He was hurt. He couldn't take it anymore. The Tate company and you were his life. When you turned against him . . ." She was choking on her words.

"You'll never know how sorry I am," he said humbly. "Perhaps one day you'll understand more. I'll understand more, then we'll both heal."

She swept on. "You know how sorry I am about Alicia and Ronnie, how I grieve for you, but I can't forgive you for what you did to Mike. Not yet. Maybe one day I can, but I will never forget."

Byron felt his heart squeeze dry as he looked at her. She had always meant so much to him, from the very beginning. The long, now chemically straightened earth-brown hair, the all-spice brown, silken smooth skin. Her straight eyebrows gave her a tranquil look, and her even features were attractively placed. But it was the dark brown, once sparkling, almond-shaped eyes under thick, lush black lashes and the beautifully curved full mouth that made her a standout. And under that coat was a body that put Coca-Cola bottles to shame.

He had to come right out and say it. "I want to see you and I want to see Tressa. I have a present for her birthday. May I come by?"

Sherrie looked at him with amazement. How dare he ask? "I don't think so," she said slowly. "Tressa has said she doesn't want anything for her birthday." Her laugh was short, harsh, hopeless. "She just wants her daddy back."

"Sherrie," he said softly, "maybe I can help. Mike and I were so much alike. If I can ease her pain, your pain."

She shook her head. "I don't think so."

"Will you think about it?" he asked stubbornly. "She'll love the present. I promise. I'll call you."

"I wish you wouldn't. . . ."

"I'd like to salvage some remnant of friendship. It could help us both."

"We can't be friends, Byron, ever again. You betrayed Mike, and I can never forget that. Had it not been for what you did to him, he might still be alive."

"I'm sorry," he said again, and they were silent for long moments. He touched her arm. "You look well. You always handled things well."

"Not this. For what it's worth, you seem to be holding up well. I wish you all the best, Byron. I think we have to realize that our estrangement is permanent."

"Don't say that. I want to help."

"I don't think you can."

A beautiful Siberian husky dog came bounding out of the woods, stopped for a moment at Byron's side, then went to Sherrie, his tail wagging furiously. The dog sniffed her and moved closer.

"Husky!" she exclaimed. "How I've missed seeing you."

The dog's slanted brown-yellow eyes shone in his long, wide-jawed head with an almost-human understanding. The cream, buff, brown and black fur shone with love and good care. She had forgotten what an amazing animal he was, and he was Byron's constant companion.

Byron's heart lifted at her response to his dog. At least some things hadn't changed. He saw her long, slender hand reach out and pat Husky's head, then stroke his neck and shoulders, and he was reminded of their recent past steeped in friendship and love.

The dog only awakened her pain, and Sherrie felt herself weakening. Her body felt cold with regret and anguish.

"You're hurting," he said. "Let me take you home. I'll send someone back to get your car."

She shook her head. "No. I have a big day ahead. Thank you, but I'll make it. Byron?"

"Yes."

She had been going to say, *don't call. I don't want to see you again save in passing,* but the words stuck in her throat. She didn't want to talk to him. The past was dead. Let it die.

"Goodbye, Byron." Her voice trembled with finality.

"Tressa's my beloved godchild," he said urgently. "I've got to stand by her. She needs someone now and you need a friend."

She laughed shortly then, tears in her voice. "A friend, Byron? I think you mean well now, but surely you can understand that after what you did to Mike . . ."

She started past him, leaving a saddened Husky who longingly looked after her. Byron's big hand on her shoulder stopped her. "Consider what I've said, Sherrie. Don't get revenge. Forgiveness is so much better."

He let her go and watched her walk away, watched until she got into her car and drove off. Was she crying? His feelings went deep for this woman and he hurt with her pain. He had to see his godchild, re-create his bond with her, even if Sherrie could never forgive him. It seemed to him the saddest day in his life since his wife and child had died.

Chapter 2

By the time Sherrie neared her beauty salon just off Connecticut Avenue in D.C., she had calmed somewhat. She drew deep breaths and willed herself to put Byron Tate out of her mind. She had a long, hard day ahead and tomorrow she would get up in the predawn hours and drive down to a spot between D.C. and Richmond for a beauty and fashion show. She had a very full plate these days.

She slowed her burgundy Volvo, selected for safety, as she got to the corner where she would turn. She slowed a bit more and looked at the big sign on her beauty shop. The large black scripted initial letters MBS never failed to excite her, even after six years of owning the salon. The words scrolled out from the script spelling out *My Beautiful Self*. The whole concept, she thought now, was dedicated to African-American women, a love offering, if you will. Giving Black America the well-deserved best in beauty care.

Going in, she was immediately surrounded by her staff. Katherine Aldano, the manager, a smartly coiffed woman in her early forties, held Tressa's hand for a moment until she broke free and ran to Sherrie.

"Mommy! Where have you been? I need a hug."

Bending, Sherrie hugged the thin, almond-colored little girl tightly and felt her heart beating rapidly.

"Where have I been? Well . . . places."

"Aunt Helena's in your office. We're not going to stay long. We've got things to do." The piping high voice was lyrical.

Sherrie smiled. Tressa's preschool was out for a teacher's conference. She would spend the day with Helena at the social service complex that Helena, a social worker, supervised. Standing, Sherrie was saddened to see that all too suddenly Tressa's little face was somber. Was she remembering her father again?

"What is it, honey?" Sherrie asked. When the child shook her head, Sherrie urged her, "Listen, reconsider having a little party for your birthday, won't you?"

The child shook her head vehemently. "No, I don't want to. Please don't make me."

"Of course I won't make you, but what do you want for your birthday?"

Tressa answered without hesitation. "I want Daddy to come back."

Sherrie bent and hugged Tressa tightly. "Sweetheart," she began, her heart breaking, "you know that isn't possible. Daddy's in heaven with God."

"Then God's mean," the child wailed. "Why did He take Daddy? Mommy, I don't feel too good."

Sherrie hugged her child tightly again, stroking her thin, fragile back. "Believe me, my love, God is wonderful, but things happen we don't understand. Do you feel sick?"

"No. I just don't feel good, you know."

"Yes, I know, sweetheart. I know." Sometimes Sherrie thought it seemed that Tressa hadn't felt *good* since Mike had died. Sometimes Sherrie thought it seemed that neither had she.

Tressa brightened a little in her mother's arms and took a deep breath. "It's so pretty in here," she said. "I like to come here."

"I'm glad. Come anytime. Come all the time." The child's mood had passed as quickly as it had come, but she knew from experience that it would shortly come again. Neither she nor Tressa was healing very well.

"Now," Katherine said, "Tressa and I have got to make sure the aromatherapy room is up and running. We're getting shows of interest and appointments from all over. Our ad people are the greatest."

Sherrie agreed and looked around her. Walking over to a long cream-colored counter, she selected a raisin bagel, spread it lightly with cream cheese and drew herself a cup of chocolate-flavored coffee from one of several coffee urns. My Beautiful Self was decorated in raspberry, rose, blush pink and cream, with both black and ivory swirled marble and plush dark mauve carpeting. She reflected now that it had been very expensive to get the salon started, but it had proved to be well worth it.

Mike had set her up, and now business could not have been better. She stayed on top of things, had the best operators, used the best products, and people were calling from as far as New York for the new aromatherapy services. Still, she sighed. How could one part of life be so rewarding and another so devastated?

In her office she found her best friend, Helena Crane, sitting in a deep, plush barrel chair. Helena looked up as Sherrie came in.

"I wondered whether you'd been hijacked." Then, looking at her friend more closely, she frowned. "You look a little peaked, love. What is it?"

Sherrie drew a deep breath, and her voice came out a little above a hoarse whisper as she sat down opposite Helena. "I saw Byron Tate at the cemetery."

"Oh dear. He's been back only a couple of days, I think."

Sherrie nodded. "He wants to see Tressa."

"And you don't want him to," Helena responded quickly.

"You know I don't. After what he did to Mike . . ." Tears filled her eyes then. "I've even thought of moving away, Helena, selling out, going back to New Orleans. I don't want to run into him, to see him."

A dark haired, tall, slender woman, Helena sat up straight, her tan face full of concern. She ran her tongue over her bottom lip. "Love, you may hate me for saying this, but I've always wondered what Byron's side of this story is."

"As far as I'm concerned, he has no side. Mike told me everything."

"Okay, then he was wrong, but he is Tressa's godfather, just as I am her godmother, and Tressa needs him. He loves the child and she loves him."

"One day she'll know the truth. She won't love him then."

"But she needs him now. Sherrie, please consider his request. You've got to think of Tressa."

"I am thinking of Tressa. He'll break her heart the way he broke Mike's."

Helena got up, went to Sherrie and stroked her shoulders. "You're so upset," she comforted. "Bite the bullet, love. Try letting him see her. Tressa is so unhappy. You know that. What could it hurt? You don't have to be around them when he sees her. He's suffered a terrible loss, too, Sherrie. Three terrible losses, because no matter what went down between Mike and him, they were bonded friends who loved each other. I think Byron Tate is the walking wounded because of these things. You believe in forgiveness. You know you do."

"Not Byron Tate."

"Even Byron Tate."

Helena sat down again and leaned forward. "Promise me you'll think about it. You have Tressa to consider. The God you serve is forgiving. I know that."

Sherrie leaned forward, putting her face in her hands. She was coming apart. "Not now," she said. "I can't let him see her now." Her mouth was bone dry, and her head ached with tension. How did you put back together something that had been so violently ripped apart?

When Helena and Tressa left, Sherrie pulled herself together and walked about her salon. Early-morning customers were in varying stages of progress. Their rose-pink capes and hoods and the matching smocks of the operators gave them a lovely sensual air. She greeted each customer, grateful that Katherine was so effective, so efficient. The dark chocolate-skinned woman with her remarkably beautiful satiny skin and close-cropped cap of black, curly hair was a wonder who never ceased to amaze her. They were good friends as well as owner and employee.

Coffee, pastries and fresh fruit with varied drinks were served all day. Soothing, piped music flowed softly—Lionel Richie, Luther Vandross and all the beautiful classical music. A blend of many marvelous scents soothed the spirit. A large, lighted portrait of Madame C.J. Walker, eminent late founder of cosmetology, graced one wall niche. It was a wonderful place to relax, to just *be*.

One thing had long bothered Sherrie. Byron Tate owned and ran Tate Supreme Cosmetic Manufacturing Company. They made the best cosmetics in the world for African-American skin and hair, and since Byron had done what he did to Mike, she hadn't wanted to use his products, but her hands were tied. He had great customer loyalty who demanded his wares. Tate beauty products still lined the walls in their stunning containers, some black glossy labels with beautifully scripted gold lettering, some cream and gold with the same scripted lettering. Everything Byron Tate did was top of line, she reflected—even his betrayals.

She was standing near the entrance and the big plate-glass windows when she heard her sister's voice. "The light of the world is here. Pay obeisance!"

Laughing in spite of herself she moved toward her sister, Mallori, and hugged her. As always, Mallori didn't really hug back, just suffered herself to be hugged.

"How is my sister?" Sherrie asked, never giving up trying to really reach Mallori.

"Your half sister."

"I'll take that, but we could be whole sisters if you let it be so."

A sharp, hard glint came to Mallori's eyes. "We had different mothers. My own never cared much and yours didn't care for me at all."

"Mallori! That's not true."

The small, fair-skinned Mallori laughed shortly, tossed back her long, light brown hair and narrowed her brown eyes. "It's true all right. Minta tried, she really did. I'll give her credit for that, but she had you and that was enough. I used to hate you, Sherrie. Do you know that?"

Sherrie shook her head. "Look, this is no conversation for the middle of the salon. Let's talk in my office. What are you having done today?"

Mallori grinned sourly. "You're sure getting away from the hatred thing. You're such a Goody Two-shoes. I'm just having a trim and a facial. I could use six cups of coffee, and I've just had one. My darling husband served me breakfast in bed."

"How nice and how like him," Sherrie said as they stopped by the coffee urns and Mallori drew herself a big cup.

Seated in her office, Sherrie felt that Mallori looked rattled. "How's the job going?" she asked tentatively.

"Couldn't be better. I'm in line for a humongous raise and a promotion to manager and my beloved husband, Gus, isn't taking it so well. I thought he'd be way ahead of where he is now at the police department, but he's dying on the vine."

"Being a sergeant isn't too bad."

"I much prefer captains and above. He needs to be in New York, or at least D.C."

Mallori was a pharmaceutical representative for a world-class company. Sharp, savvy and well educated, the only thing Mallori Dueñas lacked was a loving heart, Sherrie thought. Mallori had always been a prickly pear, but she was so full of life, so beautiful, so openly and pleasantly aggressive that you liked her in spite of herself. And she made no bones about who she was or what she was. The world, according to Mallori, owed her everything, and she intended to get it.

"How's Gus?" Sherrie asked.

Mallori shrugged. "Same old, same old. And how are you since I just said for the first time ever that I hated you when we were growing up, hated all you had."

"You had just as much."

"You were loved. I wasn't."

"Surely you don't still hate me."

"Mind if I smoke? Oh, I know all about your no-smoking rules, and I've always observed them, but with this new upcoming raise I'm feeling my oats, and I intend to cut loose in more ways than one. I've got a new lover."

Sherrie's mouth opened. "You have a husband, Mallori, a husband who loves you very much. What about him?"

"What about him? He's free to roam. I certainly don't mind. The brother I'm hooked up with lives in Baltimore, and we're burning up the city." She opened her purse and removed a cigarette case and a small gold lighter. Swiftly she extracted a cigarette, lit it and drew in deeply. After a few drags, she finished her coffee as Sherrie pushed a paper-clip dish toward her. She had no ashtrays.

Mallori shook her head. "I'll just use the cup. I wouldn't want to cause you any extra trouble." She lowered her head as she drew in a deep breath of smoke.

"You're upset," Sherrie told her.

Mallori laughed harshly. "You bet I'm upset. I'm thinking about Mike today, more than usual, if that's possible." She glanced at the large photo of Mike, Sherrie and Tressa that sat on Sherrie's desk.

Her nerves went raw, and Sherrie drew her shoulders in as if to ward off what she knew would come next.

Mallori looked at Sherrie and through her, her eyes blank. "You never manage to get used to it, do you, half sister? With Mike, for the first time in my life I had something you no longer had—*him*. I've told you before. I'll say it again. He was going to divorce you. We were in love. We were two of a kind, taking the world only on our own terms."

Sherrie protested heatedly. "You never knew the real Mike. He changed, did so much he never would have done before. But he told me shortly before he . . . was killed, that he loved me, that he'd never leave me, and he begged me not to leave him."

Mallori threw back her head, and her laughter was cruel. "Then he lied to you. He loved me, Sherrie, not you. Why do you keep deceiving yourself?"

Sherrie willed herself to calmness. "I don't think I am. Gus loves you, Mallori. Worships you. How can you mistreat him like this?" She was trying to change the subject.

"Oh, this new lover is no sop to my ego. He's someone who keeps me going." Her voice broke then. "I'm a bottomless well now, Sherrie. Dear God, I miss Mike." Her voice was raw with passion.

"He was *my* husband, Mallori," Sherrie said evenly. "Try to remember that."

Mallori shook her head. "But if he hadn't died, he wasn't yours for long. You can believe it or not believe it, but that changes nothing."

Sherrie began to get up. "This conversation is finished, Mallori. You're being cruel and I hate cruelty."

"Mike could be cruel."

"Not before he was so badly hurt. You're my sister, and I love you, but that love isn't endless." Rigid with anger, Sherrie told her, "I want you to stop throwing your and Mike's affair in my face. I'm sick of it! He was wrong and you were wrong and you know it. You're acting like a cheap hussy, so cut it out."

Mallori expelled a harsh breath. The wind seemed to go out of her sails. "Forgive me for being so obnoxious. I think a major reason I loved Mike was that he was so tolerant of my cruelty. Look, Sis, I need a favor." Mallori was penitent, pleading. "Come by our digs. Gus and I are both off today. I'm thinking of buying an incredible big rocker recliner from Matt Smartt, the furniture designer. Matt sent it over; so now

Gus is in a snit and thinks it way too expensive, but I want what I want. If you agree that it fits in with my décor, it stays."

"That puts me in the middle."

"Not really. Gus always gives in to what I want. Besides, you've got to see it. I value your taste. Will you?"

Mallori was charming now. It was a sad state of affairs, Sherrie reflected, when your sister told you your dead husband had wanted her, not you, and you knew it was true. But the Mike he had become was no longer responsible. Broken, bitter, crushed, he was killing himself long before the murderer's dagger struck his heart.

Chapter 3

Byron Tate sat at his desk in his spacious front office of Tate Supreme Cosmetic Manufacturing Company. Founded by his great-grandfather, the company had long been the premier company that brought the best in beauty aids to the African-American public. The new plant he had built was spacious, even imposing. Steel and black marble on fifty acres of impeccably landscaped grounds out from Minden, Byron always felt a lump in his throat thinking about his father and his forebears when he looked at it.

It was his first day back. Now he rocked slowly in his big, black soft leather executive chair and smiled at his right-hand man and right-hand woman, Curt Winters and River West.

"I said it before, and I'll never stop saying it. Thank you both for the way you ran the place while I was gone— increased sales, great progress on new products. Wow! Am I impressed. Maybe I should have stayed away longer."

"You're back, and we're happy about that," Curt said in his booming bass voice. A silver-haired man in his fifties, he had helped groom Byron for the job. He was his mentor. A widower with no children, he had loved him like a son. "We're no substitute for you. We just had pure, dumb luck."

Byron smiled. "I'm not accepting that. You're both the best, and I'm going to see that my appreciation is reflected in steep raises for you."

They both thanked him effusively, then River said, "You seem to be feeling much better, Byron. I'm glad to see that. I was beginning to worry before you left. I think it did you a lot of good to get away."

Byron nodded. "It did, but if I didn't have such a great right-hand man and right-hand woman, everything might not have turned out so well. Now, fill me in some more. River, how's your new perfume coming along? Will it be ready for the August ball?"

River laughed. "It better be—long before." A medium height, slender woman of thirty-eight with long, brown silk hair, she had a lovely elfin face and smooth pale skin. She had worked with Byron since she was just out of Howard and Duquesne. She had developed a line of perfumes that had some of the world's leading perfumers trying to woo her away.

River drew a deep breath and continued. "My new perfume is based on pheromones, you know. I keep wishing for ambergris to blend it, but if we were still using whale oil sperm, there'd be no more whales by now. I guess it's a good thing they outlawed the use of it in the seventies."

"Yeah," Byron said, "so what are you using?"

"I'm experimenting with rose oil, one of my favorites. It doesn't come cheap at two hundred and fifty dollars an ounce wholesale, but . . ." She shrugged. "I'm not quite pleased with the way the rose oil carries the fragrance, so I'm also experimenting with musk ambrette and musk rose oil.

"I have to be careful. Musk ambrette can cause photosensitivity and contact dermatitis. Some African-American skins are particularly sensitive. I'm probably going to wind up using musk rose oil. There're lots of good oils out there. I promise we'll both be thrilled with the result. Come by and sniff."

"I will," Byron said. "What's up with you, Curt?"

"Just running the place as best I can."

"And doing a damned good job of it."

Curt grinned. "Thank you. It helps to have a great guy to work with."

"I hope I am," Byron said. "God knows I try."

"What did you bring back from your travels?" River asked. "Although your just feeling better would be enough."

"I did more." Leaning back, he picked up a big navy, leather-covered book from the credenza behind him and put it on top of his desk. He stood it on edge so they could see the title, *Rare Cosmetic Formulae*.

Byron smiled. "Two thousand, six hundred and fifty dollars," he said.

Curt's eyebrows raised. "For one book or the volume?" he teased.

"One pop, but Lord, it has the makings of wonderful discoveries. I'm itching to develop an antiwrinkle cream from one of the formulae. It's one of the cosmetic books of the century."

"Who published it?" Curt asked.

"A German publisher. It was written by a panel of experts drawn from the world over. One of the most effective formulae is said to be a Zimbabwean white mud pack with musk oils. I think they could more than quadruple the price and it would be a bargain."

Both people said they'd be anxious to look at the book.

"Now, how are you both?" Byron asked. "River?"

River's face brightened. "I couldn't be better now that our leader is back. I'm burning the midnight oil developing my new perfume and working with Curt to run Tate properly."

"Have you thought about a name for this new perfume wonder?" Byron asked.

"Not yet. I've put it in my creative womb, and I'm expecting something good."

"And your personal life? How's that coming along? You were a little unhappy when I left."

She didn't answer for a moment. "On target. I've got so much going on."

"Good. And you, Curt?"

"Lord, the sky's the limit." Curt laughed. "D.C. has discovered our products in a big way. The beauty salons are burning up the phone lines ordering. You didn't ask, but I can't complain about my personal life."

Byron nodded. "That's all good. I'm happy for both of you. The African-American community deserves the best and the best is Tate cosmetics."

River's head went up suddenly. "Funny. Michael and Sherrie Pinson used to say that all the time. They were great fans. Of course, Michael worked with us, but Lord, they both were such fans. . . ."

Byron's eyes got sad. "Yes," he said. "They were."

Their conversation become desultory then. River and Curt left to begin their work.

At his desk, Byron rocked and thought about going to the company gym, but he decided to work out later. His secretary, Marcia Keely, came in, gracious and smiling. A woman in her midfifties, cinnamon-brown and energetic, she moved with effortless grace.

"I just can't tell you how good it is to have you back," she said. "All the pieces come together now."

Byron laughed. "You flatter me."

"No, I don't. It's true. Now, how's your appetite this morning?"

"Well, I got up late, grabbed a glass of orange juice and a small cup of coffee and hustled out. Why do you ask?"

"Well, I got up at five and made my famous buttermilk biscuits that Hal loves, and I'm wondering, how does a huge biscuit topped with extra-sharp melted cheese and a thick slice of Canadian bacon, with a pot of wild plum jam and great Colombian coffee or fragrant chrysanthemum tea grab you?"

"Hey, I'm drooling at the thought! My stomach's standing at attention. Bring it on!"

Laughing happily, Marcia turned and went out.

Byron got up and went to the window. Marcia had taught his wife, Alicia, to bake buttermilk biscuits. Alicia. And Ronnie, his six-year-old daughter. They had been a happy, close-knit family until that fateful late November night when a very early ice storm had caused the car Alicia and Ronnie were traveling in to go down a steep embankment and crash into a big tree in a ditch. He wiped a tear from his eye and shook his head to brush aside the thick cobwebs of memory.

He and Alicia had been close companions; they were not impassioned lovers, but she said she was well satisfied with what they had. Their life together filled space and time in his life, but he was haunted by what might have been with someone else. Sherrie. Her hatred of him had torn his heart out this morning. He had met her in New Orleans before Michael Pinson had. They had dated, kissed lightly, and he had been blown out of the water by those kisses. His kisses had not seemed to matter as much to her. Her father had just died of cancer and he had been loathe to push her, so he had held back, waiting for a later time when she had healed more.

Then his best friend, Michael, had come to New Orleans and Michael hadn't waited. He had pursued the beautiful Sherrie with ardent persuasion, and she had fallen hard.

He and Michael had been friends since high school in D.C. Swimming in a Maryland creek, he had been seized with a cramp and nearly drowned. Michael had managed to save his life. After that, they were blood brothers. Both had attended Howard University, majoring in chemistry. The same age, both had matriculated further at Massachusetts Institute of Technology, both still majoring in chemistry. Byron had earned a doctorate, Michael an MS. Michael had actually begun full-time work at Tate before Byron had, but Byron had worked there part-time summers since he was a child.

The accident killed his wife and child and had devastated him, but he had already been devastated by the falling out between Michael and him. How could it happen? But it had. He had asked Michael to leave the company that had come to be Michael's life. He'd had to do it and even now he didn't want to think about it.

Then Michael had been murdered. His immensely charming, life-filled former buddy had been found in his car only a few miles from his house, stabbed to death through the heart. It was a cold case now, except as Lieutenant Danielle Steele often said, Minden had no cold cases; they never stopped working on them. There had come to be gossip about Michael, gossip about other women, drinking. Even drugs. He had inherited money and was trying to found a company of his own. Before he died, Michael had seemed harried, wired on the few occasions he'd run into him. He still grieved the loss, and his heart hurt for Sherrie who had loved her husband so.

Marcia came in with a big wooden tray. The food was tastefully served on china dishes. He always used the same big coffee or tea mug of sky-blue Royal Doulton china.

Setting the tray on a table near his desk, Marcia said, "Dig in and enjoy! I'm prejudiced, but I defy you to find better."

Once he had finished, Byron felt a sense of satisfaction come over him. His stomach felt soothed. He was a man who loved good food. Getting up, he lifted the tray and carried it out to the kitchen where he found Marcia.

She came toward him. "I never manage to train you to be a properly uppity, old-fashioned, chauvinist boss. We're supposed to carry your dishes."

Byron laughed heartily as he set the tray in the sink. "I enjoy working along with my staff. We're all kings and queens here. We run a happy shop."

"You can say that again," Marcia amended.

"Listen, I'm going to walk over the plant a bit," he said then.

"Fine. Some of the employees are having a meeting in the

conference room, so don't go there. They'd be intimidated in spite of themselves."

"I'll stay clear."

Tate Supreme Cosmetic Manufacturing was meant to be and was a beautiful place in which to work. Furnishings were for maximum accomplishment, beauty and comfort. Fitness rooms, a nursing station, a small library and a resting room all added to the comfort of the place. Piped music of varying melodies filled the air. Dr. Annice Jones helped with personal problems the staff may have been experiencing. Walking, Byron congratulated himself on setting up a good place and doing a good job. Too bad the emptiness in him kept getting deeper. Otherwise, he had it made.

In one alcove, oil portraits of his father, his grandfather and his great-grandfather hung. His great-grandfather, Claude, had been a Tuskegee graduate and later a confidant of George Washington Carver and Booker T. Washington. His grandfather and his father, David and Paul, respectively, had been Harvard graduates. All three had been illustrious men, and Byron was their only heir, his younger brother having died in childhood.

Byron felt himself fill with pride. His heart always expanded when he thought about his forebears, his heritage. He would make it somehow, but now he wished he were not a man who craved one woman, one romantic dream.

Employees came up to him, warmly welcomed him on his first day back. He was immensely proud of the enveloping spirit of warmth and caring that permeated his company. If only it reached into the rest of his life.

As he rounded the corner by the conference room, Marcia came out, closed the door and leaned against the edge of it. She caught sight of him.

"I think your employees have something to tell you," she said.

"Oh?" He wondered why she glowed.

Flinging the door open, she beckoned him in, and a number of employees greeted him with a banner proclaiming, OUR HERO! WE LOVE YOU FOREVER!

Happy laughter welled from Byron's heart and soul. Deep love, affection and admiration permeated this room and the people in it.

The credenzas were filled with luscious food, and a large punch bowl of pineapple-papaya-mango punch stood by. Other employees came in, and he was hugged again and again as Marcia grinned. It was the beginning of a great party.

Chapter 4

As she walked along Minden's Main Street late that afternoon, Sherrie reflected that it had proved to be a good day
after all. Business had been brisk. Everything had gone like
clockwork, and the discomfort over her run-ins with Byron
and her sister, Mallori, had eased. No, she amended, she still
felt Byron in her bones. She wouldn't forget what he had
done to Mike.

Still she hummed to herself "Everything's Coming Up
Roses," as she walked along. She was meeting Helena and
Tressa at Scarf's drugstore and famous soda fountain. Tressa
adored the drugstore's soda fountain as did so many people in
the surrounding area. People came from Baltimore and D.C.
to sample their wares. Tressa would spend the next two nights
with Helena. The thought of her little girl warmed Sherrie's
heart.

Ahead of her she caught two sights at once: Helena and
Tressa getting out of Helena's car, then Byron coming toward
them. She was close enough to hear Tressa screech excitedly,
"Uncle Bye!" and go flying toward him. Byron squatted as he
reached the little girl and hugged her tightly. He had shaved
his beard. Sherrie hastened her steps as she got to them. She
was surprised to see tears streaming down Tressa's face. The
child seemed unaware of Sherrie.

"Pumpkin!" Byron exclaimed. "You're a sight for sore
eyes. I'm so glad to see you."

"Oh, Uncle Bye, I love you." Tressa quickly stopped crying.

"Day after tomorrow's my birthday. I'm so glad you're back. Did you bring me a present?"

"Tressa," Sherrie admonished, "where are your manners?"

The child paid no attention to Sherrie. "Manners have long flown," Helena said, laughing. "This is serious birthday request time."

"You bet I brought you a present. Two in fact. I'm waiting for one to come, but the biggest one is here."

Sherrie couldn't help being happy that Tressa seemed livelier than she had in a very long time. Her little face was glowing.

"Will you bring it by?" Tressa asked. "Please?"

Byron looked up at Sherrie, seeking her approval. Suddenly he nodded, getting no response from Sherrie. "I'll bring it by if it's okay with your mommy."

"It's okay," Tressa said. "She wants me to have a good birthday. I haven't been feeling too good."

Byron looked at the child closely. "I'm really sorry to hear that. Maybe I can help." He patted Tressa's shoulder and stood with her in his arms. Looking levelly at Sherrie, he asked, "How about it, Sherrie? I wouldn't stay long. My present is guaranteed to make Little Miss Muffet feel a whole lot better."

Tressa's thin arms went around Byron's neck and the two held each other tight as Sherrie drew a deep breath.

"All right," she said reluctantly. "For a very little while. I'll be tired from my short trip south." She stopped, her mouth tightening. She didn't need an excuse not to entertain Byron Tate in her home for any length of time.

Reluctantly, too, Sherrie accepted Byron's offer to treat them all to ice cream flavors of their choosing and they all went inside to Scarf's.

"I can't stay long," Sherrie said. "I've got to go by Mallori and Gus's, and I've got to get to bed early in preparation for a long day tomorrow."

Helena looked from Byron to Sherrie and smiled inside. These two were attracted, she thought, even if they didn't yet know it.

* * *

It was early evening when Sherrie stood outside her sister's patio entrance. She tried to collect her riotous thoughts caused by her second encounter with Byron for the day. It was beautiful out here with stars beginning to come out and a new moon growing. She didn't want to go inside.

She caught her breath as she heard raised voices and wondered if she should leave. Mallori and Gus often battled fiercely. Mallori was sadistic, liked to draw emotional blood, and Gus was thin-skinned where Mallori was concerned. The voices grew more strident, and she stood transfixed, unwilling to go in, unable to walk away.

Inside the den, Mallori and Gus squared off angrily.

"You're not going out of here tonight," Gus yelled.

Mallori laughed nastily. "Like hell I'm not. I'm late, I'm late, for a very important date," she chirped in a singsong voice, and her levity infuriated her husband.

"I'm your husband and I love you. You owe me some respect."

"I owe you nothing. My bill with you is paid in full. I've given years of putting up with you going nowhere, when I married you, thinking you were going to forge ahead. No, Gus, you owe me my dream."

"I've tried," Gus said brokenly. "You haven't helped. Being a sergeant keeps plenty of people happy. They support a family, kids. Why can't we?"

Mallori laughed scornfully. "With my newly promised raise, I'll make nearly twice what you make, and I don't want kids, Gus, not with you. Can't you understand that I've been bleeding ever since Mike died? He would have gotten a divorce and we would have been married. Then Happy City and kids, yeah. But not with you, Gus, not with you."

"Careful," Gus warned.

Mallori's voice got softer then. "I'm not just being mean,

Gus. Mike rang *all* my bells. No one ever did before, and I don't think anyone ever will again."

"You're a verbal sadist," Gus grated, his lean, tan face reddening. *"Por que?"* But why? He was Puerto Rican and sometimes he thought the culture gap between him and Mallori was what caused their problems. But no, his wife was cruel as the grave, and he knew she wasn't going to change. Aching, he said, "Be careful that one day your own tongue doesn't cut your throat."

Mallori laughed nastily again. "Oh, so it's veiled threats tonight, is it?" She yawned. "You're wasting my time. I've got to make myself beautiful."

As if they hadn't quarreled, he said tenderly. "You are beautiful, and I keep wondering how you can be so beautiful outside and so ugly inside. Mallori, I used to feel some sympathy for you where Mike was concerned. I thought just maybe he was your one love of a lifetime, the way you're mine, and you couldn't help yourself. But this new guy, you don't love him; you're just using each other's bodies. You're acting like a slut."

"Sure, call me names. Name-calling's the refuge of the hopeless, the dispossessed."

For the moment, Gus ignored her taunts. "I know who the guy in Baltimore is," he said evenly. "I've had you followed."

With a sharp intake of breath, Mallori's eyes raked him furiously. "Now why doesn't that surprise me?" she asked sarcastically. "I'm sick of this, sick of you. I want a divorce, Gus, and I want it now. Your magic wand's quit working!"

His fingers were hot steel gripping her arms as he pulled her to him, breathed fire on her face.

"No!" he shouted. "There'll be no divorce between us. Damn you, Mallori."

Rigid with alarm, Sherrie knocked hard, then knocked and waited. She quickly knocked louder, demanding entrance. Someone had to interfere and who better than Mallori's sister? Her heart hurt for Gus, whom she liked, and the voices were quiet. She heard no movement.

At her fourth knock, Mallori opened the door and stood there. "Sherrie?"

"Yes, it's me. Let me in." Her voice sounded far cooler than she felt.

"How long have you . . . been out here?"

"Long enough." She wasn't going to lie about it.

"You heard everything?"

"Enough," Sherrie said.

Mallori's laugh was shaky. "Good, you can be a star witness in my divorce fight. Can I count on you?"

"I hope it doesn't come to that," Sherrie said as she came in. She took off her coat and put it, her purse and her tote on the sofa.

Gus stared at her for a moment as if in a trance. "Hello, Sherrie," he said dully. "Sorry to scare you with our battle. Were you out there long?"

"I've already asked her that question," Mallori said sharply. "She can't be a witness for both of us."

"I'm warning you, Mallori. Cut it out," Gus told her.

"You're still threatening me," Mallori said, "when I have a witness? You're foolish, Gus, but then you always were."

"I'm a cop, and cops can be dangerous. Danger is our business. Watch your step or you may be sorrier than you dream." Gus turned to Sherrie. "I've got to leave now. My mother didn't raise me to be a batterer."

Mallori got in his face. "Know this, brother. I'm not afraid of you. When I lost Mike, I lost everything. The devil himself doesn't scare me anymore."

Gus grabbed her by the arms again, but she didn't flinch.

"You evil woman," he grated, hot tears choking him. "Mike was your sister's husband. Have you got no shame?"

Mallori stood her ground, and her eyes were bleak. "No, I have no shame where Mike is concerned. Sherrie came to understand that. Didn't you, Sis?"

Seething with anger, Sherrie shook her head. "No, Mallori, I don't and I never have understood. I've told you Mike was hurt beyond the telling, bitter. He never would have taken up with you if he hadn't been. I've asked you to stop talking this way about my husband. Keep it up and I'll stop seeing you."

Mallori drew a deep breath. "I'm sorry. I promised to stop, but I've got to say this: Mike and I were attracted from the get-go, but I was married to Mr. Wonderful here." Her voice was scathing.

Raw anger took Sherrie. "Let it go, Mallori! We're not having this conversation any longer."

"Fine," Mallori said flippantly. She looked at Gus and a smile curved her mouth. "You're leaving. I'm leaving. I guess we'll have to bid you good night, Sis."

"Good night, Sherrie. I'm out of here." Gus snatched his uniform coat from the back of a chair, slung his holstered gun on and went out, slamming the door with a vengeance.

After Gus left, the two women stood in the middle of the floor. Mallori's face bore a strange, twisted smile. "Could I offer you something to drink? I'm going to have a stiff Scotch."

"No. Nothing. And I don't think you should be drinking now either."

But Mallori already stood at the wet bar pouring her drink, which she upended swiftly, making a sour face. "You heard me tell my beloved I'm meeting someone, so I'll have to be on my way."

"Mallori, you're playing with fire, and you're going to be burned. Surely you've got to know that."

Mallori looked at her with half-closed eyes. "Gus is harmless, all bluster. He loves me. Nothing's going to change that."

Sherrie looked at her sister with disbelief. "Hatred is the other side of love," she said tiredly. "Why don't you know that?" The negative sides of the day were beginning to take their toll. "We're sisters," she said. "I would have stopped speaking to you, put you out of my life when I found out about you and Mike, but I have no other family except a few cousins I'm not close to. I thought we could salvage something since Mike is dead. Mom always urged us to be friends."

"Don't throw your mother up to me," Mallori said with sudden fury.

"I'm not and you know it. Even if you choose not to believe it, she loved you, or tried to, but you never let her. Dad loved you, too, but you were too busy playing the heller, and Dad worked hard in his shoe business. He had little time left over. You've always been determined to be miserable, to take the world by the tail, twist it and throw it against a concrete wall. Why can't you be happy? Why do you hurt other people so?"

"Ha!" Mallori scoffed. "Believe me, I would have been happy if Mike had lived."

Sherrie shook her head. "No. Not even with Mike would you have been happy. Mike was a man who belonged to me, and you've always seduced or tried to seduce every man who belonged to me. Let it go, Mallori. For God's sake, let it go and let's try to salvage something of our relationship."

Mallori gloated as if she didn't hear Sherrie's plea. "Mike and I were soul mates," she said. "We used to laugh about how I took boys away from you and he took girls away from Byron."

"You've got to change," Sherrie cried. "You're driving Gus to the wall. Don't make him hurt you. Please."

Mallori laughed scornfully. "I can take care of myself, and I plan to live a whole lot longer. God isn't ready for me yet, and the devil thinks I'm too hot to handle."

She laughed harshly then as Sherrie stared at her. "End of conversation," Mallori said abruptly. "I have to go, Sis. I have a really hot date waiting in the wings. I'll call you tomorrow. No, you're away tomorrow. The next day then."

Outside in her car, watching Mallori drive away, Sherrie reflected that Mallori had called her "Sis" a number of times tonight. Mallori seldom called her that.

Chapter 5

At one o'clock two mornings later Sherrie turned off the main highway and onto the long, winding road that took her past the Tate company, then Byron's house and on to hers. His estate had bright floodlights in the back and softer front lighting. Both the company and his house were beautiful buff fieldstone, imposing, with perfectly manicured grounds, planned and built by one of D.C.'s finest architects.

Back from the road, between her house and Byron's lay a long, deep ravine with a block-wire fence on either side. A huge oak and a smaller sumac stood on Byron's side. People called it Bottomless Canyon because you stared down into unending blackness. Just thinking about it gave Sherrie goose bumps.

Sherrie felt pleasantly tired from today's meetings and the night's banquet. She had taken her best operator with her, and they had won first prize in the hairstyling category. But the past events still hung in her mind like bothersome insects that she could not swat away. Mallori and Gus and their tangled marriage. *And yes,* she thought, *say it, Byron Tate.*

Byron's estate and her house were less than two miles apart. Mike had wanted to build nearby. Now she wanted to move away and often began plans to do so, but the house held dear memories of the life she'd known with Mike—precious memories. The indecision tore at her constantly.

A soft smile lay on her face as she thought about Tressa. As much as she didn't want Byron near her daughter, she was delighted at the happiness the little girl had shown with her Uncle Bye two afternoons before. Tressa hadn't been happy like that since Mike died. A lump filled her throat then. How was she going to keep Tressa away from Byron? She was so sad when she was away from Uncle Bye. Helena seemed to be on Tressa's side, which nettled Sherrie because Helena knew the score. She thought then she would talk to Dr. Annice Jones about this. The psychologist had such a levelheaded, down-to-earth approach to problems, and Sherrie knew her own brain fogged up where Byron was concerned.

Whenever she neared her house, she always felt lifted. She and Mike had a good architect, but they had taken a hands-on approach. Much smaller than Byron's, their house was beautiful by any standard. Constructed of dark red, patterned brick with a contemporary style and lush plantings, it was the home of her dreams.

Coming into her driveway and toward her garage, she frowned. The house was dark. Mrs. Hall, her housekeeper, always left a few lights on when Sherrie was coming in late. A couple of floodlights lit the yard so she wasn't afraid. Pulling into the garage, she lowered the doors by remote control and collected the items she would take in with her. Other packages could wait until the next day.

Turning on lights in a small room just by the entrance, she continued to frown. A sense of deep unease hit her as she walked into the living room and gasped. The room had been savaged. Books and papers were strewn everywhere. Credenza drawers lay overturned on the floor and books were thrown about. Blinding fear hit her then, and her stomach churned. Was someone still there? A hard chill shook her as she saw through her dizziness that the big oil painting of Mike had been ripped from the wall and slashed to ribbons. "Oh my God!" she gasped and reached into her purse for her cell phone, dialing 911. Thank heaven, she thought, that the operator was efficient. Willing herself to be calm, she told the operator what had happened and gave her the address.

"Ma'am," the operator finally said, "I think you should leave, drive away from the house. We'll have someone there immediately. You may have interrupted something in progress. Will you do that?"

"Yes," Sherrie said dully, "I will."

Parked a short distance away with her motor running, she heard the shrill scream of the sirens and several police cars pulling up to her house within fifteen minutes. She drove back and into the driveway.

Lieutenant Danielle Steele, a friend, was leading the police team and Sherrie could have cried with relief. The burglars or simply vandals had all apparently gone, their work finished. Sherrie couldn't look at Mike's slashed painting without wanting to throw up with fear and anger. Her own portrait smiled down from the wall, unharmed. Why? And who? A memory of Gus came to mind, his anger at his wife and her adoration of Mike. Hotheaded Gus had been drinking, she thought, but even if he had slashed the painting, he would have no need to tear up the rest of the living room.

"It would seem they were looking for something," Lieutenant Steele said. "I'd guess a lot of people knew you'd be away."

"Yes, a lot of people knew," Sherrie told her.

Fanning out, they found the whole house in disarray. Sofas in the basement family room had been slashed. Her favorite Royal Doulton collection of rare crystal giraffe figurines had been smashed to bits. Sherrie fought back tears that had first rushed to her eyes at the sight of Mike's desecrated portrait.

The bedrooms upstairs had been thoroughly searched and vandalized.

"Have you any idea what they'd be looking for? Do you have a safe here?" Lieutenant Steele asked.

"Yes," Sherrie answered, "but I don't keep a lot of money on hand." Going into the den, they found the safe gone.

"Was it a large safe?" Lieutenant Steele asked.

"No," Sherrie answered. "I've never needed a large safe. And Mike never needed a larger one. Who could have done this?"

"I wish I knew," Lieutenant Steele said sadly.

The photographer, the fingerprint man and the crime analyst, along with three other police people, were all over the house and out onto the yard near the house. Lieutenant Steele went back downstairs.

"They tried to destroy my home," Sherrie said to an officer in disbelief. "Who would do this?"

"We intend to find out," the officer said grimly.

Stricken, Sherrie leaned against a chest of drawers with everything dumped onto the floor and tried to steady herself when Lieutenant Steele called her downstairs and into the living room. They stood in front of a curved wall corner.

"Was this built along with the house?" Lieutenant Steele asked.

Sherrie shook her head. "No. The year before Mike died I went on vacation to St. Maarten. He'd always hated the flat, sharp corner here and while I was gone he had someone add the curved corner. He had it built as a surprise to me, although I never minded the sharp corner."

Lieutenant Steele studied the wall, her eyes narrowed, then nodded. "I'll have more to say about this when I come back and talk with you tomorrow—well, it'll be today now. Can you spare me a lot of time today?"

"Yes, anything to help get to the bottom of this. Dani, I feel so, so violated."

Lieutenant Steele hugged her. "I know. Believe me, we'll find out what this is all about."

Lieutenant Steele thought a long moment before she said, "I may as well tell you now. I think the wall your husband had added has a flat room behind it, and if I'm right, then something could be hidden there. These people were looking for something I'm pretty sure. I want to bring in a carpenter to take the wall down. Do I have your permission?"

"Just do anything you need to do," Sherrie told her.

Sighing, Lieutenant Steele said, "You've got a mess on your hands to clean up. Do you have someone in mind who can do it after we finish sifting through?"

Sherrie nodded. "That part, at least, is easy. Mrs. Hall, my housekeeper, has a bunch of great relatives who're master cleaners. They'll get it done in a couple of days."

"Good."

The door chimes sounded and a policeman who stood nearby raised his eyebrows. "Would you like me to get that?" he asked Sherrie.

"Yes." Tears still choked her voice.

The policeman opened the door and Byron stood there, deep concern on his face. "I was passing, and I wondered what had happened," he said.

"A break-in," Sherrie told him. "You can see the results."

Without hesitation Byron came to her, his countenance hot with angry sympathy. Without thinking, he hugged her tightly. They had once been close friends. He would always be her friend. Her soft, now-fragile body against his brought up still sharper anger in him at who would cause her this grief. He hugged her more tightly than he knew.

In his arms, Sherrie relaxed against him. As he had thought about it, she reflected that they had once been close friends and she needed someone. For the moment, she forgot her fury at him and lived solely in the present. When he finally released her, saying, "God, I'm so sorry," she felt strengthened, more empowered than she would have dreamed.

"I'm going to leave an officer on duty here with you tonight and perhaps tomorrow night," Lieutenant Steele said. "I'll be back for a part of the day." She knew Byron well and said to him, "Keep an eye on her, will you?"

"I certainly will," he promised gravely.

The door chimes sounded again. This time the officer

answered and a medium-height man with very white skin and a mop of carrot-red curly hair stood there. Nap Kendrick.

"Why, Nap," Lieutenant Steele said, "what brings you by?"

The young man in his early thirties shrugged. "I happened to be passing, and I saw all the cop cars and wondered what was going on and if I could help."

Lieutenant Steele looked at him easily. Everybody knew Nap. An ex-postal worker now on disability because of a back wrenched on the job and improperly healed, he was available for errands. He had no close friends of which anyone knew and had never married or fathered children. He worked for Sherrie's friend Helena at Helping Hands. Considered an odd duck, he kept mostly to himself and seemed remarkably satisfied to have such a narrow life.

"I can't think of anything at the moment," Lieutenant Steele said, "but you never know. You might want to check with me at headquarters today sometime. Meanwhile, I've got to ask you to move on because we can't have anybody who's not a family member or a friend of the family here."

Nap's eyes flickered over Byron. "It's just that I work part-time with Ms. Helena Crane and she's a close friend of Mrs. Pinson's. She's like family, and I know Ms. Crane so well— like I said, I work with her."

"I know and thank you for offering to help. I'm sure you understand," Lieutenant Steele said more firmly. Nap saw her resolve and backed away, going out the door.

"I'll be sure to come to see you," he said over his shoulder to Lieutenant Steele.

The police were there the rest of the night and into the morning. Lieutenant Steele insisted that Sherrie get some rest. They would be there for most of the day sifting and packing evidence.

At the curb, Nap got into his white Chevy Blazer and drove a short distance up the road and parked. He could see Sher-

rie's house from there. His master would want to know what
was going down, what he had helped go down. The master
had been a real devil tonight. Furious, coveralled arms slash-
ing and smashing. There had only been the four of them. The
master. Nap. Li'l Al. And Poke Willman, a hired drifter from
New York who had once been a mob figure before he was
kicked out.

Sherrie Pinson was like his mother, he thought, with his
mouth tightening. She was a proud woman, secure in herself, but she hadn't looked so proud tonight, surveying the
wreckage of her house.

He had hated her from the beginning. Reeling with shock
that a second strange woman could look so much like his beautiful, now-dead mother, he had known he would hurt her *when*,
not *if* he could. He had bided his time. With incredible luck he
had met the master who hated her too. He didn't know why the
master hated her; it was enough that it was so.

When he lived in Philadelphia there had been a younger
woman who looked like his mother. He had stalked her,
choked her, left her for dead, but he'd read the papers, learned
she hadn't died and he'd fled the city.

No, Nap no longer questioned what the master did. The
master's strength was Nap's strength and he felt great about
that. Sometimes it seemed evil worked where good didn't.
The master was a high-level diamond smuggler who had paid
Nap beyond his wildest dreams. Savvy, suave, the master was
good to him like his father.

He wondered then what would have happened if Sherrie
Pinson had come in. But that wasn't likely. The master had
known how long she'd be gone and Poke served as lookout.

Still, Nap's mind kept pressing, what would have happened
if the woman had come back? She might have been hurt, and
that would have been fine with him.

Nap sighed. His mother was a beautiful brown, like Sherrie Pinson. His own too-white face sickened him the way his
mother had always said it sickened her. He and his beloved

father looked alike. His carrot-topped head drew too much attention, and his bright blue eyes filled him with loathing.

He laughed shortly. No, she hadn't stabbed or shot his father, but had worn him out with her unending hostility. His father with his sick heart. As a child growing up, his mother often stood with Nap before mirrors. "You complain I don't love you," she'd say. "Well, look and you'll see why. You look like your daddy, talk like him. You're him all over again, and he's disappointed me too often. Done nothing. Is nothing. A no-good bum." His father had been in the room as she'd said it often enough, and the last day, he'd keeled over in a fatal heart attack.

Chapter 6

Around eleven that morning, Sherrie tossed and struggled in a frightening dream. Mike was drowning and she swam toward him calling, "Stay afloat!" She reached him as he slipped under the waters for the third time. Her cry of pain swept over the waves as she came awake to her ringing phone. It was Byron.

"Sherrie, I'm sorry if I woke you. You sound really bothered. Can I help in any way?"

"Thank you, but I don't think so just now. You're kind."

"Was I right? Are you even more bothered than you were last night?"

She found herself wanting to tell him. "I had a terrible dream."

"Do you want to talk about it?"

She hesitated. "I can't. Not yet. It was . . . about Mike." Her voice went down in depression.

"I'm terribly sorry. If you want to talk at any time at all . . ."

"Thank you again. I've got to get up now. Danielle and other policemen will be by to sift evidence and question me."

"Sure. Remember what I said. I'm here for you. I'll be here."

Sherrie hung up and held the phone a few minutes. She was so mixed up. The night before she had gone into Byron's arms as if she belonged there. His touch had felt so comforting. He had taken away some of the fear. But he was Mike's enemy, and so hers too. He had indirectly caused Mike's death. She could never forget that. He was Tressa's godfather and they adored each other. He had made her unbearably sad little girl happy.

She was angry at herself for telling him about her dream, for sharing herself with him. Yet she felt a sharp, hungry need for him. When was it going to end?

Byron lay quiet in his bed for long moments after he hung up the phone. He was going in late. Sherrie didn't sound like a woman who hated him. She had clung to him the night before and let him comfort her. If only he could tell her what had really gone down between Mike and him. But she had a child to raise and she needed to keep the love she bore Mike. He sighed deeply. God, it was such a sorry mess. He hated the thought of her torn-up house, what had to be her fear.

He needed to walk a careful line—offer all the help he could, but not crowd her. Do what he had assured her he would do: Be there for her.

Lieutenant Steele came at ten. Sherrie noted her somber face, but did not comment on it.

"Come in," Sherrie said. "Have some coffee with me."

"I could use another cup. Did you get any sleep?"

"A little. I had a bad dream about Mike, but I don't want to talk about it yet."

Lieutenant Steele looked at her sharply. "I understand. Is there someplace we can be alone? I need to talk with you."

"No one's here. Tressa's in school and staying with Helena. Mrs. Hall is rounding up relatives to help me clean up this mess, and if she comes in, we can talk in my bedroom or in the den."

"Good."

Noting the tenseness of the other woman, Sherrie ventured, "Has something else happened?"

Lieutenant Steele wet her lips. "Let's have a cup of coffee first."

Sherrie poured the Colombian coffee. She knew Danielle

took her coffee black with natural sugar. She liked thick skim milk in hers and natural sugar. "I've got great pineapple tarts. Could I tempt you?"

Lieutenant Steele smiled slightly. "Hit me with one. Have you had breakfast?"

"I couldn't eat anything heavy. Later perhaps."

The women ate in near silence with the sound of spring birds chirping on a nearby tree limb and bright sunlight coming through the kitchen windows.

When they had finished, Lieutenant Steele looked down at the table a long while. "Sherrie," she began, "I know how much you loved your husband."

"Love, not past tense."

"Yes. A little after eleven the carpenters will be here to open the wall, and we'll see what we find. I hate being the one to hurt you, but we've discovered evidence that Mike was going high up in a diamond smuggling ring."

Sherrie's head jerked up with shock. "No," she protested, "Mike wouldn't . . ."

Lieutenant Steele's eyes were kind, tender on her friend. "I've done a lot of digging. This information has been late reaching us. A man in state prison is singing like a nightingale to save his hide. A man I helped send up—Buck Lansing—is helping me with this, trying to get his sentence cut. Maybe it's not as bad as we think, but it's bad enough. Did Mike drink heavily? Do you know?"

Sherrie laughed harshly, tears in her voice. "My husband did everything wrong in the last year of his life. He was crushed, Dani, savaged. Byron Tate forced him out of Tate Cosmetics and he couldn't take it. Yes, he drank heavily. That much I know. Oh God, there were women . . ."

"Women? Do you know who they were?"

Sherrie laughed mirthlessly. "Begin with Mallori."

Lieutenant Steele looked up, her mouth a little open with surprise. "Your sister, Mallori?"

"Yes, my sister, Mallori. According to her, he was leaving me and they were going to be married."

"Did you confront him? Did you have reason to believe her?"

"Yes, I had reason to believe her and yes, I confronted him. He cried, said he was so mixed up, he couldn't help himself, that he felt empty, desperate in his own private hell. I threatened to leave, and he begged me to stay. He pointed out what an idyllic courtship and marriage we had had up to then. Mike could be very persuasive."

"And you loved him. That makes such a difference."

"I love him." She had said that shortly before. Now that love coiled itself around her heart and squeezed it nearly dry. Was Mike guilty of what Danielle had just said he was? She couldn't see it, but then she couldn't see his behavior in the year before he died.

Sherrie thought a moment before she went on. "Mike was ambitious. The rift between him and Byron left him hungry to best him, to have more money, more clout. He was setting up a rival business of his own. Mike was a wealthy doctor's son, and his father gave him plenty of money before he died. Mike set me up in business; he was lavish. But by the time his father died there were bad foreign investments and there wasn't nearly the money he had counted on. He was hurt about that. Of course, as the sole survivor, I thought he got a tidy share, but he didn't think so."

She paused a moment. "I don't want to believe it, but a straight-thinking part of me tells me what you've said is likely to be true, given his frame of mind."

"We think the diamond smuggling may tie in with his being murdered. He may have betrayed someone. They can play rough."

"You said he was high up."

"Yes. Mike was a brilliant guy. He would have made it his business to know everything about whatever he went into. He was charming, and as you said, persuasive. He would have been invaluable."

Lieutenant Steele leaned forward. "There's something else," she said. "Your accountant, Tucker Weeks, is involved here. He and Mike were such great friends. We're still tracing Tucker, but he's been as crafty as Mike was. Just be careful. We're not sure just how high up he is."

Sherrie felt so stunned she could hardly breathe. "People like the ones we're talking about here know how to hide their tracks well, I would imagine. Will we ever know who killed Mike?" She sounded wistful.

"You're right. It's going to be hard. They're hard-nosed, but so are we. Our intelligence tells us Mike was going deep into diamond smuggling, and it can be dangerous. The Minden police force is one of the finest in the nation. If it can be done, Sherrie, we'll do it." She took her friend's hand, squeezed it. "I'll be talking with you off and on all afternoon."

Each woman had another cup of coffee, with Lieutenant Steele switching to raspberry-chocolate. Sherrie sat digesting the latest news. She had picked up a few things off the floor in the kitchen, but it was still in disarray. And in her mind's eye she could still see the slashed portrait, had seen it the rest of the night. She had laid it facedown on the sofa, glad that Tressa hadn't been with her.

Lieutenant Steele's eyes went very sad then. "I'm going to ask you to be very careful. There may be a tie between what Mike was involved in, his murder and this break-in."

Sherrie felt a wave of icy cold wrap around her. She couldn't speak.

"You haven't gotten any strange phone calls, any threatening letters?"

"No."

Lieutenant Steele shook her head. "That's good. It's times like this when I hate our budget constraints. I need more evidence to assign you an officer, but I'll work on it. We have so much going on. Let me ask you something else: You spoke of bad blood between your husband and Byron Tate, yet he came by to offer help. . . ."

"We were the closest of friends once. He still tries to be close. Perhaps one day I can forgive him."

And, looking at her, Lieutenant Steele wondered if Sherrie hadn't gone much further on the road to forgiveness than she knew.

They heard the sounds of Mrs. Hall letting herself in and the middle-aged, salt-and-pepper-haired woman spoke to Lieutenant Steele and came swiftly to Sherrie's side, hugging her tightly, rocking her.

Mrs. Hall looked around her in consternation. "My Lord, I never would have believed . . . But never mind, I've contacted all the relatives I need and we'll have this place back ship-shape in a couple of days. Lieutenant, you're going to need to poke about?"

"Yes, we are, but you can begin cleaning up tomorrow. We should get through here by late afternoon."

"Then we'll start late this afternoon. It isn't healthy to have to look at this evil mess. Will you be able to find out who did it?"

"There's always a good chance we will. We have networks linked to networks. We're nothing if not thorough."

Mrs. Hall sighed deeply. "I'm glad Tressa wasn't here. She'd be a long time getting over this. I'm going to look around. You said Mr. Pinson's portrait was slashed. What a sick human being, if he could be called human."

The carpenters came at the time Lieutenant Steele expected them, shortly after eleven. They set to work immediately.

Beforehand, Lieutenant Steele told Sherrie, "If we find something in there, I'll want there to be just you and me to look at it. Will you tell Mrs. Hall that, and if we find anything, I'll send the carpenters outside."

"Yes. Danielle, I'm so scared, and I'm so glad you're the one investigating."

Lieutenant Steele hugged her. "So am I, love. So am I."

Sherrie went out into the kitchen and told Mrs. Hall what Lieutenant Steele had requested.

"I understand," Mrs. Hall said. "I intend to cooperate all the way through. Anything you need from me, you've got. Always. And Sherrie, I'm sorrier than you'll ever know."

It didn't take long for the carpenters to break the curved wall down. Sherrie stood transfixed as she stared at narrow shelves and a lone, medium-size suitcase that sat on one of them. Stepping forward, Danielle tried the suitcase and found it locked.

"Do you know of a possible key?" Lieutenant Steele asked.

"No. Just break it open."

The carpenter got his tools and popped the lock. After he left, Lieutenant Steele opened the lid of the suitcase and drew in a sharp breath. Stacks of banded crisp green bills filled most of the case. There was a small chamois bag tucked in one corner.

"So I was right," Lieutenant Steele said.

"Good Lord," Sherrie breathed. "How much do you think is there?"

"From my experience, I'd say between two and three hundred thousand dollars." She loosened the drawstring of the bag, scooped up hard rocks and exclaimed, "Rough, uncut diamonds, worth a small fortune."

Sherrie felt sick with disappointment. This man was the father of her only child. He had been her husband, lover, friend, and she had loved him above all others. "Dear God, Mike," she whispered to herself, "what had you become?"

Lieutenant Steele got on her cell phone then and asked for additional officers. Wanting to busy herself, Sherrie went to the kitchen to find the two carpenters drinking Mrs. Hall's special lemonade and grinning happily. She wondered if she would ever smile again.

Moving restlessly back to the living room, she found Lieutenant Steele seated on the sofa, examining the money and the diamonds. Finally she put the bag back in place and closed the suitcase as Sherrie sat beside her.

Reaching over, Lieutenant Steele took her friend's hand. "I keep saying it, but I'm so sorry. You don't deserve this." Faint tears stood in her eyes.

Sherrie took a deep breath, trying to comfort herself. "They say that God sends us nothing that we cannot bear." Then fiercely, "I'll get through this, Danielle. I've got a little girl to take care of."

Lieutenant Steele squeezed her friend's hand. "We'll be getting started now. I think that's my crew pulling up outside. We'll be in your way, but overlook us. Why don't you try to eat a little something more? You need to keep up your strength."

Dully Sherrie wondered why she kept feeling Byron Tate's arms around her, holding her. Why did she keep feeling and, yes, needing his massive strength?

Chapter 7

On her birthday that following Saturday, Tressa was a happy bundle of activity. All day her little body thrummed, and by very late afternoon, a bit before dark, she was joy personified. Byron had called to say he had a bit of car trouble and would be along shortly. Sherrie and Helena were in the family room with Tressa who delightedly played with the huge stuffed panda Helena had bought her at the Washington Zoo. Balloons were set about, and the odor of white and red carnations was rich and spicy.

Sherrie had bought books and games; she was big on birthdays. At the last minute she had ordered Tressa's favorite chocolate fudge cake and bought Ben and Jerry's chocolate chip ice cream. The little girl who had been so unhappy lately had undergone a nearly complete metamorphosis. Now she sparkled.

Tressa came to Sherrie and leaned against her as Sherrie stroked the thin shoulders that felt boneless. Tressa held out her hand with her new ring, an aquamarine birthstone set in eighteen-karat gold, another present from Helena. "It's so pretty," she said.

Helena looked at her godchild and smiled. "Well, if you really think so, then come give me a hug."

Giggling, Tressa moved to Helena's side and hugged her. "Thank you, Aunt Helena," she said. "I love both my gifts." Then she fretfully turned to her mother. "When is Uncle Bye coming? He said he'd be here."

"Give him time, love," Sherrie said. "Don't be so impatient."

"Okay." Tressa moved to an alcove of the family room to play with the panda, and Helena moved closer to Sherrie.

"You're looking a little peaked," Helena said. "And with all you've got on you, I don't wonder. Oh, Shere, to have had the break-in and be told what Danielle told you about Michael . . . It's a killer trip to lay on you."

"It just feels unreal," Sherrie said slowly. "That there may be a tie-in really worries me. Danielle wonders if I'm not in at least some danger. I didn't tell you that."

Helena looked at her friend with alarm. "Danger?"

"Illicit diamond dealers don't fight fair. I guess if they think Mike had something that belonged to them, they'd want to recover it. I don't know what's going down, Helena. These are some of the bleakest days of my life—second only to when they found Mike dead. I got through that; with God's help, I'll get through this." Then in a choked voice she said, "But I keep wondering how."

"Have you talked with Byron again?"

"He's called several times. He's really tried to be helpful."

"I've always considered him a good guy. I only wish I knew his side of the story with Mike. Please don't get upset at my saying this."

Sherrie nodded. "He shook up the sled at the top of the mountain, and it smashed Mike at the bottom of the slope. I can't forget that. Mike changed, Helena. You know he changed. He would never in this world have been involved in something like diamond smuggling. He was a quintessential good guy."

"I always thought so."

The musical door chimes rang and Tressa leaped out of the alcove, crying, "I'm going to let Uncle Bye in!"

"Wait!" Sherrie admonished her. "It may not be Uncle Bye. You're such an impatient birthday girl. I'll go with you."

They found an out-of-breath Mallori at the door. Tressa looked at her, tilting her head to one side. "Hello, Aunt Mallori. I thought you were Uncle Bye."

Mallori laughed, bent and hugged Tressa. "And hello to you too. I'm not Uncle Bye, but I have something for you." She held out a shiny red-and-white bag from a ritzy department store, saying, "Happy birthday."

Tressa took the bag, thanked Mallori and ran back down to the family room as Mallori stood. "I've been racing for a couple of days now. Lord, I'm beat. Look, Sis, I'm so sorry about the break-in."

"That was Wednesday night. It's Saturday now. I haven't heard from you," Sherrie said evenly.

Mallori sighed. "Oh Lord, I've been out of town, and my new man is an ardent pursuer. My time isn't my own anymore. I really can't stay, but I've been thinking about what you said about us being closer. I'd like that." She sounded wistful.

Sherrie hugged her. "That's good. You're changing. Now will you change enough to go with Gus and talk to a marriage counselor?"

Mallori shook her head quickly. "No way. At some time I'll be moving out, but what the hell, there's no rush. Listen, I'll only be able to stay for a little of the refreshments. Then I've got to run."

"Mallori, we were talking about you and Gus. You're seeing another man and Gus is hotheaded. That's a dangerous combination."

Mallori smiled prettily. "Trust me to handle Gus. Haven't I always?" She suddenly became aware of the missing portrait. "You seem to have straightened up everything, but where is Mike's portrait? Did the creeps steal it?"

"It was badly slashed. The police took it for evidence."

Mallori's eyes went wide and she said nothing for a minute, then she swallowed hard. "Slashed. Someone slashed Mike's portrait? Gus told me about the break-in. He didn't tell me that, and I know it made him happy."

Mallori got very quiet then and Sherrie could almost see her brain working. Consternation and horror and, yes—Sherrie was certain—recognition lay on her sister's face. Mallori got around. As the wife of a police sergeant, she heard plenty.

"Can you think of anyone who might have done this?" Sherrie asked.

Mallori shook her head too quickly, and her voice went hoarse. "No. No one." She drew a deep breath and changed the subject. "I passed Byron Tate's car on the way over. It seems he's having car trouble."

"Yes, he called. He's coming over to bring Tressa a gift."

Mallori looked at her coolly. "You're letting him come here after what happened—after what he did to Mike? Sherrie, how could you?"

"He's her godfather and they love each other. Tressa's been very unhappy. He's helped her so much. She's happier now."

"Still, I hate the thought of him having the nerve to be around you and Tressa."

"He came by the night of the break-in. He was helpful then too." Mallori didn't know about Mike's being a suspect in drug dealing.

"I'd say limit the contact. Stay clear of him, Sis. He'll destroy you the way he destroyed Mike. Surely you know that. Listen, I'm going to have a bit of the ice cream and cake I'm sure you have, just to mollify Tressa, then I've got to go."

Sherrie looked at her sister carefully. She had seemed a little rushed when she came in. Now she seemed positively wired, and Sherrie was certain this had begun when they talked about the slashed portrait.

In the kitchenette of the family room Tressa scooped up ice cream for Mallori and cut her cake, then with Sherrie's help took it to her. The rest of them would wait for Byron, Sherrie decided, shrugging as she wondered why she waited to serve the rest of the refreshments.

Again and again Tressa went back to the chair where her present lay. The soft yellow dress with darker yellow rosebuds scattered all over would go wonderfully well with the little girl's skin and hair.

"Is this dress easy care?" Sherrie asked.

"The easiest. I checked the label," Mallori said. "You and Mrs. Hall are home free."

Mallori had gone by the time an apologetic Byron arrived with an oversize dark blue package. This time when Tressa answered the door with Sherrie, she was not disappointed. She flung her thin arms around Byron and hugged him with all her might. "Oh, Uncle Bye," she squealed. "You came! And that's my present? It's so big."

Squatting, Byron thought that this precious child always hit him where he lived.

"You bet it's big," he said, "and you bet it's beautiful. All the way from Russia. Now hurry on and open it."

Tressa moved off with her big but lightweight package in tow. "Aren't you coming?" she asked. "I'm going to slide it down the banister."

"In just a minute," he told her. She didn't seem to want him out of her sight.

Drawing a deep breath, Byron looked around him. He hadn't been back since the night of the break-in. "How're you holding up?" he asked gently. "You look a little tired." His eyes lingered on her with warmth and concern. "I keep saying it, but I have to. If there's anything I can do to help . . ."

"Thank you. You've already helped me more than you know. As for my being tired, the shop is busier than ever, and the police have a world of questions. I'll get through this, but you've been great."

Again Tressa and Sherrie served the ice cream and cake and took it back to the family room where Tressa's newest acquisition—a Russian nesting doll—sat on a chair in all its glory. The doll was nearly Tressa's almond color, with brown eyes and short, curly earth-brown hair. The doll's features were like Tressa's. As the grown-ups ate their refreshments, Tressa sat on a hassock in front of the doll.

"I had it specially made for you," Byron said. "Most Russian nesting dolls are white. This one, as you can see, is brown."

"And she's so beautiful," Sherrie and Helena both said.

The doll was beautiful. Setting aside his ice cream and cake for the moment, Byron showed them the doll's intricacies. Inside the big doll a smaller one was nestled, then inside that was another smaller one, all alike down to a slender, delicately fashioned, perfect wisp.

"It must have cost you a small fortune to have this made," Sherrie told him.

"She's worth every penny. Dmitri Borodin, Russia's finest doll maker, did me the honor. He worked from a photo of Tressa. I ordered it nearly a year ago."

"It's certainly a work of art," Helena said admiringly. "You have great taste."

"Thanks. I want her to be happy."

When he said it, Sherrie felt a lump in her throat.

Tressa left her dolls long enough to come and stand at Byron's knee. "You said there'd be another doll later."

"Tressa!" Sherrie admonished her, smiling. "You're getting greedy in your old age."

Tressa threw back her head and her eyes nearly closed with giggling laughter. "I'm not old. *You're* old. I'm just six today."

"So you are, and I certainly feel old when I'm traipsing around after you."

Byron pulled Tressa onto his lap. "Let's play handcar," she chortled.

"Okay," he said, agreeing to a game his father had taught him.

As Sherrie and Helena took the dishes to the kitchenette, Byron positioned Tressa on his knees facing him, took her little hands, one in each of his and held her. She leaned far back, then came forward again and again, saying delightedly, "Handcar! Handcar! Handcar, babee. Handcar!" She never got enough of the game.

When the two women finished putting the dishes in the dishwasher, Helena said she had to go. "Nap's running a puppet show tonight for a bunch of kids. He's a whiz with them—the puppets and the kids."

"He's a talented man," Sherrie said.

"Yes, he is. I only wish he could find himself."

Shrugging, Sherrie offered, "Perhaps in time."

With Tressa in dreamland, Sherrie found she didn't want Byron to go. What was with her? she wondered crossly. Her daughter had clung to him enough, requesting a bed-time story from one of her new books. He had graciously acquiesced, reading in his rich, warm baritone voice, act-ing out the characters, making Tressa laugh. Sherrie wanted to tell him about Mike: the diamond smuggling possibil-ity and what the police had said. She liked that he made Tressa laugh the ways he did. She wanted him out of her life. And she wanted him to stay.

When he did say he was leaving, she found herself sud-denly telling him what Danielle had told her about Mike. She couldn't keep it from him. He didn't seem surprised. "Did you guess?" she demanded. "Did you know?"

"I knew a lot of things were going on with Mike," he said quietly. "I didn't know exactly what, but I knew enough."

"Is that why you let him go? Turned your back on him?"

"No. I wasn't sure of that. There were other things."

"Then what? I've said it a thousand times. Mike changed when he lost you. He was a strong man, but not as strong as you. He needed others. He needed you. You were closer than most twins, Byron. What happened?"

Byron's sigh came from his heart. "One day I'll tell you, but not now. You've got too much to contend with now."

His eyes got dreamy then as he told her, "I remember a long time ago when I visited relatives in New Orleans. I met you and fell hard. Remember?"

"Yes, I remember dating you, but you didn't, as you say,

'fall hard.' We talked, sat in our garden swing, took in a few movies. . . ."

"We kissed a few times."

"Lightly. I thought you had a girl back home. You were a prize catch."

"Your father had just died, and I didn't want to come on too strong."

"You were so thoughtful, so kind. You brought me flowers and candy."

"I was smitten, then Mike blew into town, and you fell hard and not for me."

She stood there bemused. She hadn't known. From the beginning the charismatic Michael Pinson had been her passion. Now she was sick with disillusion and despair.

They were still standing and Byron moved closer; she didn't move away. A sweet torpor crept over her at his nearness; at his muscular, fit body; at his warmth. His pale blue-gray eyes were haunted under the high, square olive forehead, and his curved, sensuous mouth watered with desire for her. He reached out and held the back of her head in one of his big hands, his other hand splayed against the middle of her back. His lips on hers were gentle, tender. The kiss lasted a couple of minutes, but she pushed him away.

"Don't punish me for loving you," he whispered.

Her breath came too fast. What had he just said? Loving her? Now? He had never spoken of love in the time she had known him before Michael had swept her off her feet. She held him responsible for Mike's fall from grace. She turned her mouth away.

"This can't happen again," she told him. "I won't let it happen again."

He stared at her a long moment, not understanding what stormed through his mind, his tense body. She was here, and he loved her, had known that from the beginning. Dead somber, he caught her to him fiercely. "If you won't let it happen again," he said, "then I'm going to kiss you now the way I've always wanted to."

She found she had no will to fight him as his big hands roamed her back. His mouth and his tongue claimed her like the alpha male he was. Shocking passion gripped her, racked her body, and she answered him kiss for kiss. Then easing after long moments, he told her huskily, "Shere, I'm sorry. I had no right to force myself on you. I was wrong. So wrong."

But she clung to him and couldn't let him go. Her soft arms fastened around his neck, her firm breasts pressed against his chest as he groaned, lifting his head from hers only long enough to tell her, "I love you. I've always loved you."

His words were like honey to her spirit, sweet, soothing the hurt she had known so long. Flames licked at her belly even as passion filled her heart. Blind with desire, she began to open to him, letting him deep into her heart. The soft, spicy scent of carnations and his masculine aftershave filled her nostrils. It was quiet, so quiet she could hear the steady beating of both their hearts as they clung to each other.

Byron was raw with wanting her. Every cell of him sought to take her, make love to her until they were both spent with ecstasy. He had always wanted her. Now he needed her with a desperation that frightened him. And he knew at least a part of her saw him as the enemy. He longed to put an end to that, but she had a child to raise, and she needed to hang on to every shred of respect for Mike she could. At least he wouldn't be the source of disappointment in her child's father.

She tried to pull away and couldn't, went even closer until she shook with suddenly wanting him inside her. Her longing struck through to the marrow of her bones.

Slowly, reluctantly they finally pulled apart and stood facing each other, still close. Byron took her face in his hands, as her slender hands pressed the back of his. "You're not angry with me for kissing you like that?"

She didn't hesitate. She felt both calm and turbulent. "I'm not angry. It was something we both wanted. I'm so mixed up, Byron. I am still angry at what happened between you and Mike, but you say you'll tell me more and I'll wait for you to do that . . . and I know so much more now."

"I hate having you caught up in something like this," he said harshly. "You don't deserve this, but bad things do happen to good people."

"Thank you and thank you so much for helping Tressa and me."

"I want to do everything for you."

His words warmed her, buoyed her. Gravely she thought this was the beginning of . . . what? And what was going to be the end?

Chapter 8

Ten days after Tressa's birthday, Sherrie went in to My Beautiful Self early. By eight o'clock customers had begun to trickle in, and the air was rich with the aroma of German meat-and-vegetable pies in the oven of the well-equipped kitchen. This odor mingled with the first-rate perfumes and cosmetics supplied by Tate. The buzzer sounded and Dora, the young doorkeeper and general helper, let two people in, a customer and Tucker Weeks, Sherrie's accountant. Sherrie greeted the customer and an operator took over. Katherine came from the back. Tucker, a tall, slender man with light brown skin and fashionably styled soft brown curly hair, hugged Sherrie lightly and whistled at Katherine. Joking, he pawed the floor.

"The Queen of Sheba," he teased. "Girl, if I weren't taken, I'd give you a run for your money. You're top shelf in the beauty department."

Katherine and Sherrie looked at each other, smiling; that was Tucker most of the time when he came in.

"Be careful," Katherine said. "Remember my husband's six-feet-four and he's an ex-football player. Also, he's got a temper."

Still teasing, Tucker mockingly cringed, but said, "I'd risk it."

Looking at him, Sherrie remembered Lieutenant Steele's words but stayed calm, asking, "Since when are you taken? You're not telling us everything."

He touched her shoulder. "*You* took me over—my heart, that is—not too long after we began working together." His eyes got somber then and Sherrie frowned. Tucker had a thing for her, no doubt about that. He dated many women and was considered a prize catch, but he had never affected her that way.

"We'll always be friends," Sherrie said easily, "and you're the best."

Tucker looked at her with longing. "Poor consolation, babe."

Katherine moved away and Sherrie asked him, "What brings you by so early?"

"Just wanted to tell you in person the good news about your great cash flow and because I always want to see your beautiful face and great body."

"Flatterer. I'm glad the cash flow is good. We certainly try hard enough. We run a topflight show here, and it isn't always easy. We spend, but we're also good at saving."

"Plus, you're raking it in. Congratulations on the way the aromatherapy room is picking up steam."

"It's going to be one of our best moneymakers." He looked at her and said, "Have a late bite with me at Scarf's. They've got ground venison burgers, and they're fabulous. You don't get out enough."

Sherrie nodded. "Why not? But I can't stay out long."

He bowed, lifted her hand and kissed it as she laughed.

"A minute with you is worth a day with another woman," he said gallantly. Tucker looked at his watch. "My sister's coming by. She's supposed to meet me here, and I want to introduce you."

As if on cue, the buzzer sounded and in a minute Dora escorted one of the most beautiful women Sherrie had seen. This was Jasmine Hill, retiring topflight model, a woman in her thirties she'd seen on television, in newspapers and magazines. She was as smooth as she was gorgeous. The woman had long black hair some women would envy. Dressed in a simple white pantsuit, her flawless beige skin, burnished with good health and the best the cosmetics world had to offer, she glowed.

"I'm just in for a facial and a trim," she said in a deep, throaty cultured drawl. "Your place is beautiful. If I weren't moving here, I'd insist you move to New York."

Sherrie laughed. She found she didn't altogether like this woman. Her smile never reached her eyes, and she was imperious to a fault. Sherrie had read that she was recently divorced. She found herself saying, "You know, I feel we should pay you for coming in. You'll be a walking ad for our work."

Jasmine accepted the compliment; she was used to headier ones.

"Become friends with this woman, Jazz," Tucker told his sister. "One day you may be sisters-in-law."

"Tucker!" Sherrie exclaimed.

"Don't be embarrassed," Jasmine reassured her. "My brother's a Romeo. I hope I can get started soon. I'm in a bit of a rush."

Sherrie got an operator and the beauteous Jasmine moved off. Giving Sherrie a sly smile, Tucker said he'd meet her at two.

Sherrie stood with her back to the door, pouring a cup of green tea and squeezing a quarter of a lemon into it when a hand touched her shoulder. She turned to face Gus.

"Hey, Gus Dueñas," she said, "good morning." She pronounced it *Daway-nyas*. "You look like you've lost your best friend."

"Buenos días," he said. "Try wife."

Lionel Richie's moving voice serenaded them with "Lady" as Gus's shoulders slumped. "I've always liked that song," he said.

"It's one of his best. What's going on, Gus?"

"You mean what's going down."

"Do you want to talk about it? We can go to my office."

He shook his head. "I'm in for a scissors cut. Can you put me in a corner? You don't seem to do unisex."

Sherrie chuckled. "We have a few male customers, but we don't advertise it. The ladies like their privacy. The men we take are special. Sure we can work you in. You're on a later shift?"

"Yeah, three to eleven."

"We've moved away from the subject. What's going on between you and Mallori?"

"I'm thinking of moving out. She's kept threatening to—"

"I'm sorry to hear that. Gus, would you be willing to see a marriage counselor? I hear Dr. Will Casey is very, very good. He's retired, but he sees a few people."

Gus's voice broke as he said, "God, Sherrie, I'd try anything." He was silent a long while, his eyes bleak. "I came home and found her and this cat coming out of the apartment. I know him, Shere. He's a Baltimore cop. We've swapped case info a number of times, and he's a real bastard. A noted player. A *sinverguenza*."

"*Sin-ver what?*" Sherrie asked. "Spell and translate, please."

Grinning wryly, he spelled the Spanish term for her. "It means the worst of the scoundrels."

He drew a deep breath and went on, "Anyway, he was slick and not a bit upset. I don't know how long they'd been there or what went down."

He seemed to choke on his words, and his voice was guttural. "I told her if it happened again, I wouldn't be responsible. He grinned, told me to take it easy. She laughed at me. The hell of it is, Sherrie, I feel like I'm losing it. I could feel myself taking Mallori out, taking this guy out. . . ."

"Gus, get it under control."

He smiled crookedly then. "You help me, Lieutenant Steele helps me, Captain Ryson. I've got good friends. Don't worry. I'll make it. I'll come around to talk sometime soon. You're getting busy now, and I'm drained."

"You do that, and like you said, soon. Have you eaten?"

"Nope. What're you offering?"

"German meat pies. Danish pastries. Doughnuts. You're in luck."

"You're a godsend. I find myself starving. Hit me with a meat pie, and thank you."

Dora got an operator for Gus and went to the kitchen to get a hot meat pie for him before asking him his choice of drinks. Sherrie stood near the door, pleased at the morning's beginning when the door buzzer sounded. Sherrie answered it to find River West.

"River," she greeted her, "you're always one of my late customers."

"Oh, I'm by early because I made a quickie appointment yesterday, and I've got something special I want your opinion on."

"I haven't had a chance to look over my list for the day. You're always welcome. Now which would you like to do first, opinion or appointment?"

"Could we talk in your office?"

"We can."

In Sherrie's office, Sherrie asked Dora to bring River the strong, black coffee she favored. River opened her purse and took out a slender vial, opened it and moved it slowly back and forth near Sherrie's nose as they stood.

"Oh good Lord, this is heavenly," Sherrie said enthusiastically.

"Like it?"

"It's wonderful! Rich. Affecting. It'll make strong men weak."

River giggled, overjoyed.

"Is there a story behind this perfume? If so, please tell me."

The two women sat on tub chairs side by side. Dora brought in the coffee and River sipped it and began.

"I've really caught it with this one. African-American women are apt to have trouble with hyperpigmentation with so many products. At Tate, we bend over backwards to find safe products. I've worked my can off, but I think I've got something. I'm finishing in time for it to be well advertised and distributed by the August ball. Byron is so pleased."

At the mention of Byron's name, Sherrie flushed. Why did she still feel his kiss? Shouldn't it have faded by now?

"It mimics pheromones," River said, "you know, the substance that all animals produce to attract the opposite sex."

"Yes."

"Lord, so many perfumes have up to two hundred substances. This one has one hundred ninety. Count them. I had gone with rose oil as a base, but although it's a favorite, I was never satisfied. Then I tried sandalwood and voilà, it worked like a charm. I don't know what took me so long. I tried so many. Do you really like it?"

"Love it. No wonder some of the world's best companies keep trying to lure you away from Tate. You're superb."

"Thank you. Now, I need further help."

"Name it."

"Name—that's it. I need a winning name for this great perfume."

"Let me put it in my creative womb. I'm sure together we can come up with something good." Then, unexpectedly, her mind spun enthusiastically as she said, "How about Black Magic? That's what it is."

River looked radiant. "Thanks a lot, Sherrie. I really appreciate this. Now, I've got to get my trim and get back to work." As always, her curly brown hair looked lovely.

River left then as Sherrie found herself thinking about the slender woman. Fit and attractive, her pale skin was bolstered by the best that Tate offered. The company created perfection in creams and lotions, and she used them to her advantage.

Sherrie thought then about something she hadn't let herself think about too much. Byron. He had called every day after Tressa's birthday as she had grown more rattled and confused. She couldn't get the sheer feel of him from her mind. The image of his big, fit and muscular body seemed to press in on her constantly and, make no mistake about it, she reached for him, responded vividly to him. Then he had backed away a bit, said he'd give her time to think things through, but he wanted her to call him if she needed, wanted anything at all. That was sweet. His declaration of love had been shocking, but she didn't lie to herself. It lifted her, even as it scared her. Hurt and disappointed at what she'd been told about Mike, she still reeled with shock and heartbreak. But thoughts of Byron struck through like rays of sunlight. Mike had betrayed her badly before he died, had hurt her beyond belief. Would it never end?

And Tressa. Her daughter constantly asked about her uncle Bye. She called him, demanded to know when he was coming by again and why couldn't she visit him.

Sherrie got up and went back out into the salon. The place was full. She spent the rest of the morning greeting customers, selling cosmetics, giving the expert advice on beauty for which she was famous.

At twelve-thirty she went back to her office for a brief rest. She had hardly gotten settled with the *Post* style section when Dora knocked and stuck her head in the door. "You have a visitor," she said, "a Mr. Winters. Are you free?"

Sherrie's breath caught with surprise. "Send him in and please hold my calls."

The first thing she noticed was that Curt Winters looked bothered. He was his usual debonair self, but definitely bothered.

"Hello, Curt. I'm glad to see you." She offered her hand. He took it, held it in his firm grip a minute before he said, "I'll try not to take up too much of your time since it's the first day of your workweek. I'm here on a mission, a meddler's mission, but a necessary one."

"Oh? Please have a seat."

Curt sat down in a chair beside hers and leaned toward her, one fist in the other hand. "It's about Byron—and you. And yes, Mike."

Sherrie sat up straighter then, listening.

"Byron loves you, Sherrie. He has for a long time, and I think you love him."

He didn't wait for an answer as Sherrie flushed hotly. "You blame him for what happened to Mike, but he'd never tell you the truth. He doesn't want to break your heart. Mike had gone bad before Byron asked him to leave. That's why he asked him to leave. Top men in a company are monitored carefully, Sherrie. They have to be because they can take a company under if they're headed in the wrong direction, doing wrong things.

"We began to find out things about Mike more than a year before Byron let him go. We couldn't prove anything, but there were shocking allegations of something about diamonds we were never able to pin down. Mike seemed to be involved high up. It might have been to pay back money he'd been embezzling from Tate."

"Embezzling?" Sherrie's voice was hoarse. Her shoulders hunched involuntarily. Lieutenant Steele had told her about the diamond smuggling only.

"Yes. We found he was stealing money from Tate. It was a mess. I thought it would kill Byron. At first Mike denied it, until he couldn't. He agreed to leave, said he'd pay back the money. . . ."

"And did he?"

Curt shook his head. "No. Byron paid it back and refused to prosecute. I wanted to, as much as I cared for Mike. I trained him. I was mentor to Byron *and* him. Mike was half my heart; Byron is the other. As you know, I am a widower. I have no children."

Sherrie put her head in her hands and wept unashamedly. Curt stood and put his arms around her shoulders. "I'm sorry," he said, "but you needed to know. Byron has wanted to shield you, but there are some things we cannot be shielded from. He feels you need to love Mike as best you can because of Tressa. I feel you will know how to handle this, that you will find ways. Meanwhile, you *and* he are hurting. You and Byron can help each other."

The crying eased, and he handed her a Kleenex tissue from a box on her desk.

"I've hurt you, I know. Will you be all right?"

"I'll be all right. And Curt?"

"Yes."

"Thank you."

"As I said, it's something you need to know. You're a gutsy woman, Sherrie. You'll pull through this. You've always had strong faith in God. It pulled you through Mike's death and it will pull you through this. I'm going to stay a few minutes longer. Call Byron. Talk with him."

She nodded, thinking he couldn't know how much she wanted to call Byron.

Sherrie didn't call. The salon was hectic that afternoon, and she busied herself. She also rushed for lunch with Tucker. And in the back of her mind, she wondered what she would say to Byron. His kisses had blocked their being to each other what they once had been. There was new territory, thrilling, exalting, heady, and she wasn't sure she was ready for it. But they had to talk. The next day perhaps. Certainly soon.

At lunch, Tucker was in rare form. He told her his latest droll jokes, and she found herself thinking that he was her enemy.

He leaned toward her. "We have the place almost to ourselves. Too bad there isn't a dance floor. Sherrie, have dinner with me soon. I want to press my case."

Sherrie felt nervous. She always did when he got too close.

"Please don't push me away. You and Mike and I were so close after Byron betrayed him. It didn't take me long to fall in love with you after Mike was gone. I'm not going to bite my tongue about it."

"We're friends," she said honestly. "But I'm not in love with you."

"You could be if you stopped holding me off."

Frowning, she thought about what Curt Winters had told her about Mike, and about Byron.

Tucker watched her with a puzzled look on his face as Byron's face and virile body rose in her fantasy. He said he loved her and she was attracted beyond the telling. "I have to be blunt," she said. "We're friends, Tucker. We can never be more."

"Doesn't my loving you mean anything to you?"

Her eyes on him were kind, sympathetic. "You need to find someone else. You're such an attractive man. You have lots of choices."

He threw up his hands. "You're my only choice."

"Tucker, please."

"Okay. I'll stop. I don't want to badger you, but remember what I've said. I've said it before. We work well together. We make a great team."

"I've got to run," she said. "The lunch was delicious, and thank you."

"You're very welcome. Have dinner with me soon."

"I'll certainly think about it."

She left and, walking back to her salon, reflected that Byron had knocked all other men from her mind. Was she falling in love with him?

She was thoroughly tired that night when she got home to find Tressa in a fretful state. Tressa was in her room desultorily playing with the Russian nesting dolls. She didn't look up as Sherrie entered the room.

"Hi, sweetie," Sherrie greeted her.

"Hi, Mommy." The child still didn't look up.

"How's everything going?"

Tressa shrugged.

"Aren't you feeling well?"

Another shrug. Sherrie sat on the floor beside her daughter, taking her in her arms. Tressa was unresponsive. "Can I call Uncle Bye?"

Sherrie glanced at her watch. Seven-thirty. "Well, it's a little late, honey. Your bedtime's at eight, and you've got to have your bath. Is tomorrow okay?"

To her surprise, Tressa meekly said, "Okay, but tomorrow for sure."

Sherrie pulled Tressa to her, hugging her tightly. "Scout's honor," she said.

It hurt that her child looked so sad. She knew then that she would call Byron the next morning. Curt was right. They had to talk. Perhaps he would meet her for lunch.

Chapter 9

Sherrie spent a restless night as erotic dreams of Byron filled her thoughts. All right, she thought, he was a fine specimen of manhood. Kind. Gentle. Caring. A body to make her reel. She smiled. He wasn't all gentle. That long, impassioned kiss among the lighter kisses had been anything but gentle. It still burned her to think about it.

She rose early, a bit weary from tossing, from the fantasized lovemaking about Byron, and took a long, warm bath. Tressa was sleeping late. Mrs. Hall always took her to school. In the bathtub, enveloped in water softened with baking soda, lemon verbena essential and patchouli oils, she heard Mrs. Hall close the front door and leaned back.

In her mind's eye she chose the outfit she would wear that day. A dark heather-rose dress that fastened on the side with round dollar-size buttons rimmed with gold, artfully cut and carefully fitted. She had not worn it before. Lacy rose undergarments. She smiled. This was a seduction outfit. What if he was too busy for lunch. She got out of the tub, dried off, smiling all the time. She certainly hoped Byron could have lunch with her. She shivered a little with anticipation and some sudden fear.

At My Beautiful Self, Sherrie waited until things settled a bit before calling Byron, but it was still early. He was in his office.

"Good morning," she said. "I won't keep you long."

"You can, you know, any time."

"Thank you for being kind. Byron, there are things I need to discuss with you. Could you have lunch with me today?"

He thought a moment, and she held her breath. Then he said, "Lunch would be fine, but I've got a far better idea."

"Oh?"

"Yeah. I'm knocking off early, and I'm making my famous Texas chili. Topflight and spicy, stick-to-the-ribs. Remember?"

"I remember. It was wonderful, something to write home about."

"Okay. You're properly enthusiastic. Take that with scalloped, sour cream potatoes; a garden salad that's got black olives, thin sliced onions, pimentos, the works; and my crisp corn-bread cheese sticks. And what would you like for dessert?"

So he assumed she was coming. She stroked the wide, eighteen-karat gold bracelet on her arm. "Surprise me." And she was going to have dinner with him.

He chuckled. "You bet I'll surprise you—pleasantly."

"I can't stay too long. I need to be home by seven-thirty to put Tressa to bed."

"Not a problem. Could you come early? Around four-thirty. You used to say Katherine's so good about taking over."

"I can do that."

"It gives us more time together. Are you driving?"

"My car's in the shop. I took a taxi over. I can take a taxi there."

"No. I'll pick you up."

"But . . ." she began, starting to say it would be too much trouble.

"No buts. I'll be there around four."

The day passed for Sherrie in a haze of excitement. Katherine teased her. "Seems to me you've got a scorching date."

Sherrie grinned impishly. "Mildly warm."

"Uh-uh. Mildly warm doesn't light you up like that." Katherine hugged her. "I'm happy for you."

Byron was prompt in picking her up that afternoon, and Sherrie enjoyed the ride. His fieldstone mansion had always filled her with awe. It was that beautiful. She reflected that it could so easily have been a mausoleum, but it was in every sense a warm, comfortable home.

"Where's Husky?" she asked, missing the big Siberian dog.

"I assume out roaming the grounds with Joe. Once he knows you're here, he'll come running. He's your slave, like his owner."

"It's reciprocated."

Entering the front door with her, Byron smiled inside. One day he would carry her over this very threshold. It had to happen.

Stella, the housekeeper, hugged her. Sherrie was one of her favorite people, and she had missed her.

"I'm so glad you're coming around again," Stella said. A woman in her sixties, with an American Indian–African American heritage, she had long, coal-black hair braided and worn in a coronet and soft black eyes; Stella had once been a beauty queen. She had been with Byron for many years. Her husband, Joe, drove for Byron and pretty much ran the estate.

The smaller kitchen with its pale yellow fittings was full of spicy odors. The kitchen windows overlooked a distant view of the Chesapeake Bay and had been one of Sherrie's favorite spots when she, Mike and Tressa came to visit. Byron led her to the stove, lifted a pot lid, picked up a tablespoon and let her sample the chili, blowing on it first.

Velvety rich, the chili quickly claimed her taste buds.

"Really, really good," she complimented.

"Just really, really good?" he teased.

"Okay, spectacular."

"Now that's more like it. I didn't work over a hot stove much of the afternoon for lukewarm kudos."

They stood close, and his nearness was making her dizzy.

Her dreams and fantasies of the past night had come back to haunt her. Did other women fantasize the way she did? She had read that they did, but she had never been all that much bothered before.

They ate in the small dining room, again looking out on the bay. It was a calm, peaceful setting with low-lying bright sunlight and fresh breezes coming through the open, sparkling windows.

"I never can get over the beauty of this place," she told him.

"It is nice. I've always enjoyed it." He reached for her hand. "Sherrie, I've missed your coming here. I'm glad you decided to make it this time."

"I'm glad too. Did Tressa call you this afternoon?"

"She did, and we had quite a chat. She wants to know about her doll to come."

"My daughter's gotten to be something." Then her voice was anxious. "Is she running on empty, Byron? I know I am sometimes. She seems so impatient for everything."

Byron thought a moment. "Maybe it's an emotional virus. I know I'm impatient these days, especially for one thing."

She looked at him closely. "Which is?"

He grinned crookedly. "I won't say right now. You look beautiful, Shere. You own rights to that color." Her all-spice–brown skin was like silk and her dark brown almond-shaped eyes shone under sooty lashes. She looked happy. Did he have anything to do with that? he wondered.

"Thank you!" she told him. "You look good, you know. Very good."

"Do I? If I look good to you, I'm glad. I've got music I've selected for you, and I've got a lot of things to talk with you about. As you know, the music room, too, faces the bay, and we can be comfortable. Come back soon when it's warmer and we'll go out on the deck and watch the moon and the stars. The galaxy."

"I'd like that."

She leaned back. The meal had been scrumptious. She had eaten a bit too much.

"Did you enjoy your dinner?"

"It was delicious. If you ever need a job as chef, I'd consider you."

"Just consider?"

"Okay, hire you."

He grinned. "What perks would I get?"

She was caught up in the spirit of his edgy teasing and she answered boldly. "I think you'll be pleased."

His eyes got dreamy, swept hers and both grew very, very warm. She broke the spell. "I keep wondering about the dessert."

"Ah, the dessert. Well, it's from a recipe you once gave us. Peach Delight Frozen Wonder."

"Oh, good. I always found it yummy."

"I've embellished it with crème de cacao. Let's see, very ripe, very sweet peaches, slices of wine cake, whipped cream, heavy cream, then the crème de cacao. Prepare to drool, I warn you."

She had an idea. "Why don't we eat it later? Do it full justice?"

"Great thinking."

In the well-appointed music room, Byron turned on Dvořák's "Symphony No. 8," beginning with a single selection of the third movement.

"You always liked classical music," she told him.

"Yes. My taste in music is catholic, but the classicals soothe me, let me think, make me think. You always liked them too."

"Uh-huh. That piece is one of my favorites."

"I remember."

They sat on a deep cream glove leather sofa side by side.

She wasn't sure if she should say it, but she began, "Curt came to see me yesterday."

"He told me. Is that why you called?"

She shook her head. "Not altogether. Tressa is so desperate for your company. She really loves you, and she misses her father so much. Byron, thank you for bringing some joy back into my daughter's life. She was so sad."

He took her hand, squeezed it. "I love Tressa, and she feels my love. And what about you, Shere? What have I been able to bring back into your life?"

The room swam a bit as she looked at him. He was so close, and his nearness filled her with all kinds of turbulent feelings. Slow heat was like a blessing spreading through her body. She was going to be honest with him.

"You've brought back a lot," she said slowly. "I can't begin to tell you how much I appreciate the way you've stood by me, helped me . . ."

"I kissed you deep and hard one night, a savage kiss. We haven't talked about that. It shook you up."

"In more ways than one," she said quietly. "Byron, I'm not going to lie to you. Your kiss affected me. I've never stopped thinking about it." She sighed. "But I'm torn up. I want more, but I need time to think, to get myself together."

He answered without hesitation. "And I'm willing to give you that time. I'll settle for my fantasies and seeing you if you'll let me."

"I want to see you. Tressa is dying to see you."

Byron smiled. She kept talking about Tressa, and that was fine, but he longed for a time it would be herself she talked about dying to see him.

She wanted him to take her in his arms and kiss her the way he had the night of Tressa's birthday. His soot-black, curly, close-cropped hair; the steady blue-gray eyes; the sensuous mouth that carried his hot kisses were all mesmerizing her. She wanted to stroke his muscular arms and put her head on his wide shoulder and nestle there.

"So Curt came to see you," he said.

"Yes. He told me about Mike's embezzling money and your paying it back. I'm sorry I was so wrong about you."

"You couldn't know."

"Curt said you'd be upset about his telling me."

"I don't ever want you hurt—by anyone or anything," he said fiercely.

"It helped me. I've been hating you when that's not the way I feel in my heart."

"I'm glad. In addition to the embezzling, I think Mike was trying to pay that money back *and* he wanted his own company. Our styles of what we sought for the company were so different. He wanted global input. I wanted to stay closer to home. Mike had big dreams, Shere, believe me. And he had the moxie to make them come true. It was my company, but we were a team, closer than brothers. It nearly took me under to let him go."

"He lied to me all along, but I loved him. Now, that's all in tatters."

He hugged her gently. "I'm sorry. You never deserved this, and I never want to see you hurt again."

She cried then with his arms around her, as she had the day before with Curt. These were old tears she should have shed for Mike, but she'd had to be strong for her daughter.

Byron's heart hurt for her. She had had to be so brave. Now Sherrie felt the depth of his caring, and it warmed her, lifted her, and she calmed as he stroked her shoulders and her back. After long moments she drew a little away.

"Thank you," she said solemnly. Her eye fell on a large framed photo on the table beside them. It was of both their families at some earlier time, and she said, "As I told you at the cemetery, I'm being selfish. You had a great loss and so much pain. If I can comfort you, if you ever want to talk . . ."

He took a deep breath. "I'll take you up on that one day soon, but just now you're my top priority. Are you all right? Feel better?"

"Oh yes. You said there were a couple of things you wanted to talk with me about. Mike was one . . ."

"Are you sure you want to talk about anything else just now?"

"I'm sure. I think it will help to get away from talking about Mike for a while."

He kissed her forehead, and he seemed so dear. "Okay. It's about the August ball. Remember a few years back when you were cochairman to my chairman?"

"How could I forget?"

"That ball was a smashing success. You've always believed in using natural ingredients for beauty products. I've always believed too, but you were really gung-ho. We put out our new line with your slogan: Natural Tate products for natural African-American beauty. The line has been selling like wildfire ever since. You know Margo Hilliard?"

"Yes."

"Her husband is with the state department and he's being assigned to India. She was cochairman for this year. Now she has to give it up, and I want you to take her place."

Sherrie thought a long moment.

"Oh, I know it will be hard," he said. "My Beautiful Self is taking seven-league-boot steps, and you're really busy, but I'll get you all the help you need. River and Curt are deeply involved. Marcia's all wrapped up with this. I hope you'll say yes."

"It would mean a lot to you, wouldn't it?"

"I can't tell you how much. You have a gift for working with people, for pulling things together. I need you."

Without thinking further, she said, "Of course I will."

He hugged her then, holding her again, his eyes closed, rocking her a little. "You've made my day, my year." They smiled at each other. It was going to be fun, she thought, working with him again.

The gorgeous liveliness of the third movement of Dvořák's "Symphony No. 8" swept through the air again. He took her hand, kissed it.

They ate the delicious dessert in the warm, homey kitchen.

When they had finished he said, "I'm going to get your coat. I want us to walk outside a bit."

Husky met them out back and came to her, wagging his tail furiously. Delighted, she bent and smoothed his thick head fur. His long, golden eyes reflected the intelligence of a human being as he nuzzled her leg.

"Hey," Byron teased him. "Don't steal my thunder."

A little while later, they had walked to the edge of the spacious grounds. The sun was setting and a fiery ball lay over the bay.

The sun lit the windows of the magnificent fieldstone house, a three-story edifice that reflected a passion for beauty and charm. The house was timeless, outstanding.

Surrounded by a tall, massive black iron fence and heavy matching gates, it had always reminded Sherrie of an English estate. Back from the bay view a large forest stretched. There were 225 acres of land.

They stood behind a tall, wide clump of lush evergreens near a tulip bed with red and white tulips growing in profusion. Shielded from both the road and the house, she involuntarily moved closer to him.

"That setting sun just takes my breath away," she said.

"Yeah. It's even more beautiful with you here."

She ran the tip of her tongue over her bottom lip. Aching inside, she wanted him to kiss her again—deeply, the way he once had. They stood for long moments, saying nothing else before he murmured, "I've got to get you home before Tressa's bedtime."

She glanced at her watch in the dimming light. "We've got time." Didn't he want to kiss her? she wondered. A soft breeze fanned her hot face. It was cool.

He stood with narrowed eyes, and his big hand closed around her upper arm. "I'm going to kiss you," he said.

She laughed shakily, the laughter catching in her throat. "You're an alpha male, Bye. Do your thing."

She had called him "Bye," he thought, and she hadn't in a very long time.

He laughed with delight then, a deep, excited laugh, but he told her, "I won't kiss you now the way I did recently." He paused briefly, then went on. "And that's because I want you to kiss me the way I did that night."

She shook her head. "I can't always show my feelings the way I'd like to do. Your kiss was wild."

He chuckled. "I'm pleased you think so. I meant it to be."

"What makes you think I could ever kiss you that way? Am I capable? Can I?"

"You can. You will," he assured her.

His confidence thrilled her. "How can you be sure?"

He took her face in his big hands and drew her close to him. His hot breath on her face was mesmerizing her. A startling vivid fantasy leaped to her mind of them lying together, then him inside her, engorged and throbbing. She nearly groaned aloud.

"Because something in you began to open up that night, to open to me. I began to feel you in my heart and soul, and I loved every second of it, but I was forcing you."

"I never felt forced. I just felt . . ." She hesitated.

"Loved? Because that's what's going on with me."

"Yes. I felt loved."

"And did you like it?"

She laughed a little. "I loved it."

His hands came away and he took her in his arms. "I'm not going to give in to my desire to kiss you now."

"It's my desire too." She flirted with him.

"Good, but I want to hold back, let you get hungry, starved, the way I feel. Do you like the thought of that?"

She laughed throatily. "I'm not sure I like being so hungry, so starved."

His face got solemn then. His body tensed. "I'll see that it doesn't go too far, but you've got to come to me."

She drew a deep breath. "Okay. When I can, I'll come to you."

"And our time together then will be as beautiful as anything God ever created. We're going to be good together, Shere. I just feel it in my very bone marrow."

It was time to go back then and, strolling to the house, Byron looked up the road. "It's only a little over two miles," he said wistfully. "I'd like to walk you home, but I understand there was a robbery recently of someone walking along this road about this time, so we'll have to drive."

In the house she hugged Stella and Joe good-bye.

"Now don't you be a stranger," Stella said. "Like I told you, we've missed seeing you."

"Believe me, she'll be back soon," Byron assured them.

Chapter 10

Driving along slowly in Byron's black special-model Porsche, they were mostly silent until Sherrie said, "I really enjoyed my visit."

"Then you'll come back often?"

"I will."

"I can't tell you how much that pleases me."

They were passing Bottomless Canyon and Sherrie felt a mild shudder as she glanced at the fenced-in ravine. "I keep thinking what it must be like to fall into something that deep," Sherrie said.

"There's no danger with the fence."

"I know, but I can't help thinking about it. Has anyone ever fallen in, or"—she couldn't fathom why she added—"or been pushed?"

Byron chuckled. "You're morbid tonight. Not that I've heard of."

At home, Tressa flew into Byron's arms, yelling, "Uncle Bye! Uncle Bye!" as if she hadn't seen him in months. He picked her up, holding the thin frame against him as her little arms wound around his neck.

"We had mango ice cream for dessert, and I helped make it. Do you want some? I'll get it for you. Do you?"

"Well, I've just had dessert . . ." he began as Tressa's little face fell. She brightened when he said, "But I'd sure like to sample that ice cream you helped make. You didn't need sugar. Those little fingers would give it all the sweetness it needed." He kissed her fingers.

"Oh you," Tressa said, the way Sherrie often spoke.

Sherrie laughed and said to her, "Listening to you is sometimes hearing myself."

Mrs. Hall came in with her coat on. "I'm leaving now, and I'm getting absentminded. This small package came for you late this afternoon. The mailman mumbled something about a busy day. He wasn't being pleasant. I laid it on the pantry shelf because I thought about the hairstyling show, and I intended to put it on your pillow so you wouldn't miss it. Somehow I forgot, but I guess there's no harm done."

Sherrie shook her head. "None whatsoever."

As Tressa busied herself dishing up and serving her uncle Bye a small dish of ice cream, Sherrie examined the small package. There were large initials, FMHYH, and there was a Richmond return address on the label. She, too, guessed it was something regarding the beauty show she had recently attended near Richmond. Putting the package on an end table, she turned her attention to Byron as he ate his dessert.

"How are my baby's culinary skills?"

"She'll be a chef if she wants to be," he said.

"Got some for your poor old ma?" Sherrie asked Tressa.

The child jumped up with alacrity. "Big or little?" she asked.

"Make it a little dish," Sherrie said, ruffling Tressa's hair. "Tomorrow when I get home, I'll pig out."

In the meantime, Byron held out a spoonful of his dessert for Sherrie to taste. Rolling it over her tongue, she found the mango flavor delicious. "*Hmmm,*" she said. "I'll say, a chef."

Afterward, Tressa kissed them both good night and went to her room to bed. Before she left, she looked suddenly bothered.

"What's wrong, honey?" Sherrie asked.

Tressa shook her head. "Nothing." She was getting a mind of her own.

Sherrie unwrapped the package and lifted a videocassette box. "I guess I should be going," Byron said. "You probably have things to do."

She looked at him quickly. "No, please stay, at least a little while. Watch the tape with me. I think it's about us winning first prize in the hairstyling contest."

"Fine. I'll stay."

"Good. I can use the company. Your company."

"Mommy," Tressa's plaintive voice called from her doorway.

Moving quickly, Sherrie got up and went into Tressa's room, turning on the lamp on her night table as her daughter got back in bed. "Yes, sweetheart."

"Is Uncle Bye still here?"

"Uh-huh. Why?"

"Can I talk to him?"

"*May* I."

"Okay. May I?"

"Yes." She went to the door and called Byron, who came in, going to the bed.

"Nightmares?" he asked.

"Am I going to die like Daddy did?"

Startled, Byron assured her, "You're not going to die, Tressa."

"God took Daddy to be with Him. I want to stay with Mommy and you."

"And you will. Count on it," Byron told her.

"Will Mommy die? And you?"

Byron sat on the bed and gathered the child in his arms and hugged her tightly. "It's all right, Tressa. We're all going to live and be happy."

"Aunt Alicia and Ronnie died. I was a little girl then."

"Yes, they died."

"Why did God take them and my daddy?"

Byron expelled a harsh breath. "Sweetheart, we don't know

all the answers. We just have to have faith that we'll live. All of us." His voice was soothing, but husky with stress.

In a small voice, Tressa asked him, "Could you live here with us?"

"He has a house of his own, honey." Sherrie smiled a bit.

"I know, but he could live here *and* there, couldn't he? I want him here."

"I'd like that," Byron said heartily, "but it may not be possible. We'll talk about it later. Now you've got to get your beauty sleep."

"Okay. Am I going to be beautiful like Mommy?"

"You already are, pumpkin. You already are."

"Uncle Bye, I love you."

"And I love you."

"My eyes are going to sleep now. Nighty night."

Byron kissed Tressa's smooth forehead and downy cheek, saying, "Good night, angel."

Then Sherrie kissed her cheek, squeezed her little hand and the child was sleeping. Sherrie turned out the lamp and they went out.

Back in the living room, she opened the cassette case and took out the tape, slipped it into the DVD-VHS; the TV was already on.

They settled back on the sofa, facing the TV with Byron's arm around Sherrie's shoulder. She thought it felt so comfortable. She hadn't spent an afternoon and evening like this in a very long time.

At first the tape rolled—blankness. Then an image appeared, ringed in raspberry, rose, pink and cream—My Beautiful Self's colors. Later she knew she focused on that to slow seeing the main image. It was an excellent drawing. A human heart with a dagger plunged through it and rivulets of blood flowing. All in color. Beneath that picture were the words: *From my hand to your heart! Be warned!*

"What the hell?" Byron exploded, his voice raw with fury. He moved to take the remote control from the sofa cushion and cut it off, but Sherrie stayed his hand. "No, let it play. There may be more." Her voice was hoarse with stress.

And even as they spoke, weird laughter filled the air. Laughter from hell. A man's laughter. Vicious. Bloodcurdling. Bone-marrow chilling. The personification of evil. "My God," she whispered.

The laughter went on only a half minute, but it seemed much longer. Then the blank tape was all that was left. Sherrie rewound and played it again. Listened, stunned and unbelieving. And she silently mouthed the words, *From my hand to . . .* That drawing was seared onto her brain, that laughter enslaved her memory.

When she would have rewound it the third time, Byron stopped her. "No, Sherrie. Don't. We've both heard enough. What is Danielle's number?"

Sherrie told him and he called. Lieutenant Steele said she'd be on the way immediately. She lived only a few miles from Sherrie.

As they waited, Byron held her for the second time that afternoon and night. At first he felt enraged and helpless, then strength flooded him. In his mind, she was his woman, if not formally, and he would protect her. The animal who did this was going to pay; he'd see to that. Then he thought, no, not animal. Animals behaved more honorably. They couldn't help what they did. Humans had a choice.

Sherrie looked dazed as she pulled herself together. Finally she said in a small voice. "Mike was stabbed with a dagger. Remember?"

His breath quickened. "I remember. Sherrie, try not to focus too much on that."

She laughed hollowly. "You know a psychologist contended in a recent book that there are no coincidences."

"There must be a few."

"Danielle said I might be a target, a fallout from what Mike was doing in the diamond smuggling ring. He had hidden the money, the diamonds. They'll want to know where that money, those diamonds are."

"It's small potatoes to them. They're big outfits."

"There may be other things we don't know about. Byron, I'm scared." She was icy cold. Her teeth were chattering. He gathered her into his arms, held her tightly. She was out of tears, and delayed fear gripped her body like a plague. She was as cold as, yes, say it, the grave. *From my hand to your heart.* The words spun themselves out in her brain, wouldn't stop repeating.

Byron pulled away a bit. "I'm going to get you some Tylenol to soothe you."

"No. Please don't leave me. Just stay with me. Will you?"

He pulled her close and kissed the top of her head. "You know I will."

Lieutenant Steele was there in a half hour. Her husband, Whit Steele, the gospel singer, had driven her over. He sat in the den with Byron as Danielle questioned Sherrie, who strove valiantly to hold herself together.

"Do you think this is the work of the diamond smuggling gang?" Sherrie asked immediately.

"It could be. We'll try not to draw any conclusions too quickly."

"Who else could it be?"

"I don't know. I'll need to hear that tape. Can you bear to hear it again? You could go into the den with the men while I listen."

"I want to listen. Byron didn't want me to keep listening, but I'm trying to understand. I need to understand. I want to know if I can remember anything that might have brought this on, if there's anything I might have done."

"I don't think you had anything to do with it. You're just caught in a web of circumstances." She caught Sherrie's hand. "I'm going to put the tape in again."

"Go ahead," Sherrie said dully.

Listening, Lieutenant Steele winced with horror at the drawing and especially at the horrifying laughter. Before, Sherrie had been largely numb. Now hairs rose on the back of her neck and her spine felt icy.

"I'll need to take this tape with me."

"Welcome to it."

"And the package it came in."

Sherrie got up and handed Lieutenant Steele the package wrapping. "Ten twenty-five Trudy Lane, Richmond, Virginia," Lieutenant Steele read. "I'll get this checked out first thing."

"The initials," Sherrie said quietly. "Notice they spell out 'From my hand to your heart,' and the colors are those of my beauty salon."

"I noticed. Sherrie, you're going to need help with this. The break-in. What we've found out about Mike's ties to a diamond smuggling ring. These guys play rough. Human life often means little to them—even their own. I would recommend Dr. Will Casey or my sister-in-law, Dr. Annice Jones. I don't want this to take any greater toll on you than has to be the case. Will you talk with one of them?"

Sherrie nodded. She had met Dr. Jones through Helena and liked her. She thought now that this would be her choice.

"How did the package come to you? FedEx? If so, we can easily trace it."

Sherrie shook her head. "No. Mrs. Hall said the mailman brought it later than usual."

Lieutenant Steele sat up straighter. "Was the man wearing a postal uniform?"

"I think she said he was."

"He might have been an imposter. Postal uniforms are easy to rent in costume shops. Someone doing something like this would do everything to cover his tracks. We'll get to the bottom of this," she said grimly. "Also, your home will be under surveillance at least part time. I told you before we have a budget crunch, so I can't assign a man full time. . . ."

"Could this be a prank? Someone who dislikes me? Some kind of business quarrel? There are other salon owners in hot competition." She was clutching at straws and knew it.

Lieutenant Steele shook her head. "I doubt it. Tomorrow, I'm going to cast a wide net over this whole matter, and I expect to come up with many fish. We've already got more and more info about the diamond smuggling ring. We have names, backgrounds now. I think we can be ahead on this. And Sherrie?"

"Yes."

"Be very, very careful. Call me immediately when even the smallest thing happens. Watch your surroundings. Are you comfortable with a gun?"

"Yes. I've taken shooting instruction."

"Good. I'm going to get you a temporary gun permit, and I want you to get a permanent one. Will you do that tomorrow?"

"I will, Danielle; Mike was stabbed to death with a dagger. The hand in this drawing held a dagger."

"Yes. There could be a connection." She suddenly thought of something. "Do you know of anyone who draws particularly well? This was a drawing."

Sherrie thought a long moment. "I can't think of anyone. I'll keep trying."

"This is a particularly good drawing. Perhaps an artist, but many people who aren't artists have excellent talent." She took Sherrie's cold, damp hand. "You're very frightened, and I'm sorry. You have every reason to be."

"Talking to you helps. Knowing how topflight you are at this sort of thing."

"I'd better be this time. Talk to me now about how you feel, what sensations you're having. Dredge up anything that could be useful. Anything you've seen, heard. I want you to keep a journal of everything that happens. Any car or person you think may be following you."

"Very well."

Slipping on a pair of gloves, Lieutenant Steele got up then and took the tape out of the machine, put it in its case, then into the package wrappings.

The detective had been there more than an hour and a half when she and Sherrie walked to the den where Lieutenant Steele's husband and Byron sat. With tears standing in her eyes for her friend, Lieutenant Steele told Byron, "Take good care of her. Be with her all you can."

"Believe me, I'm going to do just that," he said, moving to put a protective arm around Sherrie's shoulder. His heart was bursting with rage at the devil who would threaten her this way.

Chapter 11

In the old tan brick building that housed Helping Hands, the Minden agency that provided assistance, social worker Helena Crane walked along the second-story corridor. She had just dialed her friend Sherrie and gotten her answering service. Leaving a message for her to call her back as soon as she could, she put her cell phone back in her pocket.

She was worried sick. Sherrie had called her the night before and told her about the vicious tape. She had wanted to go over, but Sherrie had said no, that Byron was there and would stay late and, if needed, would stay the night. She had felt greatly relieved.

As director of Helping Hands, she was proud of her shop as she called it. They managed to help a lot of people. Co-operating with Melanie Ryson, who ran the only other helping agency in the city, she knew that their places helped to make Minden, Maryland, the great city it was to live in.

"Boo," said a male voice behind her.

She turned to face Nap Kendrick who grinned at her. "You're walking in a daze," he said. "I saw you from another angle."

"Hello, Nap. What're you up to?"

"Not much. I thought I'd sort those files you told me about. Got time to show me exactly what's to be done?"

"Yes, but first, could you fix the straight-backed chair near my desk? It seems to be wobbling."

"Sure. I'm your jack-of-all-trades. Hey, you look like

you're going to some nice place for lunch," he said, then added slyly, "with someone you're sweet on."

Helena blushed. "You're just too perceptive. I'm having lunch with a friend."

"Ah-ha. I know you so well, like you so much."

Helena walked on up the corridor with Nap. She was having lunch with Curt Winters, the second luncheon date they'd had recently. He was a nice guy, she thought. Attractive too. Helena closed her eyes, envisioning him, and she felt a small thrill. "Hey, teenager," she said to herself. But no, she was no teenager. Women her age of thirty-nine got dizzy over males too, males they were coming to care about. Helena had been engaged twice in the past fifteen years, broken engagements, and she was wary. Curt seemed different. Mature. Caring.

They reached her office and went in. She hoped Sherrie would call soon.

Inside the office, she sat behind her desk and Nap sat backward on a straight chair facing her. "I'm moving on in a minute," he said. "Just want to chat a bit."

That was unusual for him, Helena thought. Nap was usually taciturn. He kept to himself, but he seemed to love the children to whom he showed the puppets. She asked him, "Have you got any new puppet shows planned?"

He shrugged. "A few—down the road a bit."

She nodded. "You do a really great job, and Nap, I just want to tell you how glad I am for your help around here. You've got a lot of talent. I'd like to see you go back to school. You're gifted with your hands in so many ways. Are you artistic?"

He shook his head quickly. "Nope." He didn't seem to want to talk about it anymore.

Suddenly she felt a need to ask him. "Are you close to your mother and father?"

"My dad's dead. Heart attack. My mother's dead too. She used to hit me with anything she could pick up." Bitterly he thought, she beat him because he kept on living.

"I'm sorry. She was probably upset over something else."

"Don't defend her. She was just a mean woman who hated me. Gee, you've got beautiful skin. Great color—like an Indian summer peach."

Helena smiled. "It's just skin, but thank you. Your skin is nice. You're so fair. Clear. Smooth. But you can't take too much sun or you burn."

"I hate my skin," Nap blurted. "My mother always called me clown white and said I look like Ronald McDonald. I wish I had brown skin. I think that color is the prettiest there is."

"All skin is beautiful, Nap," she said gently, feeling sorry for the child he must have been. "We have to learn to like ourselves."

"Yeah," he said. She reflected that his skin was clown white. It wasn't unattractive, just odd. She didn't think she had ever seen that color before.

"Who're you helping these days?" She wasn't prying. It was simply a conversational question.

He looked alert. "Well, you, Miss River, Mr. Curt, Mr. Tucker and"—he grinned here—"Miss Mallori." He rolled his eyes. "Lord, that is one fat-to-death woman."

Helena smiled. "Fat-to-death" meant beautiful and the term was growing obscure.

"She is," Helena agreed.

She returned to her original topic. "As I said, I think you could go far if you went back to school. You're just over thirty."

"Yeah." He hung his head, mumbling. "Never did care much for school."

"You're smart enough. You catch on to everything so easily. You're the best helper I've ever had."

Nap turned scarlet. "Thanks. Guess I'll take the chair now. It won't take long to fix."

"Okay, and we'll do the folders after lunch."

Nap grinned at her conspiratorially. "Sure thing and happy lunchtime, Ms. Crane."

"Thank you."

"Bring me a doggie bag if you get something really good."

"I'll do that."

Nap left and Helena sat, thinking that he was a real enigma. God had given him so much talent and he wasn't using it. That always bothered her. Nap was good with kids, good with office work, good at fixing things around Helping Hands. Great with the equipment. She shook her head, wanting to light a fire under him.

She hunched her shoulders, fretting. Why didn't Sherrie call?

Nap had his own cluttered office. Cluttered, he thought, like his mind. Much smaller than Helena's, there were photos everywhere—on the walls, on tables, on his desk. He thought wistfully he'd like to be a photographer, but every time he tried to focus, his mind began messing up.

Nap looked at the broken chair. He sat down and pulled the chair to him, shaking it a bit. He could fix that wobble in a hurry. He leaned far back, his legs stretched out, his hands behind his head. Thinking. Suddenly straightening up, he swiveled around and faced his desk, got a pencil and began doodling.

Chapter 12

At My Beautiful Self, it was a slow day from the beginning, and Sherrie welcomed the respite. She had just settled in with a cup of latte in hand when Tucker walked in with his sister, Jasmine, who looked glamorous and beautiful as usual. Sherrie felt a mild pang of envy.

"I'd like an aromatherapy session, and I don't have an appointment. Can I beg my way through?" Jasmine asked prettily.

Sherrie smiled. "You're in luck. We're not busy today."

She went to summon an operator, and Byron walked through the door. He and Tucker greeted each other with nothing more than civility. As Byron went toward Sherrie, Jasmine spotted him and languorously came back, saying, "Byron Tate! Why haven't I run into you before now?"

She threw her arms around him, kissing him on the mouth as he looked only slightly uncomfortable, Sherrie thought.

"Jasmine! How are you?" Byron asked.

"Everything's copacetic now that I've seen you at last. Promise me you'll come by to see me, have lunch, dinner." Lowering her arms, she dug into her purse and came out with a card. "This is my address."

Byron moved a little away, his eyes seeking Sherrie's. "Lord, but I'm up to my ears in business these days and I'm caught up, too, in other things." He moved to Sherrie's side and Jasmine quickly caught on.

Jasmine gave Sherrie a dazzling smile. "Byron and I go

way back. He took me to my senior college homecoming ball. Wouldn't you say we were an item, Bye?"

Byron smiled and said evenly. "That was so long ago."

Her head a little to one side, her eyes beguiling, Jasmine courted him. "I never forget someone as special as you. I hope I'll see you later. I'll be in touch."

She turned and walked down to the aromatherapy room, and Byron caught Sherrie's hand. Tucker had busied himself in Sherrie's office.

"I came by because I just couldn't stop thinking about you," Byron said, his eyes caressing her. "I have something to ask you, an invitation you can't turn down. I wanted to be looking at you when I asked."

"Okay." Her eyes were shining. Already she had forgotten the threat of Jasmine.

"You've been to cherry blossom festivals in D.C.?"

"Not often enough. I love them."

"Go with me this year. You. Tressa. Me. We'll make a day of it. Take lots of photos. Have lunch at a fabulous Caribbean restaurant I know about. Take in the sights. You spoke of wanting to go by Caitlin's art gallery to spend some time. Now's your chance."

"That sounds wonderful. I'd love to go."

"Then we've got a date."

Sherrie pursed her lips, teasing him. "Only if the glamour queen doesn't enthrall you by then."

"But I'm already enthralled. I thought you knew."

Looking at Sherrie, Byron felt his heart beat faster. Lord, he thought, the woman was in a smock, yet he saw only the tender outlines of her naked body. She wondered why he grinned so wickedly. She wanted to be in Byron's arms, if only briefly, feel his lips on hers, his hard body pressing in on hers. She sighed.

"What is it?" he asked.

"Nothing really. I'm happy, even if I am still scared."

"That's why I came by too. I'm going to check on you

often, see you're all right. I love you, Shere. I'm never going to stop saying that. You'll tell me, as well as Lieutenant Steele, if anything else happens?"

"You know I will. I keep saying it, but I'm so grateful for your help."

"You don't have to be. It goes with my love for you."

She felt warm then, secure deep inside although she knew she wasn't. The laughter from hell was still in her ears, would not go away.

"Call me," he said urgently, "and I'll call you. Considering the circumstances, God only knows what's going on. What Mike was involved in may well be sending its poisonous tentacles out to clutch at you and damn it, I hate having you frightened. You take things well, Shere. You're a brave, wonderful woman." He whispered, "My woman."

Sherrie smiled then, delighted. His words sounded so sweet.

Bending, he kissed her cheek, her brow. "Keep in close touch," he said.

"I don't want to be a nuisance."

"How could you be? You're a part of me now, and I can't be a nuisance to myself."

"You're a nice man."

"And you're the love of my life."

After Byron left, Sherrie paused at the door of her office, reluctant to face Tucker's banter. She took a deep breath, turned the knob.

As she went in, Tucker sat on a chair and looked at her long and hard, unsmiling. Shivering, she remembered Lieutenant Steele telling her about Tucker and the diamond smuggling ring. "Well," she said, "how are things looking today? Cash flow still good?" She sat in a chair beside him.

"You've had few bad ones since I started with you. Sherrie?"

"Yes."

"Byron Tate was by this morning. I saw him pick you up the other afternoon, whisk you away. Listen," he blurted, "Tate's going to destroy you the way he destroyed Mike. Don't be a fool. Don't let him do that to you."

But even as Tucker spoke, Sherrie was thinking. His words were similar to Mallori's, but she was feeling Byron's deep, deep kiss. Their kisses. She was hearing Curt Winters's voice and what he had told her. Mike had betrayed her on so many levels. Why hadn't she known that in some part of her? Oh, she knew about Mallori and Lord, how that had hurt, but she had blamed Byron. Now she knew another side of the story, a side Tucker didn't know. Or did he?

"Tucker," she began slowly, "we're friends, and I appreciate your concern, but I've always been pretty good at paddling my own canoe, taking care of myself."

"Tate's out of your league, honey. He'd do anything, say anything to make Mike look bad, even though the poor guy's dead. You know Mike and I became very close after Tate kicked him out."

"And do you know why that happened?"

"Because Tate had his own fish to fry. He's not the black knight you see him as."

"And Mike certainly wasn't."

"Are you turning against him too? Has Tate done that to you?"

"He's done nothing except be helpful."

Sherrie got up and sat behind her desk and Tucker got up, came and sat on the edge of her desk, leaning forward.

"It's no secret to you the way I feel about you," he said, drawing a deep breath. "We could be good together, Shere." He shrugged. "You don't love me now because you don't let yourself, but we could be the best couple going. At least I didn't betray Mike the way Tate did. There's nothing I wouldn't do for you."

"Tucker, don't. We're friends. We can never be anything else."

"Don't you feel at least some love for me?"

"I'm sorry," she said slowly. Then, "No, I'm not sorry. We can't help the way we feel."

"I don't want you to deny what you feel for me."

"I'm not. I wouldn't."

Her hand lay on the desk, and he covered it with one of his. "If you ever change your mind, when, not if, Tate hurts you, come to me, and I'll help you heal. I've got it bad for you, Sherrie, really bad."

And looking at this attractive, debonair man, Sherrie felt she didn't altogether want to trust Byron Tate, but deep inside she did trust him. Their families had long been friends. They knew each other. She didn't lie to herself, ever, even when the truth hurt. She had immediately faced Mike and Mallori's affair, and it had cut her to the bone, but she had forgiven him, blaming Byron for letting him go. Now she knew that what she felt for Byron was growing rapidly, racing along. She needed him and, yes, she wanted him.

She wondered then what else Tucker had said because she hadn't listened very carefully. What would he say if he knew about the frightening tape? If Lieutenant Steele's sources were right and Tucker was connected somehow with the diamond smuggling ring, was he even indirectly a part of what lay behind the tape? Smugglers were often cruel, heartless because they had to be. Her head hurt just thinking about it.

But she said, "Thank you, Tucker. I'll keep what you've said in mind."

Chapter 13

Washington, D.C.'s Tidal Basin was gorgeous at cherry blossom time. Byron, Sherrie and Tressa arrived there at 5:30 one Saturday morning in April. There were fewer people than the crowds that would throng in later, and the air was warm and misty.

"It's beautiful! It's so beautiful!" Tressa kept saying, and indeed the pink-tinged white blossoms on thousands of Japanese cherry trees lived up to all expectations. The trio had caught the blossoms in all their splendor, and soon Byron and Sherrie had cameras at the ready. Tressa posed and strutted as they laughed. Then a passerby was engaged to take photos of all three. The Potomac River was mirror-calm and birds twittered happily. Daylight saving time had just come in the Sunday before that week.

The Polaroid photos were quickly theirs and they all admired them. The one of Tressa mugging was all their favorite.

The sun rose with coral and gold rays fanned out across the horizon, and Sherrie found her heart fairly ached with the beauty of the scene.

After taking many photos, they walked down to Hains Point to watch the rippling waves from the guardrails, and Tressa continued to be delighted. Early sailboats were on the water.

"One day," Tressa asked wistfully, "could we go on a boat, please?"

"Next time for certain," Byron told her. "We've got a full day for this time."

Mollified, Tressa took his hand. "Uncle Bye," she said softly, "I love you."

Byron bent and picked her up. "And I love you, pumpkin."

Sherrie looked at the two favorite people in her world and her heart constricted with momentary anxiety, then expanded with hope.

They were an attractive group with Sherrie in her cream-colored, wool reefer coat, Byron in a greenish-blue Harris tweed jacket and dark brown trousers and Tressa in a navy light wool coat with a narrow white collar.

A soft breeze began when they had walked along for a while. Looking back at the thousands of clusters of cherry blossoms, Byron thought nature was outdoing herself this year. He came for most years, but he had missed the year after Alicia and Ronnie's deaths.

"I remember," he said to Sherrie, "you once said you didn't care much for pomp and circumstance, and God knows I don't, so I didn't opt for the Cherry Blossom Festival Parade."

"You have a good memory," Sherrie murmured. "This is perfect."

They walked back to the Tidal Basin and sat on a bench with fallen blossoms dotting it. Byron brushed most of the petals off, holding a few in his hand. When they were seated, he got up and sprinkled the petals in Sherrie and Tressa's hair as Tressa squealed. "What are you doing, Uncle Bye?"

Byron laughed. "Spreading beauty over the already beautiful."

"Grown-ups talk funny sometimes," Tressa commented.

Sherrie took a few petals from her hair and put them in a small Ziploc bag in her purse. "I want to press these," she said, "keep them forever."

Byron's breath caught as he looked at her with her eyes shining and peace lying on her face like a benediction. His chest hurt with loving her.

"Who's hungry?" he asked around nine.

"Me! I'm hungry!" Tressa yelled.

"Hey, pipe down," Sherrie said, laughing. "We're both right here."

Tressa buried her face on Byron's knee, giggling, then whispered, "I'm really hungry."

They walked back to his car and drove a short distance away to northwest Pennsylvania Avenue where they found a big hot dog stand and ordered half smokes, which Tressa loved.

"Load mine with onions," Sherrie told him. "You two will just have to tolerate the consequences."

"Not a problem. I carry breath mints," Byron said.

They bought bottles of orange juice and packages of trail mix and sat on a park bench munching. The sun rose steadily, bright and beaming.

"Byron," Sherrie said, "you think of everything. Thank you."

"For what?"

"For this trip. For bringing us at the most beautiful time . . ."

"You're welcome." His eyes were narrowed, the corners creased with smiles.

They spent the rest of the morning at the Tidal Basin just soaking in the atmosphere. By then, they had scores of photos and memories stored for a lifetime.

"We're going to one of my favorite restaurants in D.C. for lunch. Ever hear of the Caribbean Gem in Adams Morgan?"

"I've been there and like it very much."

"Carry-what?" Tressa demanded.

Byron reiterated, then spelled it for her and helped her pronounce it as she gravely tried and succeeded. Suddenly she announced, apropros of what they didn't know, "I'm six and my teacher says I'm smart."

"Six. Smart. And pretty too," Byron teased her. "It's enough to turn a young boy's head."

Tressa giggled. "You're talking funny again. Will I talk funny when I grow up?"

"Yeah," he said, "I expect you will. You've already got the gift."

The little girl looked as if she were about to comment again, but thought better of it.

Caribbean Gem was one of Adams Morgan's trendiest ethnic restaurants. Serving delectable, plain Caribbean food and drinks, graced by a calypso band and waiters in colorful uniforms, it was owned by Raymond Peterson. Ray came forward, beaming as they came in. His accent was heavy, his voice wonderfully deep.

"Ah, Dr. Tate. I welcome you. We are at your command."

The two men shook hands and Byron introduced Sherrie. Ray bowed and kissed her hand.

"How beautiful your two ladies are," Ray murmured. "Candy for my eyes."

"Thank you. I agree with you."

"You're kind," Sherrie murmured.

"What've you got that's outstanding?" Byron asked.

"The jerk chicken turned out unusually well today. I would also suggest the candied yams, mixed vegetables, collard greens—none better—and our delectable corn bread. Try the fruit punch. Our freshly made pecan ice cream and dirt cake for dessert. Believe me, you'll have a feast. Are you here for the cherry blossoms?"

"We are, and I want you to help me make this a day to remember," Byron answered. "Have you seen the cherry blossoms?"

"I make time to go daily. They are one of God's springtime gifts to us."

Ray seated them and they made desultory talk as they waited. Their server took their orders, graciously smiling. Dressed in red and black, the man had beautiful white teeth and a splendid smile. Tressa sat agog as she stared at the calypso band on the small stage as they played Bob Marley tunes and songs as old as "Rum and Coca-Cola."

"Now that one," Ray said, "is for men of my time, not for the likes of you young people. But I still get a kick out of it."

"We're not so young," Byron said, "and you're not so old."

"That is a compliment I'll treasure. It makes my day."

The meal was served quickly as one of the calypso band members came over and bowed low at their table, saying "Welcome, happy people." Tressa was enthralled. The meal Ray had recommended was excellent, as delectable as he had promised. The jerk chicken was delicious, the candied yams smoothly glazed with a tangy lemon-vanilla flavor and the collard greens with ham chips were superb. The corn bread came in crisp sticks, split and buttered. They took salad from the big bowl of mixed greens, tomato wedges, cucumbers and red and green peppers.

"This fruit punch is just the best," Sherrie said. "Do you think he'd give me the recipe?"

"I think so. I'll ask," Byron said.

In just a little while the lunchtime crowd filed in and the air was festive. Everyone seemed so laid back. It was Saturday, a day for relaxation. They stopped short of being too full and ate their pecan ice cream and dirt cake, which was chocolate cake with chocolate fudge icing.

Byron placed his hand over Sherrie's, wanting to lift it for a kiss. Later, he decided, because it was crowded and still people were coming in. They wouldn't tarry too long. When they asked for the check, Ray came over.

"Was it all you expected?" Ray asked.

"Everything and more," Byron told him.

"Then you must come again—and often."

"We will," said Byron.

Ray held out a small bunch of mixed flowers. "These are for you," he told Sherrie. "You and the little one. You have helped to make my place a happy one today."

Surprised, Sherrie took the flowers as Byron grinned. "Thank you, my friend. This is a happy day for us."

Ray gave Sherrie the simple recipe for the fruit punch as soon as Byron asked. She vividly imagined it and committed it to memory.

"Now if you forget," Ray said, "simply call me. My recipes are for the public. We don't keep secrets. Our magic is in the making. Good luck!"

Midafternoon, they climbed the flagstone steps and walked into Costner's Art Gallery, a buff brick town house in Adams Morgan, and were greeted by Caitlin Costner, a customer from Sherrie's salon and an old friend.

"Oh, I'm so happy to see you all!" Caitlin exclaimed, hugging all three. A nutmeg-colored woman of rare beauty with earth-brown hair and light brown eyes, Caitlin was serenity itself. She owned and ran the art gallery, and business was thriving. "Why didn't you call?" she asked.

"No time," Sherrie answered easily. "I know this is a busy time of year for you and you'd have gone to too much trouble. We were in town, so we dropped by."

Caitlin's head went a bit to one side and Sherrie noted that she seemed sad. "Are you here for the cherry blossoms?"

"Yes. Have you seen them?"

Caitlin shook her head. "Not this year. I've been too busy. We're mounting a new exhibit just finished. You've heard me plan for the Black Eagles showing?"

"Yes. You were so enthusiastic."

"You'll be too."

Caitlin led them back to the main room and there were the marvelous photos of all the Tuskegee Black Eagles airmen mounted and gazing down with magnificently conquering countenances. Warriors before their time, deprived of much of their glory, but knowing it now that few were left.

"Oh Lord, this is wonderful," Byron complimented her.

Sherrie concurred.

"Thank you. It's been quite a job. Listen, this can't be much fun for Tressa. I've set up a nursery for the kids. She'll be at home there. I'll take her. Wander around. Enjoy!"

Caitlin left then with Sherrie still wondering at the sadness on her face. She hadn't made an appointment in a few months; she sometimes did her own hair. Alone in a small alcove, Byron drew her close, kissed her lightly. "My special dessert," he said.

"Greedy," she teased him. Then, sobering, "You've been a love. I care a lot about you."

"Yeah," he answered, "I'm greedy where you're concerned. I can't settle for your caring. I want you to love me the way I love you."

Sherrie closed her eyes and drew a deep breath. "Let's go slow. I need time. Can you understand that?"

He smiled. "I'll wait, but I can't stop pressuring you because I'm too hungry for you."

Out on the highway going home, Sherrie felt happy remembering the day. With the warm sunshine shining through the open car windows, they sang nursery rhyme songs to Tressa's delight.

"I had a great day," the little girl enthused.

As Byron drove, Sherrie leaned over and put her hand over his on the steering wheel. "Thanks for everything," she said simply.

He turned slightly. "You're very welcome. I'm the one who had a great time."

Chapter 14

On Tuesday morning, Sherrie sighed as she sat across from Lieutenant Steele, who asked, "How are you holding up? Any more trouble?"

"No." Sherrie shuddered a bit, remembering the tape. She knocked on the edge of a nearby table. "Thank heaven for that. Do you have any more information about Mike?"

Lieutenant Steele nodded. "Unfortunately yes. The circle is closing. We're finding he went from drugs to diamond smuggling. We're getting very useful info from our informants at state prison about others who may be involved."

"Tucker?"

Lieutenant Steele nodded. "Are you being very careful? Letting me know everything?"

"Yes, of course, but I can't stop being spooked."

"I can understand why. We have police watching your house. I don't think it was a prank, that tape. It was very well done. Professional. Just be careful and watch your back."

"As for the money and the diamonds," Lieutenant Steele continued, "they've been bagged as evidence and are in our safe at headquarters. The diamonds will be appraised. Where contraband is found, the courts decide who gets it. We certainly don't expect anybody to claim it. Maybe there's some way you can keep it. At least some."

Sherrie shook her head slowly. "The break-in seems a long time ago. If I get it, I'll give the money to Helena to use at Helping Hands. She needs it."

"That's kind, worthwhile. Let's do lunch soon. I asked you to come by this morning because I want us to get used to being on each other's turf. This may go on a while. How was your weekend?"

Sherrie smiled. "First, yes, let's do have lunch this week or next. I'm glad you asked me to come in. I spent the weekend in D.C. with Byron and Tressa looking at the glorious cherry blossoms."

"Wonderful. I usually go, but this year . . ." She shrugged. "We're busier than usual. How's Byron? Tressa?"

"Both couldn't be better. We had a marvelous time. I'm going to make it an annual event. Danielle, thank you for your help with this and for being my friend."

Lieutenant Steele smiled. "You're such an easy woman to be friends with."

At Tate Cosmetics, Byron Tate leaned far back in his chair, his fingers interlaced as he watched Marcia slump in hers.

"You're not feeling your best," he said to Marcia, who sat on the other side of his desk.

"I have reasons."

"You've been my secretary for a long time, and this is the first time I can remember seeing you down. Can you say what it is—what's bothering or bugging you? If it has to do with me, I'll straighten it out in a hurry."

Marcia smiled wanly. "You know you're a wonderful boss. No, it isn't you." She hesitated a long moment, then drew a deep breath. "It's my marriage, Byron. It's falling apart. I'm falling apart."

"You sure seem together to me."

"You know my husband has an eye for beauty. Hal was a coach and he notices bodies. I'll be fifty-six my next birthday. The wrinkles are coming in. My hair is gradually thinning, early. I've read that usually starts in the seventies. I never used many cosmetics. Crisco's been my beauty cream. . . ."

"Crisco!"

"It's always worked for me."

"And here I was thinking you were one of our best ads."

"I've let myself get flabby. . . ." Her voice trailed off. Her shoulders had a dejected stance.

Byron tapped the side of his head. "I'm thinking as you talk. I whip up a mean batch of specialty creams, potions, lotions I'd like you to try, and I want you to talk with Sherrie—soon. Get the works. Put your heads together and the bill comes to me. Aromatherapy. Facials. Massages. I said the works. Understand?"

Marcia's smile was a little wider. "I read you loud and clear. I wonder why I never thought of that. I guess I'm just not a beauty salon woman."

"Well, you're going to be. I'll make your appointment."

Marcia stood and came around the desk, hugging Byron. "Thank you," she said simply and there were tears in her eyes.

"Hello, beautiful."

At My Beautiful Self, Sherrie's heart lifted at Byron's voice on the telephone.

"Hello yourself, Adonis."

"Whatever it is you like, well, that's what I aim to be."

"We're both getting an early start at work," she said.

"Yeah. I've got a favor to ask."

"Anything for you."

"Work Marcia in, tomorrow if possible, for a series of treatments. She's feeling a bit down, thinking about aging, holding on to husbands, et cetera. I think she can be stunning until she's a hundred. I've seen such women. Can you help?"

"Of course I can. Why not begin today?"

He laughed. "Because I want you personally to take her treatments over completely insofar as you can, and I've suddenly got things for you to do today."

"Today? You didn't mention anything."

"I'm mentioning it now. You know I cook up a mean batch of beauty stuff."

"I remember."

"I want you over to my house this afternoon for company and moral support while I do a batch of magic creams and lotions for Marcia. I've already begun. I told you about my special, expensive rare formulae book. Do you have anything for thinning hair?"

"Sure have. And this is my own concoction. Marcia can make it up herself after I get it started. Oh, this is exciting!"

"You bet it is. And aromatherapy? She needs a lift."

"Aromatherapy it is, a whole round. She'll be our new Mrs. America. Oh, Byron, by the August ball, she should be shining. I'll drive over."

"I'd pick you up, but I'm right in the middle of something."

"I'm fine with driving. See you after twelve."

Around one, Sherrie worked with an ebullient Byron in his personal kitchen niche.

In a big white chef's apron himself, Byron got Sherrie a smaller one. Sherrie closed her eyes. It brought back memories of times Byron, Alicia, Mike and she had concocted cosmetics here.

"I've got the lotion finished," he told her. "Now help me mix a moisturizing cream."

Testing, he set the blender to high speed and turned it off. "You know, if only women knew that the best cosmetics are those we can whip up for ourselves. It is a bit of trouble and you have to find a supplier, but a few good books give info on the whole procedure."

"Skin care adds so much. What particular cream are you mixing?"

"A liposome wrinkle cream, or antiwrinkle cream." He had two one-pint canning jars, a two-quart pot, a thermometer and several measuring cups and spoons all assembled.

The copies of pages from the formulae book lay on the table and they followed them closely. Eleven ingredients were required, all available from suppliers. As they measured, they read aloud.

"One cup emollient alginate base at two percent," Byron began and measured.

"One half teaspoon vitamin C powder, then one tablespoon aloe vera," Sherrie added. And so it went until all eleven ingredients were whirring at high speed in the blender.

"Always the thrill of something new, helpful, beautifying," Byron said. "When I can help make a woman more beautiful, I wouldn't trade what I'm doing for anything."

"Nor would I."

They stood close together, and his nearness moved her. In a T-shirt, his strong biceps and pectoral muscles were well developed, not bulging, but there, turning her on. She touched a bicep and smiled, desire rising in her breasts and belly.

"Don't tempt the help," Byron said, laughing. "He has a hard time keeping his hands off you."

She wanted to say, *Then don't keep your hands off me. They seem to belong there. My flesh is all nerve endings where you're concerned.* But she said nothing, only smiled.

Looking at her, Byron's eyes shuttered. He was so acutely conscious of her softness, the lemon verbena essential oil she wore. His loins hurt with wanting her. He abruptly drew a harsh breath. They had work to do.

"Now for another thing I think will help greatly," he said.

"What's that?"

"Alpha hydroxy acid deep moisturizing lotion."

With the deep moisturizing cream finished and bottled, they washed up the utensils and started on something new.

This one was far easier; few utensils were required. The most effective ingredient was the alpha hydroxy acid fruit juice, which was already mixed. Avocado oil, phosphoderm, vitamin E linoleate oil and a few other items all went into the high-speed blender. Byron beat his chest like Tarzan.

"Voilà! I'm going to have a happy secretary in a couple of months."

"The alpha hydroxy works fast."

"Yes, it does. Now, for a sunscreen lotion for sensitive skin and we're done. Thanks for your help."

"I really have enjoyed this."

They were done in a short while, and they poured the mixtures into Tate containers and set them on the counter.

Stella served them shrimp salad and a molded gelatin vegetable mix. They ate slowly in a nearby breakfast nook with the thrill of creation singing in their breasts.

As they sat enjoying the food and each other's company, Stella came to the arched doorway.

"Excuse me," she said, "but Husky is demanding to be let in."

Byron looked from Sherrie to Stella and grinned. "I think I know his game. Let him in. He'll come straight here."

And like a homing pigeon the dog came to the table and Sherrie's side. He sat gazing at her like a lovesick puppy as she scratched behind his ear.

Byron laughed. "I've got your number, old buddy. One of us is going to have to check out."

Sherrie held out a large shrimp from her plate and Husky wolfed it hungrily.

"Uh-huh," Byron chided. "This from a clown who ate a chopped beefsteak not an hour ago. I guess love's like that, eh, fellow? You ready to go back out?"

But Husky had stretched out, his long brown-yellow eyes adoring Sherrie.

"Please let him stay. He's so sweet."

And Husky stayed for the rest of Sherrie's visit, with Byron grumbling, "I see I've got to do something about finding you your own personal sweetie. You can't wrestle me for mine."

* * *

A little later, in his den, Byron's cell phone rang. Sherrie got up to go out to give him privacy, but his big hand stayed her.

"Jasmine," he said easily and listened for a while.

Sherrie was surprised to feel sharp jealous shards lodge in her chest. He was smiling widely.

"Well, of course you are. I value your patronage."

He was so desirable. What woman wouldn't want him? she thought. And Jasmine had it all going on. They'd be quite a pair. He talked for a few minutes and hung up, grinning.

"You seem happy enough," she said guardedly. "I could have left you alone to talk."

"No need. Hey, are you jealous?" He didn't wait for an answer. "She wanted to be sure she got tickets for the August ball."

"Oh. I'm sorry, Bye. Maybe I am jealous a little bit. She throws it all at you."

He grinned. "Maybe you should throw a little more of it my way."

"You're a rascal."

"And you're beautiful when you're jealous."

Slowly he drew her into the circle of his arms and she lay there nestled against him. Then he lifted her chin and kissed her, tantalizing and thorough, slow and soft, then deeper until finally her mouth hurt with his passion. It was a powerful kiss, but it was not that first all-engrossing kiss.

His voice husky, he told her, "Know that I'm waiting patiently for you to come to me and kiss me the way I kissed you."

Sherrie laughed. "If only I could," she said faintly.

His kiss then was harder as he held her and she tore up with wanting him. Liquid fire filled her veins as she opened to him, yearning, longing for the rapture of him inside her.

"Why don't you take a chance? I'll never hurt you."

After a long moment she said, "I was savaged. Can you understand that?"

He nodded. "Yes, I understand."

"I know now how I lied to myself again and again. Mike's affair with Mallori, with other women nearly destroyed me, but my love for him kept me with him. Byron, I can't, I won't go through that again." Her voice was hoarse with remembered grief.

He stroked her back. His heart ached with sympathy. "God, Shere, surely you don't believe I'd ever put you through that."

Anger at Mike surged through him. How dare he hurt her like this!

He stood then and pulled her to him. The voluptuous outlines of her soft body against his drove him crazy. Her soft, tender lips under his, her mouth was open to his tongue as his was open to hers, all urging him on. Desire ran like wildfire in his loins.

"Let me make love to you," he whispered. "We want each other, and I love you. I've got to make you love me the same way. Baby, give me a chance."

But Sherrie didn't answer. She wanted him inside her with every cell of her being, wanted to feel him, know him, but she still hurt too much so it could not be now.

Driving home, Sherrie felt full of conflict. Byron's kisses and his love entered and filled her very soul, but she wasn't ready for it. She had known a powerful past love, a blighted love that had seared her, made her angry and afraid.

She was nearing Bottomless Canyon when it happened. Such a short distance, she saw it as plainly as if it were real, a bloody dagger like the one on the tape. Shock waves rippled through her. Her skin went clammy, then ice cold. What the hell? she thought. The vision was gone as quickly as it had come, but she shook uncontrollably until she could force herself to calmness and drive on.

There was little traffic on the road and she managed to get home without further incident, envisioned nothing else. But she was apprehensive all evening and spent the night dreading a recurrence. She did not call and tell Byron about the vision, nor did she tell anyone else.

Chapter 15

"Relax! You're about to begin a journey I assure you will be one of the best you'll ever take."

Marcia chuckled as Sherrie and she sat in two tub chairs in the aromatherapy room at My Beautiful Self.

"I guess it's just that I've never been a beauty salon kind of woman," Marcia said, repeating what she had said to Byron. "Thank you so much for taking me. I'm a wreck."

Sherrie held up a slender hand. "You're not a wreck. You'll be one of my easy ones. You've got so much going for you." She held up a Polaroid camera from her lap. "First things first. I want to get several snapshots of you for before and after pictures."

Marcia posed as Sherrie aimed, shot several times from different angles, and let the photos develop. She held out the finished photos to Marcia.

Both women were in rose-colored smocks and the color lent a warm glow to their brown skins. Marcia shrugged as she looked at the photos. "They'll do, I guess."

Sherrie laughed. "The thing is you've gotten spoiled from being a natural beauty all your life. Now you need a little assistance the way most of us always have."

Marcia stiffened. "Is this going to work, do you think?"

"I'd bet my everything on it. Not bad," Sherrie said, placing a finger alongside her nose as she thought.

"My hair's thinning too early. Can you help that? Byron said he thought you could."

Sherrie nodded. "Yes. I mix a treatment and it's simple. Take one heaping soup spoon each of stinging nettle, rosemary leaves and sage, put them in a pint of boiling water—what we call a decoction—boil on low heat five minutes, cool and strain. Pour into a bottle. There'll be sediment, but always shake it up. That sediment is useful. Use water if you're not concerned with your hair 'going back,' as we say, or use oil if you are. Put on the scalp with cotton balls. It makes a wonderful treatment whether your hair is thinning or not. I've used it most of my life . . ."

"And your hair is beautiful."

"Thank you. It's an old Indian recipe from my great-grandmother. You've got Byron's antiwrinkle cream, the alpha hydroxy acid lotion and the deep moisturizing lotion. Use them according to directions. How's your fitness program?"

"Exercise?"

"Yes."

Sighing, Marcia said slowly, "Hal's a coach so he rides me there sometimes, but I've slacked up." Here Marcia stopped, wringing her hands. "Sherrie, I can tell you. My marriage is in trouble. I've got to do something. . . ."

Sherrie got up, squatted by Marcia's chair and put her arms around her. "You know it all begins inside, all beauty, all happiness. Think about Hal now. Maybe he's in trouble he can't talk about."

Marcia's head jerked up. "Oh Lord, I didn't want to think about that. I'll ask him right away. Oh, Sherrie, thank you."

Sherrie patted Marcia's back. "Okay. I think I want you first on the aromatherapy, then the facial, massage, manicure, pedicure, the works. Byron wants me to treat you like the queen you are."

Marcia's spirits had lifted and she chuckled. "Oh, Byron is a love."

"He's a nice man all right."

Sherrie got up and walked over to an open set of shelves

and brought back a panel board of essential oils to be used in the aromatherapy session. She explained the process to Marcia. "Select your favorite scent from this ten," she said. "Take your time." Beside each essential oil was a list of its uses.

Slowly Marcia unstoppered and sampled each aroma as Sherrie had shown her how to do. They were all so lovely and she felt herself relaxing deeply. "May I choose two?" she asked.

"Certainly. I don't recommend more than two at first, because they sometimes clash, but two is fine."

"Patchouli and rose. They smell wonderful and I need what they offer."

"Let me tell you something about aromatherapy," Sherrie said. "It's going to be one of the most useful tools you'll have. It goes back into antiquity, used by the Egyptians, Greeks, Romans and American Indians. It's like magic, awakening spirituality, psychic awareness, arousing sexual desire. There's so much you can do with it.

"You can visualize and, working with certain essential oils, get changes you wish in your psyche. Make a prayer to a deity while burning incense, see business success or a loving relationship. Later, after you're used to them, combinations can enhance all of these and that's where more than two fragrances can be effective.

"Psychic aromatherapy is a ball game in itself. It puts you in touch with yourself, gives you confidence, eases tension, pain, even gives you hope. It's been used throughout the ages.

"Check some books out of the library and read deeply about aromatherapy. My shop's only been offering it a little while, but women who come in keep coming back."

"It certainly sounds exciting."

"It is. You've chosen patchouli and rose oils. Patchouli is used to enhance sex, relieve anxiety, which you need, for physical energy, money. It's an antidepressant. Rose oil. Ah, the benefits are unending. Love, peace, sex, beauty. It's a stimulant and it, too, is an antidepressant. It's good for emotional shock, grief, anything concerning the heart. Plus, they're marvelous fragrances."

"I can't wait to get started."

"Then let's get our show on the road. I'm to work with you personally and the results are going to be outstanding, I promise."

Chapter 16

Mid-June

Nothing else frightening had happened since the videotape, Sherrie reflected as she jogged along a woodland path near her house. It was an early Thursday morning and the air was surprisingly cool for June. Mrs. Hall had baby-sat Tressa the night before while Byron took Sherrie to a movie in D.C. And Mrs. Hall would take Tressa to nursery school as Sherrie took a couple of hours off from My Beautiful Self.

She looked around her, feeling happy. Everything was going well. She and Byron had grown closer and closer, but she was still afraid. Now as she looked around her, her spirit felt more expansive. The two-mile wooded stretch where she jogged was only a short distance from her house and was across the road from scattered houses set far back. It was a bit isolated, but fairly well traveled.

A sparkle came to her eyes. The night before Byron had been sweet when he walked her in. He had stayed only a little while. "I've got to see that you get your beauty sleep," he'd said, "and too," he had teasingly leered at her, groaning, "you make me horny as hell."

"Byron!" she had remonstrated, laughing.

"Well, truth is light."

Thwack!

Sherrie started as her heart slammed against her rib cage. What on earth?

It was a few seconds before it came again. *Thwack!* Through eyes dimmed with fear, Sherrie saw that someone was throwing something at trees as she passed. There was little sound other than the *thwack*ing and a few cars passing. Even the birds were momentarily silent. Then with horror, as her vision cleared she saw a bullet pierce a nearby tree in front of her and knew that someone was shooting with a silencer. Fear had sharpened her wit and brains. *My God!* she thought. *Why am I out here alone? Don't I ever learn?*

Trembling, she looked across the road, looked at the highway. The scene was so serene.

Thwack!

With her knees nearly buckling under her, she heard it then. That laughter! Then the coarse, crude voice commanding her, "Run, bitch! Run!"

Whimpering, she tried to speed her steps and couldn't. The world and she seemed to move in slow motion. She was headed away from her house. For some perverse reason, she turned and looked into the trees. She could hear soft footsteps. Someone was running along with her, and for a few moments her vision cleared and she saw him. Average-sized body. Bushy black hair. A fleshy medium-brown face. All of it was forever burned onto her brain. Cruelly she thought of the bloody dagger she had envisioned in her car while driving from Byron's. This man was the source of the hellish laughter. Did he also have the dagger? Would he use it on her as he may have used it on Mike?

Then the guttural voice came again, angrier, more commanding. "Run for your life! I'm not playing with you!"

And with fear fueling her feet, Sherrie did run as if she had wings.

Thwack! Dear God, wasn't it ever going to stop! She was growing winded, breathless. How much longer did she have before a bullet pierced her body?

"Byron," she whispered, longing for the safety of his arms. She had run more than a half mile in the stretch. She wanted to go to the fence and climb through the bar and barbed wire, run to a nearby house, flag a passing car. But he could have read her thoughts as he barked, "Run straight ahead. Don't get any ideas or you're dead meat!"

She ran parallel to the fence and tried to think, but her brain had gone foggy even as her legs were giving out on her. Would they find her lying sprawled in these woods? She wasn't ready to die and she willed herself to think, to take some action that could save her. There was none. Zero. Zilch. She was nearing the end of her rope. No, she thought, not nearing, she was there.

Then she was dimly aware of a car stopping on the highway shoulder and someone getting out, calling her name. The shooting had stopped as abruptly as it had begun.

It seemed eons before the figure reached her and, blinded, she heard someone call her name again, someone close by, and she sank to the ground.

"Sherrie!" River said frantically. "What is wrong? Are you ill?"

"Oh my God," Sherrie whimpered, "he was shooting at me. I—I saw him." Her voice went hoarse, desperate. She needed to cling to someone and River squatted, taking her in her arms.

"Oh Lord, this is terrible," River said, commiserating with her friend. "Do you know who it was? Did you recognize him?"

"No. I never saw him before. He kept laughing, River, talking to me. It was the man on the tape . . ."

"The tape?"

Sherrie reflected that River didn't know about the tape. Lieutenant Steele had said she didn't want too many people to know. Thinking as quickly as her fogged mind would permit, Sherrie told her, "Byron and I watch fright films, and there is a tape on one of them, a frightening one."

"I see. Listen, I've got to get you home. Can you pull yourself together just a little? I'm going to call Byron, then take you home. But first, I'll call nine-one-one."

Still squatting, River duly called the emergency police line, gave them a location, then called Byron. Breathing heavily, still in a state of disbelief, Sherrie listened.

"She's not hurt, Byron," she heard River say. "She's very, very frightened, but not hurt." She gave him the location, told him she had called police and was taking Sherrie home. "Thank God I was passing," River told Byron. She listened a moment longer, then hung up.

On her knees by then, Sherrie heard River say, "I want you to take a few deep, slow breaths and try to stand. Don't be surprised if you can't. Help is on the way, but I'm going to take you home if I can. Oh, Sherrie, I'm so sorry."

Tears came then, hot and stinging, as Sherrie babbled, "I thought it was over. . . ."

"You thought what was over?"

Sherrie shook her head. "I can't talk about it. I just can't."

River bent and hugged her. "It's all right. You don't have to talk. I won't pry—ever. I just want to help."

Somehow, Sherrie managed to stand, and slowly she and River got to the fence. It took a long time for them to get through it, but finally they were in River's car. Only then did Sherrie say, "He might have shot you too. Thank you so much, River."

River smiled narrowly. "He didn't shoot you, love. Thank heaven for that. He was shooting *past* you, apparently trying to frighten you. There's so much insanity around these days. So much sheer craziness. The police may catch him, with your description, or they may never. I'd give anything to get to the bottom of this."

"Thank you," Sherrie said fervently.

River patted her shoulder. "You would have done the same for me."

Byron had been at a friend's office in Minden when the call came, but he was at Sherrie's house in a very little while. He found Sherrie and River in Sherrie's bedroom with Sherrie lying on the bed. He knelt and gathered her into his arms. "Are you all right?" he asked anxiously.

"As all right as I can be."

After a moment, he turned around as River began to leave the room.

"No, stay at least a few minutes," he said. "Again I have to thank you for saving something precious to me."

"It was nothing. I was passing."

"You risked your life."

River wet her lips. "I knew about the shots only after I climbed through the fence and talked to Sherrie. He stopped shooting shortly after I stopped, I gather. Some lunatic, I'd guess. Plenty of those around. Listen, Byron, I left a lot of things hanging when I just went out for a drive to clear my head. I went in early; thank heaven I did. I'm going to be running along. You're here now. I'm not needed."

Byron laughed, stood and hugged her. "You're always needed by me," he said.

Alone with Sherrie, Byron could not hold her close enough. Hot tears stood in his eyes.

"Don't cry," she told him. "I wasn't hurt."

"Not physically maybe, but you had to be so damned scared." He felt her heart thudding as he held her to him, said the words.

"Yes," she said finally. "There was no sound of shots. He must have used a silencer." She described the thwack she heard, remembering and growing faint with the memory.

"Byron, I saw him. He laughed the way he did on the tape." She shuddered. "What does it mean? Is he coming after me again? He could have killed me. Why didn't he?"

"Hush! Don't say that. Maybe he only wanted to frighten you. Damn him to hell for this!"

The door chimes sounded and the police were there. Byron

answered the door. Lieutenant Steele came to the bedroom door. "Don't get up," she said. "Sherrie, I'm so sorry."

She pulled up a chair and sat down, stroking Sherrie's back. "I hate having to question you when you're in such a state of fear, but it's now that you'll recall things you may want to forget later on. Please slowly tell me everything that happened, what you remember of it. My people are canvassing the woods, and I'll shortly be going back." Lieutenant Steele's mouth had set in a grim line. "Believe me, Sherrie, we're going to get to the bottom of this."

Byron paced the floor like a protecting lion, unable to be still.

"If River hadn't come by . . ." Sherrie began.

"But she did come by. I don't want to second-guess a maniac, but I think he was trying to scare you."

"Set me up maybe," Sherrie said bitterly, "so I'd be easy prey for the kill."

"Don't, love," Lieutenant Steele said. Sherrie reflected that River had called her "love" this morning, now Lieutenant Steele said the same. Byron said it often. Somebody sure didn't love her.

"I saw him," Sherrie said suddenly, just remembering again.

Lieutenant Steele's head jerked up. "You saw him." Her breath came faster. "That's wonderful."

Sherrie gave her a description and Lieutenant Steele said, "This is going to make all the difference." She stood. "I'm going back to the woods now. Sherrie, keep in very close touch. I think this is a frightening device he used, but I don't want us to take any chances. Don't ever be alone in isolated places again, do you understand? You let your guard down when nothing else happened after the tape. Please don't do that again."

Sherrie thought then that she had never told anyone about the vision of the bloody dagger. Not anyone. It was a chimera. Or was it a forewarning of what was to come?

After Lieutenant Steele left, Byron lay on the bed beside her, holding her.

"You brave, foolish woman," he said, "what am I going to do with you? You've got to be careful, Shere. Never take a chance like jogging alone in the woods until this is over. Don't you know my very life is all tied up with you?"

Suddenly Byron looked at her. "You're coming home with me," he said.

"For the night? Okay. I'll leave a note. Mrs. Hall can bring Tressa over. She'll be back around twelve."

He shook his head vehemently. "No, for a while, a long while."

"Oh, Byron, I . . ."

"Don't argue. It's a done deal. You say Mrs. Hall will be back at twelve. She'll pack your things and I'll take you."

Leaning back, Sherrie found she breathed a sigh of relief. It felt good to be wanted and cared for. To be loved. But she was still scared witless.

Chapter 17

"Good night, sweetheart. Sleep well."

Byron sat on the edge of the bed Sherrie lay in, bent over and smoothed her brow. Her body still seemed to him to thrum with fear and anxiety and he drew her to him. "I'm right down the hall. Call me on your intercom if you want or need me."

Sherrie lay still under his ministrations. He stroked her shoulders and her back, touched the lace-trimmed pale blue nylon tricot nightgown she wore. He was taut with protective anger at the devil who had put her in this state.

"Thank you," she said softly. "I'll be all right, now that I'm here with you."

"You bet you'll be all right. I love you, Shere, so much. So much."

She looked at him, her heart in her eyes. It was time to say it then. "I love you too."

Byron's heart nearly burst with joy. It was hard to tear himself away, but she needed sleep, so he kissed the corner of her mouth, tucked the cover under her chin as one might a child and went out. He couldn't take advantage of her frightened situation.

Sherrie lay thinking, only a little drowsy from the sleeping tablet he had given her. Tressa was with Helena who had cried bitter tears. She, Byron and Helena all thought it was best that the little girl not be around while her mother was so upset. Tressa had been happy to stay with her beloved Aunt Helena.

Byron's house and Byron had been a godsend. Sherrie felt safe there. After staying two days, she had insisted on going in to My Beautiful Self. She had been nervous, but things had gone well. Katherine had been vividly sympathetic, furious.

"I'd like to get my hands on the monster who did this to you," she'd said. Being at the beauty salon had taken her mind off things. And she had seen Tressa at the salon. Tressa who explained that she was playing with the nesting dolls and having fun and wondered when her other doll would come.

Sherrie thought how she was calm for periods, as if nothing had happened, then the fear struck and she wretchedly relived the terror. And yes, she'd envisioned the dagger again, the bloody dagger. In flashbacks, she'd seen something else: the hated vicious face she'd seen in the woods. A shudder ran the length of her body, then she calmed, drifting off to sleep. Only once did she cry out softly, "No!" She ran on shaking legs, pursued by a madman with a silenced gun.

Much later she came awake to the sound of loud, rumbling thunder. The luminous clock hands reflected eleven forty-five. She had only been asleep two hours and she felt wide awake.

In his room, Byron lay awake, too, and worried. A bad storm had been forecast with constant lightning strikes and fifty-mile-per-hour winds. How was Sherrie sleeping? Her face and body rose before him, making him breathe shallowly with warmth and longing to have her in his arms. His love for her strengthened and enriched him, and he thought he would protect her always, would kill for her. He got out of bed, going to check on her.

With Sherrie, the fear took her when the first arc of lightning flashed, illuminating the darkened room, to be closely followed by other brilliant flashes. Then crashing thunder shook the house, and she was on her feet, driven by demons beyond any she had ever known. Springing up, she fled her room, not stopping for a robe or slippers, pushed by overmastering terror, of what she wasn't sure.

They met in the hallway just outside his door and the lights went out. In the darkness he pulled her to him and held her trembling body tightly. "I've got you," he whispered. "Don't be afraid." Feeling his way, he led her into his room and they stood locked together.

Her face was wet with tears as she tried to talk, finally saying, "I was so scared. Byron, let me stay with you."

His heart leaped with joy. "Oh my darling, you know you can always stay with me. You get into my bed and I'll just sit in this big chair." He wished he could see her face.

She pressed even closer to him, body clad only in pajama bottoms. "No. I want you in bed, too, with me. Sweetheart, please light a candle. I want to see you."

Lightning crackled in angry, jagged streaks and thunder continued to crash as Byron found big glass-enclosed candles on a closet shelf in his room and lit them with an old cigarette lighter from a nightstand drawer, throwing shadowy romantic light across the room. My God, but she looked beautiful in the candlelight, he thought, his heart thudding with tension and with need.

He took her in his arms again and held her against his bare chest. "It's cool. I'll get you a robe."

"No." She clung to him. "Just hold me. Byron?"

"Yes, love."

She trembled as she told him, "You once said you wanted me to kiss you the way you kissed me that night at Tressa's birthday party."

She drew his beloved face down to hers and kissed him, her mouth open a little, her tongue exploring his. Her heart raced with wanting him.

After a moment, he drew a little away. "Are you sure? You're scared, anxious. I want you to be sure."

She nodded. "I'm sure. In the woods when I knew I could die, might die, I wanted you so badly. I was full of regret that I hadn't let myself love you the way I now know I do. Full of regret that I haven't felt you deep inside my body, that I haven't let you fill my heart and soul the way I know you can. Oh, Byron . . ."

Her mouth found his then and she opened totally to him as fire swept her belly and hot honey filled her veins. Byron felt his loins constrict with momentary disbelief, then flame with relentless desire. Had she really come to him at last?

Pulling away for a moment, she told him, "I love you, my darling, and I want you so bad. Come inside me. Come home the way I have."

With a prolonged groan, Byron felt the hardness of his flesh press into the wondrous silken softness of hers. His big hands squeezed her buns, stroked her back, could not get close enough to the firm breasts that strained against his muscular chest. Breathing heavily, he stripped the gown from her as she tore off his pajama bottoms. Attenuated naked flesh met then and was undone.

Nearly staggering with passion, he lifted her, carried her to the bed and laid her down. In the flickering, shadowy candlelight, the nimbus of her hair thrilled him, as did her luscious body. Her rounded breasts, her indented waistline and wide hips filled him with awe. He thought of the Bible and The Song of Solomon.

"You're so beautiful," he said.

"I'm glad you think so."

"What do you want? Tell me what you want me to do to you."

Wetting her lips, she put her mouth to his ear and whispered all the wild, delicious things she wanted. A reticent woman ordinarily, she felt raging desire melting her reserve.

"What you ask for, you get," he promised. "My darling, I want you to have whatever you want—in bed, in all our life."

They kissed feverishly and he began to wetly caress her with the tip of his tongue. Pausing at her breasts, he suckled them gently at first, then with hungry fervor, his tongue flicking teasingly over the nipples that hardened and pebbled. Her frantic hands cupped the back of his head and pressed him in to her.

Moving to her navel, he licked it lightly then patterned quick kisses over the silken flesh of her belly, going down to her female core and lingering there. His tongue flicked her lazily, tantalizing, teasing, driving her crazy as she bucked beneath him. He willed himself to hold back, but it was killing him. He wanted to be inside her so badly. He had to slow himself so he told her, "I had a peach tree once that bore delicious freestone peaches—ripe, juicy, sugar-sweet. Honey, that's the way you taste to me."

She drew a sharp breath. "That's such a precious thing to say."

Urging him on, Sherrie felt ancient fire sweep her body, felt ecstasy take her as she placed her hands on his mighty shaft. He shuddered and laughed shortly. "No, don't, sweetheart. I'll go over the edge if you do." He opened the drawer of the night table and took out a condom.

"I want to put it on you," she said. And lovingly, she slipped on the thin latex shield, smoothed it and he trembled. Engorged, still rising, he entered her then, slipped into her nectar-laden body and quivered vividly for a moment, stopping, slowing himself so he wouldn't finish. He thought of snow-laden mountains, and he groaned because it wasn't helping much. He had wanted her for too long.

For Sherrie it seemed that every cell of her body surged toward him. Her very soul was caught up with this man. With him filling her body, touching her womb, she felt herself quivering with passion like a guy wire in a high wind. She pressed his rock-hard buns into her and wrapped her legs across his back. That was his undoing as he felt an earthquake shake his body and his seed went streaming.

"Oh, sweetheart," he whispered, "I'm sorry I couldn't last for you."

"We couldn't last. I had multiples. Couldn't you feel them?"

"I did." He squeezed her tightly. "And they felt wonderful. We've got the whole night ahead of us."

Still wanting each other, they lay side by side as she stroked his lips with her fingertips. "Did I kiss you the way you kissed me that first night?" she asked.

"That and more. No wonder you held back. You took me away with you."

"I love you. I know that now. I've missed so much with you."

"Now we have it all. We won't lose any more time." He stroked her lips, tracing the outlines with his fingertips.

"Do that again," she demanded.

"What?"

"Trace my lips with your fingertips."

He smiled. "Oh, I can do better than that." He bent and kissed her, letting the tip of his tongue trace her lips as she felt wild rapture. Her medium-length fingernails raked his back, and it thrilled him. Her finger pads made concentric circles on his back and it egged him on.

"We're so good together," he told her. "I knew we'd be."

"We're better than good," she said. "We're superb."

"Heavenly."

"Byron?"

"Yes, sweetheart."

"Let's wait a little while. I want to make this last. Talk to me."

Byron smiled lazily. Talking wasn't what he wanted to do right then, but if she wanted to . . . The storm raged on, and in the candlelit room they took little note of it, they were so intent on each other.

"Okay," he said. "What do you want to talk about?"

"You. You've been hit hard with loss in the past two years. We both have, but before that, you knew little pain. You've always had the best luck, the best of everything."

Byron pondered her statement, and it brought back memories he didn't want to remember, but he meant to be honest about it.

"Am I right?" she asked then.

"Wrong. My parents certainly thought they were giving me the best of everything, but they were both busy people, very busy. My father had a business to run and my mother was a club woman from the heart. I had every material thing I could want, but I seldom saw them and had little of their time. Joe and Stella largely raised me, and as you know, I love them both dearly."

She was silent. Despite having been family friends, she hadn't known this. He continued, "In school, I had a drinking problem. I got involved with Alcoholics Anonymous in college. Mike helped me. He didn't drink then. It was another thing to be grateful to him for.

"I made it through my Ph.D. with honors, but I had a gnawing emptiness I couldn't fill. I fell in love with you, and for a time it was worse."

"I'm sorry."

"You couldn't know. I married Alicia, and it stabilized me some. Then Ronnie was born, and I felt more purpose in life. I was determined to be the parent my parents had never been, and I was far happier. From the beginning Tate had done well. So I, as they say, had it all, but you continued to haunt me. Somehow I managed to put you on a back burner, as best I could, and go on with my life. We were all friends. You and Mike loved each other, were divinely happy. Our little girls were near the same age.

"Then Mike began to go bad, and I found out. I bled for what I felt you were going through. It opened up old wounds. Then Alicia and Ronnie died. Mike was killed. . . ."

Hot tears had come to his eyes and some trickled down Sherrie's face. They held each other tightly, and the soothing rhythms of love took over. She placed a hand on either side of his face and kissed him deeply. "I never knew," she said. "All the time we were friends, I never knew. I wish I could have helped."

And her heart hurt for the child and the juvenile and the man he had been, suffering in silence. Now he was here and he was hers, as she was his. "I'll make it up to you," she said softly. "I'll spend my life making it up to you."

He smiled crookedly. "I only want to give you the best of everything, always." He hugged her fiercely. "And I'm going to do just that."

She nibbled his ear. "I got the best of everything when I got you."

Desire was like hot lava then, driving them on. He slipped on a condom and positioned her astride him, his mighty shaft slipping deep inside her tight sheath and, eyes narrowed, he gauged the depth of his penetration and smiled.

"Why are you smiling?"

"Am I?" he asked lazily.

"Yes, you are."

"I'll tell you later."

Passion had overtaken them both and they moved like gymnasts, like dancers choreographed by cheering nature. She felt him throbbing, pumping, and thrills ran the length of her body. Deep inside he knew glory the way he had not known it before. Then all at once he went deeper still and groaned. This was unbearably sweet. She was quiet, riding him easily and well. His eyes feasted on her high, firm breasts and the aureoles of her nipples. Their faces were strained with excitement, their eyes clouded with ecstacy.

Each slow, voluptuous movement brought rippling waves of enjoyment as time passed, and they knew each other in ways neither had known with others before. In the living room the grandfather clock struck two and she moved closer. His big hands fastened on her buns and drew her even nearer as if he couldn't get her close enough.

"I love you, Shere," he told her, "and you're right, I've come home."

"I love you too. No, I adore you." There was no separation now, no boundaries. They were as one.

Neither could talk above murmurs and whispers then, their feelings ran too deep. He pulled her down hard onto his erection so that she felt wonderfully impaled, with flashes of thrills permeating her entire body. She was crazy with passion. And facing her, he felt his strength go up to her, claim her, and mad with desire, he turned her over onto her back, entered and began to work her. He was no longer gentle, nearly savage, but protective, caring, mad with overwhelming love for the woman beneath him.

Eyes glazed with desire, she watched his powerful, wonderful body, watched the rippling muscles, the smooth abs and pectoral muscles, stroked his biceps feverishly. His chest was fairly hairy, but there was a thinner line of hair going down his belly and below. He was so beautiful! She couldn't bear the time she had been angry with him, had hated him. Or had she loved him all the while?

He flicked the tip of his tongue back and forth over the flat, brown mole that lodged near the valley of her breasts opposite the right nipple. "Mine," he said, claiming his treasure. "All mine."

"I'm all yours."

"Don't say it if you don't mean it."

"I mean it."

And her words spurred him on. Drugged with desire, he gave himself over to ecstasy and the body, the presence of this woman. There had been a time when he'd been unhappy, sick with grief, when he hadn't been certain he wanted to go on. Suddenly that was behind him and he felt like an African god, subject only to the greater God. He felt alive for the first time in a very long while.

They were a long way this time and, gasping for breath, she felt them winding down and chuckled inside. No, winding up, she thought, for even greater pleasure.

"Do you want a deeper thrill?" he asked.

"Oh yes."

"Then put at least one leg over my shoulder."

Lifting her legs, she tried what he suggested and held her breath with delight. He had maximum entrance then, touching her womb again, moving with loving precision. Her heart thrummed with delight and excitement. They were so intense they could hardly breathe for long moments, then they hit the zenith, and for him, volcanic explosions rocked his loins. He groaned and clutched her to him feverishly, wondering at the softness of her flesh. Sherrie felt herself going into a near trance, felt herself gripping and relaxing again and again. She went limp as powerful, undulating oceanic waves swept through her again and again, carrying her to a shore she wanted to re-visit many, many times. Again, she felt the multiple orgasms, and he teased her.

"You come on strong."

"You bring me on. I've never had them before."

"Never?" he asked, incredulous.

"Never. Thank you."

"Thank *you*." He lay, still inside her, still throbbing, still with fire and honey in his veins, and she wanted to hold him there for a long, lovely while.

They slept then with the winds still howling and the rain sluicing down. The thunder and lightning had stopped when they woke up and there was only the patter of light rain against the windowpanes. He came awake first. Reluctant to bother her, he felt the urging in his loins too strongly to resist. Leaning over, he lightly ran his tongue over her lips and she roused.

"What time is it?" she asked sleepily. All the fear she had known in the past days had been swept away. She was safe in his arms.

"It's five o'clock." The room was dark. There was a bat-tery-operated digital clock, with a luminous dial on the night table. He had put the candles out.

He relit the candles, and they made their way to his bath-room. "A shower together about now would be nice," he said, carrying a candleholder that he put on a table near the bathroom door.

"That appeals to me."

In a few minutes needles of warm water stung them both. Stepping outside the circle of falling water, she took lemon verbena bath oil from a shelf, rubbed it over them both and smoothed it down his body, then hers.

"You feel slippery, like a seal," she said.

"And you just feel good."

She stroked his wet shaft. "I couldn't do this last night," she told him. "You were too near the edge."

"I had waited so long to make love to you, to have you for myself."

"You have me now. What's stopping you?"

"You'll pay for that remark. I'm going to run you ragged."

Laughing she said, "I've had a couple of hours sleep. Bet you can't run me ragged."

"I'm sure going to try."

With wet hands, they explored each other's slippery bodies and thrilled to the touch. He reached over and got a condom from the medicine cabinet, spread her legs and entered her with the warm water streaming down on them. Her breasts felt alive with joy and passion as she felt him deep inside her body. Her womb quivered with ecstasy at the beloved guest. Every cell of her wanted him and every cell of him reached to possess her.

Their kisses were still drugged; they could not get enough of each other. With seeking hands they caressed and stroked and petted. He kissed her wet face, throat and shoulders, suckled her slippery wet breasts and bent to put his tongue to her navel.

"Ah, you're a lover, all right," she told him.

"With you, I can't help myself. Shere, you're fantastically responsive."

"Am I? I mean to be. I feel responsive to you."

"I'd like to lock you up, make love to you night and day for a couple of weeks."

Sherrie grinned. "Only a couple of weeks? I could use a month."

"I'm going to see that you get it."

Then they were silent again because feeling had gone too deep for speech and waves of engrossing ecstasy washed over them, leaving them both gasping for breath. His kiss was hard, impassioned. He tongued the wetness of her upper body. "Your breasts drive me mad," he said.

"You drive me mad."

Constant thrills swept them as they made brief comments, made love, grew swiftly accustomed to each other's bodies, minds, spirits.

"I love you," he told her.

"And I love you. I love the way you feel throbbing inside me. I love the wicked, wonderful way you make love. There's some kind of magic going on here."

"It's coming from you. You're the magic one."

"I think we both are magic. Love's like that."

"Our love anyway. Let's get out of the shower before we're prunes. I've got one more round I've got to know with you. Forgive me for being so greedy."

"That makes two of us."

Drying off with the huge bath sheets, they rubbed on lotion and more lemon verbena essential oil and kissed, this time his tongue lazily going over her face.

"What did you have in mind?" she asked.

At his suggestion she got on her knees and he backed her with her torso and the side of her face touching the plush carpet. Sheathed, he entered with tantalizing slowness, bit by bit, until she was gasping with ecstasy. Her body begged him to go on; she bit her bottom lip with fervor and moaned softly. And hearing her, he closed his eyes, then quickly opened them because he wanted to see the gorgeous, rounded curves of her brown buns, her back, her shoulders. He was thirty-eight and in the midst of the discovery of his life. In fantasy he pounded his chest as he stood on the tallest mountain proclaiming his passion and living his love for this woman.

She had thought that with her legs over his shoulders she

had known the full measure of him, but no, this was the fullest measure and it filled her with awe. How could anything be so magnificent, so simply superb, so sublimely good? Everything in her yearned for him, needed him. Her face was grave, her vision clouded, and she knew that if they loved each other a lifetime, this was the moment she would best remember. She had come to him belatedly, never realizing that she loved him. Now she knew and it filled her heart and soul with wonder.

Byron still felt the awe in his chest that he had known when she first kissed him the night before, came to him and kissed him the way he had only dared dream she would. Now that dream was reality and his world was complete. They were still slow, making love, feeling their way in to each other's hearts and souls. This time they came together and both felt passion eddy in their vividly excited bodies, felt tension drain away and peace, contentment and fulfillment wash over them like a magic trance.

Chapter 18

A week later Sherrie's mood had evened out. She no longer felt so spooked, but she knew she could no longer pretend that what was going on might be coincidence. She was definitely targeted. Was whoever was doing this just trying to frighten her? Or did the person mean to hurt her? Kill her as he had killed Mike? She was determined to go on with her life as best she could.

She was meeting Byron at Roland Hill's Dress Designing Studio on Connecticut Avenue not far from her shop. Roland, a thin, wiry, chocolate-brown man in his thirties, hugged her. "Girl, you're a sight for sore eyes. Have I got plans for you."

"I'm meeting someone here," Sherrie said.

"And from the looks of you, I'd say that someone matters. I always make all the time you need. You've brought me more business than anybody. Bring him on. How is Tressa?"

"Tressa's fine. Now she wants a designer dress."

Roland threw back his head, laughing. "I like to get them started early." Sherrie was pleased that Tressa was with her again. Roland went out and Sherrie continued thinking. Byron had insisted that they stay with him.

"I can't stay indefinitely," she'd protested to Byron.

"Why? I've got plenty of room. Neither one of us has to worry about gossip. You feel safe here, and I don't want you away from me. We'll talk about this later. Besides, we're in the middle of August ball plans. It's great to have you close at hand."

Byron, ushered in by an assistant, came to her, kissed her cheek. "Getting everything set up?" he asked.

"Yes. I'm excited." Her face was flushed, and Byron thought she was beginning to look really well again. Still, an air of indefinable sadness lingered on her countenance and he still felt angry about what had happened.

Roland came back and shook hands with Byron. Roland had only two other helpers and he mostly dealt with customers. He said to them, "You know how I love to cook? Well, I have fig newtons that are my very own concoction. You must try them. And tea? Coffee? Herbal tea?"

Sherrie chose herbal tea and Byron black coffee. Roland brought the refreshments back on a silver tray with delicate cutwork china plates and plain china mugs. Sherrie bit into the fig newton.

"You outdid yourself," she said. "These are delicious." Byron concurred. "Fig newtons are one of my favorites," she said. "Do you share recipes?"

"For you," Roland murmured, "anything." He turned to Byron. "I hope you know what a treasure you have in this woman."

"Believe me, I'm well aware," Byron told him.

Pacing the room then with his hands behind his back, Roland blew streams of air before he went behind the curtain to emerge a short while later bearing a large white sketch pad. An assistant brought in a tray with three glasses of champagne.

"What are we toasting?" Sherrie asked.

"You. Me. And the August ball."

Byron laughed delightedly. "Wonderful. Thank you."

They sipped the champagne and Roland sat down in a half circle with them, showed them his drawings. The sketches took Sherrie's breath away they were so stunning.

"They're beautiful!" she exclaimed.

"Then you're pleased?"

"Oh good Lord, I'm beyond pleased. I love them. What do you think, Bye?"

Byron smiled. "I think it's going to be a fabulous gown for a fabulous lady."

"Thank you both," Roland said gravely. "Study the lines. Tell me what changes you'd like, and we will begin the second stage. You'll be even more pleased when you see the fabric."

He left them then and they studied the design.

"I don't think I'd change a thing," Sherrie said.

"It's a masterpiece, all right. Is Roland getting the recognition he deserves?"

"I don't think so. But he's becoming more widely known. He has plenty of business. He's from New York's Pratt Institute."

"He's good. Really good."

Roland came back then with a bolt of midnight-blue fabric. "Feel the exquisite texture of this," he said.

Stroking and lifting the midnight-blue silk chiffon, Sherrie felt a sensual wave steal over her.

"Beautiful design," she said, "sensual fabric."

"Yes, sensual," Roland stroked the fabric. "I went to New York, ordered it specially from Hong Kong. I always see that you have the best."

"And I thank you for that."

To Sherrie's surprise, Byron asked, "May I hold that, please?"

"Be my guest," Roland said.

Byron took the bolt of fabric and laid it on his knees. He held a layer up and studied it, stroked it, enjoying the feel. "This has got to be one glorious dress," he said.

"Oh, it will be," Roland promised.

They kept the silk chiffon a long while as if it mesmerized them. "Why are you taking so much time with it?" Sherrie asked.

Byron looked at her, his blue-gray eyes lazily caressing her, making her shiver with delight. "First of all, it goes on my woman and I'm interested in anything that does. And I've got further plans."

"Plans?"

"I'll say no more. Curiosity . . ."

He stopped then and she wondered if he had been going to finish with the phrase *killed the cat,* but thought better of it. Even normal conversations were difficult now, she thought.

Roland looked from one to the other. He was always immensely pleased with anything that hinted of romance. Ball gowns and weddings were his specialty and he had the soul for his profession. He pursed his lips.

"I will need you to begin fittings next week. This will be an intricate undertaking. I meant this gown to be perfect."

"That's fine," she said. "You set the time, and I'll be here."

Roland took the fabric and the sketch pad back to his office.

Sherrie felt pleased, with a growing sense of happiness. "With the ball gown underway, I'm beginning to really feel the pull of the August ball. I think this will be one of the best. I just feel it in my bones."

Byron looked at her, smiling. "With you and me at the helm, with River and Curt's invaluable input, how can it miss?"

"How are perfume sales going?"

"River's Black Magic has already gone over the top. By August, sales will be phenomenal."

She smiled shyly. "I'm going to try some out on you."

"You don't need it. You're my all-time black magic."

Sherrie laughed. "And you're mine." Her heart expanded with his love, with the things he did to her and with her those nights when they were alone. He had proved to be a fantastic lover.

Now he said, "Roland does wedding gowns, as you know. They should be exquisite too."

"Yes." She felt her heart slow, then speed up.

"Response, please. When will you be interested in one?"

She looked at him nervously. "Oh, Bye, I have so much going on . . ."

"And I have so much going on in my heart. I'll never stop asking you, Shere. Pressing you. I'll never hurt you."

She sighed then. "You wouldn't mean to, but people . . ."

She stopped. She had been going to say *people change,* the way Mike had changed. But Byron wasn't Mike. Could he change too? Mike had once been all she could have wanted, then he smashed her heart to bits, shattered it, and it never stopped hurting, even if Byron had taken away a lot of the pain.

Roland came back, shaking hands with them both. "I'll look forward to seeing you next week. Will you both return?"

"We will," Byron said firmly.

Their next stop was at the Lucerne Hotel in Crystal City, Virginia, where they met River and Curt. The entertainment manager showed them the huge eighteenth-floor ballroom and suite to be used by Tate Cosmetics for the August ball.

A slim man with curly brown hair and florid skin, the manager proudly showed them around. Stairways led to the rooftop where the crowd would also go if it was a clear night. Now the vast polished floors stretched out before them and Sherrie could envision what the ball would be like.

Standing with his beloved, Byron thought of his forebears, his love for and his pain from his father. His fingers encircled Sherrie's upper arm as he smiled at her, and he was remembering what they knew together in passion and in love. The manager smiled at them; they looked good together.

Sherrie told River, "Congratulations on the outstanding sales for Black Magic."

River blushed delightedly. "It's your name and thank you. I think it's a perfect fit. I'm really proud."

"What I'm afraid of," Byron said, "is that we're going to have a hard time keeping her on after this. Other companies are already baying at our heels . . ."

River grinned pertly. "I'll remember what I've had with Tate Cosmetics. I love my job there."

Byron grinned. "And we love you."

"I'll second that," Curt rumbled. "We've got a great theme, centered around River's perfume: A Half Century of Black Magic."

"It makes me so proud I almost can't stand it," River said dreamily. "But it's your choice of names, Sherrie. Take credit."

"The credit is all yours," Sherrie told her. "The perfume's incredible scent made me dream."

Byron nodded, rocking a bit on his heels. "I can see it now. This room decorated magnificently—champagne fountains, the odor of Black Magic in the air. Good music. It will be our best ball ever." He drew Sherrie close. "She's given me so many ideas."

They smiled at each other. "I don't think I told you Tucker's taking me to the ball," River said.

Sherrie was surprised, pleased. Perhaps the two would begin a romance, she hoped.

Sitting at a table, they took a long time going over menus. They had their own band—two in fact. Dancing under the stars would be wonderful if the weather held. It was going to be a big ball, with people from all over the United States and a few from Canada.

Curt and River left, and the manager showed Byron and Sherrie to a suite of rooms Byron had reserved in the Lucerne's smaller inn. The suite was large, beautifully furnished. When the manager stepped away, Byron said, "This is where we'll slip away and spend the night. Shere, I just get the feeling this is going to be one of the most important nights of my life."

"With you," she murmured, "all my nights are the most important."

He kissed her then, lightly, teasingly. "Thank you. I think so too."

Chapter 19

"I love her! I love her!"

Tressa jumped up and down, barely able to contain herself as Sherrie and Byron sat smiling nearby.

"Then I take it you like her," Byron said dryly.

"Oh yes!"

And the Spanish dancing doll was beautiful. Brown like the nesting dolls, exquisitely fashioned, she was costumed as a flamenco dancer complete with clicking castanets. Laughing, Byron got up, took the doll and showed Tressa how to wind the doll up to dance.

"Oh my!" Tressa cried as the doll whirled on a polished section of the floor. "I'm going to call her Bianca."

"That's your middle name," Byron said.

"I know. That's what I want." The child looked at Sherrie. "May I call her that?"

Sherrie smiled. "She's your doll, honey. Call her whatever you like. I think it's nifty that you give her your name. Then, too, she's a Spanish doll and Bianca is a Spanish name."

"Clara's going to love her too." Clara and her children was what Tressa called the batch of nesting dolls.

"How can she help it?" Byron hugged Tressa.

Sherrie yawned happily and stretched. She glanced at Byron and their glances meshed, caught fire. She flushed and looked down. They were all up early. Byron had brought the doll in the night before while Tressa was still asleep. Fully dressed, Sherrie intended to be in My Beautiful Self by nine.

Katherine would be there to cover a bit early and Sherrie would stay a little later.

"What do you say to Uncle Bye?" Sherrie prompted.

A smile wreathed Tressa's face as she stood before Byron, her arms upraised, asking to be lifted. "Thank you. Oh, thank you. I love you."

Byron picked her up. "And I love you more. Now take care you don't dance Bianca into exhaustion."

"Exhaus—" Tressa asked.

"Wear her out," he explained.

Putting Tressa down, he turned to Sherrie. "I can give you a ride in, pick you up this afternoon."

She shook her head. "I've got a couple of errands to run. Thanks anyway."

"It looks like I'll be leaving first," Byron said.

"Did you get breakfast?" asked Sherrie.

"No time. Dolls come first. Marcia will stuff me at the office. I see she's coming along really well, thanks to you."

"Thanks to you and your cosmetics magic. You're in the right field."

"And I've got the right woman. Well, almost got her."

"Why do you say 'almost'?"

Byron studied her a long moment. "I want to marry you, Shere. Then I'll—we'll—have it all together. I'll have the right woman."

For a moment Sherrie couldn't get her breath. "I don't know," she said. "I—honey, could we talk about this later?"

"How much later?" he demanded. "This is what you get for dragging me off to bridal salons. You give me ideas, not that I needed that." He was trying to bring levity into a situation he was completely serious about.

"We'll see," she said noncommittally. Then when his face fell a little, his eyes went bleak, she went close to him. "I love you," she said softly. "Always remember that."

"I need a lot more."

"And you deserve a lot more."

"You can see that I get it. Okay, I do understand where you're coming from, but it's hard as hell when I want you so."

There were few early customers at My Beautiful Self. Dora greeted her warmly at the door and Katherine hugged her as Sherrie walked back. "You've got company," she murmured.

"Who?"

"Your sister."

Sherrie went in gingerly. What was up with Mallori?

"Sis?" Mallori greeted her. She seemed to mostly call her that these days.

"Mallori, how are you?" If anything was wrong, she sure wasn't showing it. Her sister looked radiant. The two women sat in chairs side by side. Mallori sipped a cup of hot, black coffee.

"Being wired's my natural state," Mallori said, grinning. "I might as well do it up brown with lots and lots of caffeine."

Dora knocked and stuck her head in the door. "I notice you didn't stop for coffee, Mrs. P., and I just wondered if you wanted some."

"How about a cup of green tea, with lemon. I'd appreciate that. Natural sugar, please."

As Dora nodded and closed the door, Mallori tapped her foot impatiently. "You really are wired today," Sherrie said. "What's going down?"

"Gus is going down. That's for sure. I hope for the count of ten. I'm really sick of that man. I couldn't wait to tell you the news. I'm inviting Lenny to the August ball."

Sherrie frowned. "Mallori, is that smart?"

"Oh, what the hell? Hey, I'm being a selfish beast again. I forgot to ask you if you've had any more trouble."

"No, I'm happy to say." Sherrie knocked on the wooden desk and shuddered. Seeing Mallori, she thought of Mike, and thinking of Mike she thought of the dagger. And the monster in the woods. Mallori didn't know about the videotape. Mallori saw the look of fear that crossed Sherrie's face and got up to comfort her as Sherrie felt a chill sweep over her.

"Don't the stupid police have any ideas on this?"

"They're not stupid," Sherrie told her. "They're very smart in fact, and yes, they have ideas, but they don't know who's doing this." She thought she'd run it by her. "It could have to do with Mike, things he was involved with. Mallori, I've never asked you. How much did you know about Mike?"

"What are you talking about?"

Looking at her sister, Sherrie remembered the strange look on her face when she'd found out Mike's portrait had been slashed. She'd rushed away as if there was someone she needed to see.

Sherrie thought of that conversation. "Nothing. Forget it."

Mallori sat back down. "Well, okay for now. All I know about Mike is how we loved each other. Now you tell me this madman shooting at you could have something to do with him."

"I said forget it. We'll talk another time about this."

"I'll sure look forward to that. So you don't think my inviting Lenny to the ball is a good idea?"

"Gus has a breaking point," Sherrie said quietly. "Everybody has one."

"I've got my breaking point too. I told Gus I'm taking Lenny to the ball, and he threatened me again. He's getting crazy." She sounded anxious and Sherrie thought it was about time. "Speaking of unwise decisions, I don't think it was too wise of you to move in with Byron Tate."

Looking levelly at Mallori, Sherrie told her, "That subject is off-limits."

"Meaning you can criticize me, but I can't do likewise? You know what he did to Mike. How can you even see him, let alone cohabit with him."

Sherrie opened her mouth to deny—what? she thought. That she and Byron were lovers? No, that was too precious a time to her. "Byron isn't putting me in danger the way Gus is you. He loves you, Mallori. Doesn't that mean anything to you? I've said it before. Hatred is the other side of love. Don't push him too far."

Mallori smiled sadly. "Speaking of love, I must be getting soft in the head, but I find myself loving you more and more. I know you mean well, Sherrie, that you wish me all the best, and I appreciate that. Maybe we can get closer. I'm happier now. Lenny is a live wire. He means to go places. He's a lieutenant now. One day he'll be chief. He's getting a master's in criminal justice, intends to get a Ph.D." She closed her eyes, leaned back. "He's what I'm looking for, and I'm not letting Gus stand in my way."

"Does he love you the way Gus does?"

Mallori bit her lip. "We don't talk much about love, we just make it, but he knows I want to marry him."

"And?"

Mallori shrugged. "He tells me to give him a chance to get used to it. He thinks that in time . . . He's never been married. I'm showing him the ropes."

Sherrie couldn't resist it. "Be careful you don't hang yourself."

Mallori got up. "I've got to run. Nice comeback. And you be careful. We're getting more fools and crazies around these days, including Gus. I wish I'd realized I love you a long time ago," she finished wistfully, moving over and kissing Sherrie on the cheek.

Sherrie found Marcia in the salon waiting for her. "Just thought I'd run by and touch base with you. I've made a Saturday appointment for the works, but I just wanted to talk about a few things."

Sherrie smiled. "You're looking very, very well."

"I—ah—I'm feeling very well. And you look happy, Sherrie. Byron's good for you. You're good for each other."

Sherrie blushed furiously, and her heart danced as warm

feelings crept into the pit of her stomach, remembering. "Yes," she said only, then "things seem to be falling in place. Byron's wonder cosmetics are working for you. I love your new hairdo. You're going to be ready for incredulous stares before the August ball."

"Hal's excited about that ball. In fact, last night—" She seemed suddenly shy, and her voice was hushed, then she laughed a little. "I don't want to tell state secrets . . ."

Sherrie smiled broadly. "That's an open secret. The whole you shouts it to the world. I think you're falling in romantic love again, and oh, I know the feeling." *Thanks to Byron, I know the feeling,* she thought.

The two women took chairs in the consultation room. "Next time I'm selecting ylang-ylang and a couple of other essential oils for my aromatherapy session," Marcia said. "Those oils are wonderful. No wonder they've been popular throughout the ages."

"Uh-huh. Another thing I want to mention to you is collagen. You know we begin losing collagen around thirty and we don't absorb it from food as well . . ."

"We're working with collagen absorption treatments at Tate. We're a little late because we check everything fifty ways to Sunday," Marcia said.

"Yes, but I want you to get started on one already on the market. How far is Tate Supreme from being ready?"

"Several months at least."

"Okay. I've got something on hand I want you to try. Reputable, careful company. They collaborate with Tate as much as compete with them. This is a drink, and yes, it's expensive, but from the beauty salon scuttlebutt, it's well worth it. And it'll help with the wrinkles and any sagging. You know, Marcia, your crow's feet fascinate me. Adding character, that sort of thing."

Marcia laughed. "Hal's begun to say that. He tells me not to go overboard. He tells me sometime, 'I'm getting old, too, and I'm not doing much about it other than keeping fit and watching my diet.'"

Sherrie drew a deep breath. "Wrinkles, some deterioration—well, they're the price we pay for longevity. Hal's right. We don't want to go overboard. I think that in this country we're too afraid of aging, too locked in on youth. Youth has its place, but it's far from the whole story. I say, enjoy every stage all our lives. I know I plan to."

"And I'm getting there."

"Good. What do you know about the Pilates method of exercise?" She pronounced it *puh-lah-teez*.

"Just what I've heard from Hal who keeps up with such things and what I've been reading about in the newspapers and magazines."

"It seems to me to be a great system, good for any age, building strength through special exercises and equipment. A German boxer developed it, trained disciples. They hold that the body's main strength is concentrated between the shoulders and the hips, emphasis on the abdomen. The best gym seems to be in Baltimore for this part of the country. I've gone over a few times. I'm impressed."

Marcia nodded. "Hal's gone over a few times too. Do you think I ought to try it?"

"It couldn't hurt."

At a railing on the Chesapeake Bay, Keith Janey pitched small stones out on the water and watched the ripples spread. He was at loose ends tonight. A police informant in his early forties, his last case had ended and he was highly pleased with it. Lieutenant Steele had taken him under her wing. Once a suspected murderer, he was now a Minden Community College man majoring in criminal justice, and he was proud beyond the telling. The courses were hard between his regular stint of doing odd jobs around police headquarters, but he managed well.

Keith's ears perked up as a couple parked, got out of the car and strolled over near him. *Plenty of space out here,* he thought. *Why were they coming so close?* Then he saw that it was the woman leading. He pulled his slouch hat lower on his head as he sucked in his breath. It was Sergeant Gus Dueñas and his wife, Mallori, the looker. *Well now,* he thought.

They stopped about twelve feet from him and their voices were loud. It was as if they gave a show just for his benefit.

"You can't do it, Mallori. You just can't do it," Gus argued.

"Oh, but I am doing it," Mallori came back. "That ball is one of the most important social events of the season . . ."

"All my friends will be there. The chief will be there. Captain Ryson, all the people I know. Please, baby, have a little mercy."

Mallori's laugh was cutting. "You're always whining. We're through, Gus. Face it like a man. I'm going to that ball, and I'm taking Lenny with me. It doesn't stop you from going too. Get a date. You're a good-looking guy, Gus. You could have plenty of women."

"I don't want plenty of women. I want my wife. You."

"Your soon-to-be ex-wife."

"Why are you so cruel?"

"Why are you so much like a little lap dog after me?"

Gus drew a sharp breath. "Be careful, Mallori."

Keith shifted. He was a small man, and they didn't seem mindful of him at all. Having trouble, were they? Well, so much for the beautiful people. Keith thought wistfully that he had heard a lot of talk about the August ball around headquarters and he sure would like to go. He had ambitions. One day he'd walk into a ball like that with a beautiful woman like Mallori Dueñas on his arm and all eyes would turn to them. Yeah, he grinned mirthlessly. When would that happen?

Keith drew into himself. The woman was talking. "You're a masochist and a fool," she yelled at Gus. "What do you need with me? I only hurt you. I always have and I damned sure always will. Marrying you was a mistake, Gus, a mistake

I don't intend to live with all my life. If Mike had lived, he'd have a divorce by now and we'd be married. He was the only man in the world for me."

The man's voice was raw with pain. "You're as cruel as the grave, and maybe that's where you'll wind up. I'll never let you go. Count on it." Pleading, he asked, "Why do you hurt me like this?"

Mallori's voice was cold, clear on the night air. "Because you let me. Mike was strong, powerful, afraid of nothing. You're a weak man, Gus. Like I told you, I'll always hurt you."

"Lenny's not going to marry you," Gus said. "He's screwed over a lot of women."

"He will, you know."

"I'll make you a bet. I don't want to see you hurt and he's going to hurt you—bad."

"I can handle him. We're in love."

"You're in love. He's getting his lust taken care of."

"That's your jealousy talking."

Gus's throat constricted. "You're my wife and I love you."

"You keep sounding like a broken record, a yelping puppy."

"Don't say that again." His voice had gone harsh.

"Then don't talk about things you know nothing about. Lenny's giving me a ring—an engagement ring."

"Damn it!" Gus exploded. "You're still married to me. What the hell are you talking about?"

"Lenny and I," she said, "we do things our way." She placed slender fingers to his face. "Don't be such a big baby, Gus. Live in the real world."

He came back hard. "Your real world where people don't care about other people's feelings."

"I care about Lenny—a lot."

Gus changed his stance, began pleading again. "Baby, please don't go to that ball with him. You're going to his picnic and not to mine. I can take that because it's in Baltimore and I don't know many people there. But the August ball is here, and . . ."

"Oh yes," Mallori said scathingly, "and all your friends will be there. No dice, Gus. No damned dice. Lenny and I are going to dance the night away, wrapped in each other's arms. Like I said, get a date and enjoy your own night at the ball. I'm certainly going to enjoy mine."

Gus's strong hands bit into her arms like vises. "Damn you," he snarled, voice rising. "I tell you you're not going to make a fool of me because I'm going to stop you . . ."

"And how will you do that?" she taunted, her own voice rising. "Your magic wand's started back to working? It wasn't the last time I checked."

"Damn you, Mallori!"

Keith knew then what he'd thought was true. The woman had moved near him, probably unknowingly seeking protection in what must have been her fear.

"Nothing's going to help your case, Gus."

Gus's voice was guttural and Keith had to strain to hear him. "You'll see, baby. You'll see what I've got in mind, and it'll be too late then. I'm sorry. Really sorry."

Keith had moved a bit closer and they still seemed altogether unaware of him. He thought he could hear Gus's last words, but he wasn't sure. They were choked and maybe he was filling in from his own imagination, but he had heard enough. Lieutenant Steele was going to be interested in this. Gus Dueñas was her fair-haired boy.

Chapter 20

Things were slow at Caleb's restaurant. It was a Friday night; later, things would be far livelier. A band played soft music, danceable music. Tonight, it was Cass and the Cupids and Rafe Sampson was singing some of the golden oldies.

Sherrie and Byron sat at a table that overlooked the courtyard and the big, jumping goldfish in a large, brilliantly lit stone pond.

"While we're waiting for our order," he asked her, "would you like to dance?"

She sipped white wine. "I wasn't going to bother you, but I've got a slightly hurt foot. Otherwise, I'd love to dance."

"Hurt how? And why weren't you going to tell me?"

"You've got enough on your plate."

"I'll always make time for you. Now, what's the hurt foot about?" He looked at her with tender concern, and her heart turned over with love.

"A rushing customer accidentally stepped on it. Fortunately, she was wearing flats, but she was hefty. It's not too bad. I examined it carefully, and I'll soak it tonight."

"I think you should see a doctor first thing in the morning. Maybe we ought to go by the emergency room tonight. You can never be too careful about these things."

Sherrie smiled, flirting with him over the rim of her wineglass. "You're sweet, but far too anxious. I tell you I think my foot will be fine, but I will go in tomorrow morning if it's even very sore. You take such good care of me."

"I love you. Do you know that?"

"I suspect it, and I love you right back."

They sat for a moment gazing into each other's eyes. "You brought your briefcase in," she finally said. "Have you something special inside? You usually lock it in the trunk."

"Funny you should ask. I've got a surprise for you. I invited you out here when I know you've got a long day tomorrow because I want to give you something I think you'll like."

"A present? I love presents."

"My first real one to you, the first of many. I'm going to love spoiling you."

"You're the best gift of all," she murmured.

He bent over, picking up the briefcase when a merry voice lilted from behind him. "Imagine meeting you two here."

Jasmine, Tucker and River came up behind Byron. Sherrie had seen them when they came in, had not wanted to interrupt the precious moment with Byron.

Byron looked at Jasmine in a tightly fitted black dress that showed a lot of cleavage. As usual, she sparkled. He then looked at River and Tucker and wondered. He knew Tucker was taking River to the August ball, but hadn't realized they had anything going on other than that. Tucker and Byron eyed each other coolly.

"How are you, Sherrie?" Tucker asked softly. "I didn't get by today, but I'll be in early tomorrow."

"Fine," Sherrie responded. Tucker's air was warm, and yes, she thought, proprietary? He was acting odd. Sherrie suspected he liked rattling Byron's cage. There had been bad blood between them since Byron and Mike had fallen out.

Jasmine wiggled provocatively, shaking her hips, and said to River, "They're playing your song, 'That Old Black Magic.' Do they know about your perfume?" she teased River, who blushed. Then Jasmine held out her arms to Byron, "Dance with me, old friend." She swept an arched glance over Sherrie, "Seeing that you two aren't taking advantage of the music . . ."

"We've decided to sit these few out," Byron said easily, putting a hand over Sherrie's, causing a flash-of-fire look from Jasmine.

"Okay," Jasmine flirted. "Turn me down. Break my heart. You haven't always felt that way."

Byron didn't answer, and Sherrie wondered what really had gone on between those two. According to Byron, not much; according to Jasmine, everything. Sherrie felt the slime of jealousy oozing into her life again the way it always did when Jasmine was around and hustling Byron.

Jasmine shrugged as Tucker and River stood by, bemused. She turned to her brother. "It's really slow here tonight. What do you say we drive into D.C. for something livelier?" She shot a sultry glance at Byron. "I'll definitely see you around. Drop by my place anytime."

River's smile was warm for Byron and Sherrie. "Are you okay?" she asked Sherrie softly, and Sherrie nodded.

"I'm okay. Thanks for asking."

"Always," River said graciously. "You're looking well. Happy."

"Thank you. I am happy."

Tucker came forward, touching Sherrie's hand. "I'll see you tomorrow."

But Jasmine wasn't through. "We'll stay," she said, "if we can join you."

"That would be fine," Byron said, "but I have something special to discuss with Sherrie, so we're a closed corporation right now."

Jasmine's head jerked up. "In that case, we're out of here." Her voice was harsh, disappointed.

After the trio left, Sherrie raised her eyebrows. "I'm surprised she doesn't get sexually assaulted daily."

Byron laughed. "Hey, Jasmine really brings out your feline side."

Sherrie shrugged. "I'm not being catty, just observant."

Caleb, the owner, came over to their table. "I have a light, dry white wine that goes splendidly with the seafood," he said. "Drink up. It's on the house."

"Thank you," Byron told him.

"Did you know Mr. Sampson's got a new CD coming out, and next year another album perhaps?" Caleb offered.

"No," Byron and Sherrie both said.

"I've followed him from the beginning," Sherrie said. "I'll have to go over and congratulate him."

The older music man had slid into the old song, "You'd Be So Nice to Come Home To," and as Caleb excused himself, Byron caught Sherrie's hand, squeezed it, and repeated the title of the song.

"I'll wait until after we eat to give you your present, but you will be so nice to come home to. Sherrie, I can't wait for us to really belong to each other. To know that you really are mine in every way."

Sherrie's face was grave. "I want this, too, but it'll take time. I'm sorry, Bye."

"Don't be. I'm not going anywhere."

Their seafood platters were hot and succulent, and the white wine Caleb sent them was superb. They ate slowly, with Sherrie slipping off her shoe and rubbing her uninjured foot over the instep of Byron's loafered foot and up his leg as he grinned. "Provocative. Provocative. You'll pay for this."

"When?" she answered pertly. "And how much?"

Byron threw back his head, laughing. "Plenty," he answered, "and soon."

Dessert was raspberry cheesecake, which they both savored. Sherrie kept thinking of Byron's briefcase and his present. She hugged herself, smiling. She was like a child about gifts.

"Why are you smiling so?" he asked.

"I'm with you," she replied. "Do I need another reason?"

"Ah, you're stroking my ego with velvet gloves, and it's sending me up in flames."

She looked at him archly. "It doesn't take much to send you up in flames."

"Not where you're concerned. You look my way and nature strikes a great big match."

"You've got a way with words. What about the present?" She couldn't resist asking.

He smiled and narrowed his eyes. "Ah, the present."

He bent and opened his briefcase, taking out two small packages beautifully wrapped in dark blue sheer linen with fancy matching bows and bunches of small, white flowers. He handed them to her.

She held them a little while. "They're really too pretty to open."

"Wait until you see what's inside."

She undid the packages gingerly, smoothing the wrappings, saving them. Two dark blue smooth leather cases were revealed, and she snapped the larger, square one open and gasped. Tears came to her eyes at the beauty of a large, teardrop-shaped sapphire pendant that lay on a dark velvet bed. A wide, gleaming gold herringbone chain supported the pendant and diamonds on four sides winked brilliantly. The logo of one of the area's best jewelers was inside the cover.

"It is so beautiful," she whispered. "Oh, Byron, thank you."

"Now you know why I studied the fabric in the bridal shop so carefully. Open the other box."

Inside was a pair of large sapphire studs. A diamond was fastened just below each one, twinkling as brightly as those in the pendant.

Byron felt the satisfaction of pleasing her course through him, and his loins grew warm with pleasure. "Like them?"

She shook her head slowly. "I love them, and you're a lover."

"Which you've said before. Stick around. It only gets better."

Laughing softly, she told him, "It doesn't get much better than this."

"Oh that," he scoffed, "is just a saying. It gets much, much better, and you know it. In time, you and I are going to have a paradise on earth."

And looking at him, she saw that he had plans for them. Big plans. It bothered her that she was so far behind. She was hurt and scared and full of anxiety. Her life had been savaged, shattered. It was hard for her to trust again.

At home in his bedroom, Byron took off Sherrie's shoes and panty hose and positioned her on the bed, thinking her high, rounded breasts, the narrow waistline, and the wide, rounded hips were all driving him crazy. He didn't foresee a time he'd get used to all that glory. He got a wide, stainless-steel soaking pan from his bathroom. Bringing it back, he asked, "What do you want to soak your foot in? Epsom salts? Soda?"

She thought a moment. "I wish I had the stuff I had when I hurt my foot last fall, but it's at home . . ."

"This is your home now, love—with me."

She looked at him, her heart expanding, pounding a little. "Thank you, sweetheart. I guess Epsom salts will be good."

They soaked her foot for a half hour as they talked about the August ball, about cosmetics, Marcia's progress, River and Tucker. They touched on many things before he dried her foot carefully, put the towel aside and brought her instep to his lips, tracing it with the tip of his tongue. He looked at her and gauged the depth of her desire, thrilled to see it. "Feel better? It's beginning to show a little bruising."

"How could it not feel better with your touch?"

"Dr. Tate, ma'am, at your service." His voice was husky with need. "I've got to let you rest tonight," he said, "but know that I'll be tossing a few doors down from you. In fantasy my hands will be roaming your body, stroking all the tender spots. I'll go into your secret places and lavish my love on them. You give me so much pleasure, Shere. I've never known anything like this before."

As he talked, it was as if she were in his arms, making love, the images were so strong. "I'll kiss you good night," he finally said.

She stood when he did and went into his arms. Looking at her gravely, he walked her over to a jutting corner of the room and pressed her against the wall, feeling the voluptuous outlines of her soft body. Her breasts ached for him, and he caught her buns in his big hands and pressed her in to him as she moaned softly.

"I won't take you," he said. "I want you to rest. We've got time."

She laughed shakily. "You speak for yourself."

His laughter mingled with hers as he continued to rise against her like a mighty oak. "You can feel where I'm headed," he said. Raising her skirt he pushed aside her lacy panties and his fingers found the syrupy wetness of her as he closed his eyes. Hugging her tightly, he told her, "Now this is really good night. Sleep well and dream about me—about us doing all the good things."

Then he was gone, and she half stumbled back to the bed and sat. She wanted to just dream about him, feel his kisses, his hands on her body. This was ecstasy and torment. She didn't want to undress, she was so heavy with desire.

She thought she'd better turn her cell phone back on; she had turned it off in the restaurant. She carried two cell phones, one just for Mrs. Hall in case she needed her for something about Tressa. That one was never turned off.

Languidly she got up, got her cell phone and checked the messages. There was one from Helena, just touching base. The second one brought her to attention.

"Hi, Sis. Mallori here." She smiled at the thought of Mallori identifying herself. That low-pitched, sexy voice needed no identification. "I've never been afraid before, but I'm getting a little nervous. I think Gus is losing his mind. He's mad as hell with me about the August ball. I need you to talk to him, please, and do it soon. Call me right away when you get this. Please call right away." Then the voice hesitated before she said, "Love ya," and hung up.

The voice was wired from beginning to end, and Sherrie quickly dialed Mallori's number and got her recording. "Hello, you. You know what to do after the beep. Bye." So brief. So provocative. She stayed up later than she had intended to, calling every twenty minutes or so and getting no answer. Tossing, she called throughout the night. Where was Mallori?

Several times she called the cell phone Gus always carried and got no answer either. Only toward morning did she sleep and she came awake early. Dialing Gus and Mallori again, she only got their messages. Frustrated, she got up and looked at her foot, which had a long bruise. She would see her doctor that morning.

Chapter 21

"Tate has a new eye cream on the market, one based in DMAE. I want to begin using it as soon as possible," said Sherrie.

"That's the cream that absorbs collagen into your skin?" Marcia asked. "I've been reading about it, hearing about it here."

"That's it. I've tried it on a few customers, and it's dynamite."

Sherrie talked with Marcia on the phone as she sat in her office at My Beautiful Self.

"I'll begin using it right away," Marcia said. "I'm in a permanent state of excitement these days."

"That's always helpful. How is Hal?"

"Never better. Sherrie, I went with him to Baltimore and signed on for the Pilates exercise course. It may be my imagination, but after only a week, I'm feeling results. You really should try it. I've told Byron about it."

"Uh-oh," Sherrie said. "You know Byron is deep into fitness. I can see him and me now, all the way into the Pilates thing. Wish me luck."

"Pilates is better than luck. Hal is ahead of me on this, and he's swinging from the rafters. Sherrie, thank you and Byron. I want all the best for you both. You're so right for each other."

For a moment Sherrie couldn't speak. They were right for each other, but when could she get her act together?

For the second time, at the salon she called Mallori, then Gus. Where were they? Gus hadn't looked well when she'd

seen him lately, but Mallori was glowing. It was a bad combination—one divinely happy, the other deeply depressed.
She got up and went down the hall to the aromatherapy room
where the odors of the various essential oils soothed her.

She sat in a deep chair with her cell phone in her pocket
when it rang. She jumped, hoping it was Mallori, but it was
Byron.

"How's the foot?"

"Bruised, a little achy. I am going to the doctor's."

"I can drive you. I meant to check on you before you left,
but my dreams of you got the best of me and I overslept."

"Sweetheart, I happen to know you have a meeting with
foreign guests this morning. You're not going to have the
time. I'm glad you had good dreams."

"Far better than just good. Glorious. You forget I have excellent people in Curt and River. They can take up any slack.
It won't take all that much time."

"I insist on driving myself, but I appreciate your offer and I
love you." She didn't say it often enough; he said it all the time.

"I think I'm way ahead of you there. Call me when you get
back."

"I will." She kissed him with a soft, smacking sound and
he returned the kiss.

After she hung up, again she quickly dialed Mallori and
got no answer. Gus. No answer. A sense of dread set in then.
Something was terribly wrong. Gus's eyes had been empty,
devoid of hope when she'd last met him on the street a few
days before. He'd been like a child severely beaten for something that could never be his fault. Poor Gus, he certainly
loved not wisely, but too well.

Dread ran the length of Sherrie's body as Katherine came
rushing in, tears running down her face, bent and hugged her
tightly, saying, "Sherrie, brace yourself."

"What is it?"

Stroking her back, Katherine said slowly, "It's Mallori.
They found her early this morning. She's been murdered."

"Murdered?" Sherrie's questioned cry was harsh, incredulous. "What happened?"

"I don't know. It was just on a TV news flash."

"Oh my God. I've got to listen." She started up, but Katherine pressed her back.

"No. Sit still for a few moments. It won't be on TV again until the twelve o'clock news. WTOP will have it on the radio, but you've got to collect yourself."

"When did they find her and where?" Sherrie demanded. She remembered then that Katherine had said Mallori was found early in the morning.

Katherine repeated, "It was before daybreak this morning on a country road out from Minden, past the old Henderson place."

Sherrie knew then what she had to do. "I'm going out," she said to Katherine.

"Out where?"

Sherrie thought quickly; she didn't intend to be stopped. "I think home for a little while," she fibbed.

"I'll go with you. You'll be too nervous to drive."

"No. I'll be all right. Trust me."

Reluctantly, Katherine hugged her again and let her go. Out in the parking lot, Sherrie moved as if in a nightmare. Her body felt heavy, her spirits sodden. In her car a few minutes later she turned on the news station WTOP and heard the announcer talking about the murder, news she needed to hear. The announcer gave the location Sherrie headed toward. Reaching into her tote, she got her cell phone and cut it off.

Out on the highway, her head cleared and she drove toward the crime scene, toward her sister's body. She drove carefully, wanting to hurry, dreading the time when she'd get there. It wasn't far, at the distant edge of the old Henderson place on a major highway. She'd taken this route to Baltimore and it was familiar.

Finally, there it was up ahead. The old Henderson place, and in the flat stretch of land, she could see many cars parked including police cars. People busily moved about. She parked a short distance away and walked across the highway on leaden legs.

Lieutenant Steele saw her and, frowning, walked over to her and put her arms around her. "You shouldn't be here," she said.

"You know I had to come. Where is she?"

"They've taken her away."

Sherrie saw Mallori's white Cadillac convertible then as a bunch of police people moved around it. In her mind's eye she could see Mallori in the driver's seat with her silken brown hair streaming in the wind, irreverent, living a life that brooked no interference. That was Mallori in life. Now there was the empty convertible and a death wagon that had carried her away. This was Mallori in death.

Byron would be in his meeting, but he would call as soon as he knew about Mallori. She turned the phone back on.

Lieutenant Steele saw her dazed stare and, taking Sherrie's arm, told her, "Let's go to your car. There're a few things I need to ask, if you can bear talking."

"Anything to help."

Sitting in Sherrie's car Lieutenant Steele asked, "When did you last see your sister?"

"A couple of days ago."

"Did she seem distraught? Angry? What was her mood?"

There were tears in Sherrie's voice as she told her, "She was very, very happy. She had a new boyfriend and she was planning to go to the August ball with him."

Lieutenant Steele's jaw fell a little. "What about Gus?" she asked quietly.

"Yes, what about Gus? Mallori was winging it. She was expecting the new man to propose any day, she said. She was in seventh heaven."

Lieutenant Steele shifted uncomfortably. It was no secret that Gus Dueñas was one of her favorite people and she hated anything that hurt him the way this had to.

"Did you talk with Gus?"

"I did."

"And what was his mood?"

"Murderous, I'd say."

"Did she ever tell you he threatened her or did you ever hear him threaten her?"

"Many times. They were both hot tempered."

"Pointed threats or general ones?"

Sherrie was silent a few moments before she drew a deep breath. "A couple of months back he told her he'd kill her before he gave her a divorce . . ."

"I see."

The phone rang then and an upset Byron was on the line.

"Where are you?" he demanded.

She gave him her location.

"Sit tight," he told her. "Don't leave. I'm coming out."

Sherrie hung up and looked at Lieutenant Steele with dry, painful eyes that seemed to be out of tears.

"Listen, I'm going to need to talk with you at headquarters, in depth. Do you know anyone else Mallori might have known who'd want to hurt her? Was there bad blood between her and anybody you know?"

Sherrie looked grim. "No. Gus was enough. He's been fit to be tied. I've felt so sorry for him, and I tried to help. Mallori is a free spirit, *was* a free spirit. She has hurt people all her life."

"Did she hurt you?"

"Sometimes, but she was my sister and I loved her."

"She was your half sister, wasn't she?"

"Yes, but I felt we were whole sisters. Lately she said she wanted to be closer. Now—"

Her statement hung in the air, and Lieutenant Steele reached out and pressed her shoulder gently. "As I said, I'll need to question you at headquarters, but I want you to take care of yourself. Go home and take a sedative. No, go to your doctor and ask for help with this. You're going to need it.

You're fortunate; you have Byron to help. That was him on the phone, wasn't it?"

"Yes. I have Byron, and he's a godsend." She wet her lips. "I'll see my doctor, but I'm going back to my shop. I need to work, to be involved. I need to be busy. Can you understand that?"

"I can," Lieutenant Steele said.

Sherrie steadied then as she asked, "How was she killed?"

"Shot through the heart."

Sherrie drew a sharp breath. "Mike took a dagger to his heart. You know about their affair. We talked about it."

"I remember. I need you to be careful now, more than ever."

"I am being careful."

"You drove out here alone. It's a rural area. Isolated. It's all right to drive in the city alone, but not out here."

"There was no danger. I was coming toward a murder scene. What fool would accost me here?"

"The same fool who shot at you in broad daylight before."

"Touché. I will be even more careful."

One of Lieutenant Steele's men came up then and asked that she come back to the crime scene because they had found something new. The officer got out and went with him.

A short while later, Sherrie sat, still in a daze. The door opened and Byron was there. He got in on the passenger side and caught her to him. "Why haven't I been able to get you on your phone? You turned it off?" Only then did she begin to cry. Byron took out his handkerchief and lightly blotted her tears and held her close.

She looked at him with tear-blinded eyes. "You would have tried to stop me, and I had to come."

"Baby, I know you did, but I would have brought you."

She shook her head. "You have a business to run and my troubles are always interfering lately. I can't let that happen to you."

"And I have a life to live, and it largely revolves around you. What happens to you, Shere, happens to me, and I want it that way." He kissed her tear-stained face, nuzzled her. "What have they found out?"

"That she was shot through the heart." She mentioned that Mike had been struck through the heart. Byron sucked in a sharp breath. How well he remembered.

"Any leads as to who did it?" he asked.

"I'd think everything points to Gus." She had told him about the August ball and Mallori's new man.

Byron said thoughtfully, "She was giving Gus a terrible fit. Maybe she was rattling the new man's cage too. From what you tell me, she'd been giving Gus a hard way to go for a long, long time and he's never hurt her before."

"Bruised her. Manhandled her a bit, but I don't think he ever struck her, or she didn't tell me if he did."

"My God," he said, shuddering. "This is so unreal."

"It feels like a nightmare, but we won't be waking up."

He smoothed her hair gently and squeezed her shoulders. "Did you get a chance to see a doctor about your foot?"

"No. I'm going when I get back, but it feels okay, just bruised. Danielle thinks I should see a doctor and get more sleeping pills."

"I'll take you. You shouldn't be driving."

"How will I get my car back in town?"

"Easy enough. Joe and Stella are driving out. She'll drive your car back."

"You think of everything. You're so sweet, Bye. So sweet."

He hugged her tightly and pulled her over to him. "You're my woman, Shere. I'd give my life for you."

A little later, Sherrie and Byron sat in the doctor's office. Dr. Phil Larkins examined Sherrie's foot and told her it would be little trouble. He prescribed Domeboro astringent soaking powder that she was to use three times daily. Then he gravely turned to her. "You're lucky to have someone like Dr. Tate to look after you," he said.

"I'm the lucky one," Byron said.

The doctor smiled. These two were in love, and it warmed his heart. He had a rich life, and he wanted the same for others.

"I just heard about your sister," the doctor said gravely, "and I can't tell you how sorry I am. Were you close?"

"Getting closer. I cared a lot about her."

"Then it's going to be hard. This has to be such a shock. Now I want you to exercise gently, stretching to relieve the tension. I'd like you to get a massage and acupressure. Will you do that?"

"Yes," she said dully.

"I know a little bit about massage too," Byron said.

"Good. She can have it more frequently." Then to Sherrie, "Are you a religious woman?"

"More spiritual, I guess."

"Do you believe in prayer?"

"Devotedly."

"Then pray. You're going to need it often. I'm going to prescribe a really good sleeping capsule. I'll hold off on the antidepressants until I see how you're doing. There are times to be depressed, I feel. You've got a lot of support, and that's good. Let me see you in a couple of days, and I'm here whenever you need me."

The doctor's eyes on her were kind, sympathetic as they left. Walking down the wide hallway, Sherrie was close to Byron, gaining strength from his towering form, loving him with everything she was.

The hardest thing was telling Tressa. Early that night Tressa, Sherrie, Byron and Helena sat in Sherrie's sitting room. Sherrie felt she needed to talk with Tressa early before she heard it from someone else. When she had finished talking, Tressa looked at her with stricken eyes, but she didn't cry.

"Aunt Mallori's dead too?" Tressa asked. "Like Daddy?"

"Yes, sweetheart," Sherrie answered. Tressa sat beside her,

and she put her head in Sherrie's lap as if she was suddenly very tired. After a moment she turned the side of her face to her mother.

Then Tressa asked a surprising question. "Will I see Daddy and Aunt Mallori in heaven, Mom?"

"Not for a very long time, I hope. But one day . . ."

"Aunt Mallori was nice. I'm going to wear the dress she gave me for my birthday tomorrow."

"That's fine. She'd like that."

Tressa was so quiet, so keyed up. "Can I sleep with you tonight, Mom?"

"Yes, of course."

Sherrie had thought it best to say that someone had killed Mallori, not just that she'd died. Now Tressa said, "It was a bad, mean person to kill her."

"Yes, darling, a bad, mean person."

Getting up, Tressa bent and hugged Sherrie tightly, then went to Byron and Helena and hugged them just as tightly. She was holding on to those dear to her. Holding on to life. Then she went back to Sherrie, put her face down in her lap and cried. But she didn't ask if she was going to die. Sherrie would reassure her in a little while as she waited to see if the child would ask. She stroked the thin back and smoothed Tressa's hair, as Byron had done for her earlier.

Later, nestled in Byron's arms on the sofa in her sitting room, Sherrie felt the comfort of a cup of valerian infusion she had just drunk. She hadn't taken the sleeping capsules the doctor had prescribed. She favored herbs. They always worked for her. The herb was wonderful for soothing. She had soaked her foot in the astringent solution, and it felt much better, but there was little to be done for a freshly aching heart.

"It's times like this when I want you in the very closest circle of my life," Byron said.

"And I want to be there. Do you know how much I want to be your wife?"

He hugged her fiercely and his heart soared. "I haven't known, but thank you for telling me. We'll get there, Shere. I'm not going anywhere."

"Mallori's death, the maniac in the woods, they make me know life isn't promised to us. I want everything life has to offer for us, but I . . ."

He kissed her face, put his finger on her lips. "Don't try to explain. I understand. Just stay with me. Let me have as much of you as I have. I'm convinced we were meant to be."

She began to say something else when her cell phone rang. Getting it from the end table, she was pleased to hear River's voice.

"I've wanted to call, but I thought I'd give you time to settle a bit. Sherrie, I'm so sorry about Mallori."

"Thank you. I'm sorry too."

"I won't talk because you can't be up to it. Know that if there is anything I can do, you have only to ask me. Promise me you'll do that."

"I will and thank you so much."

Hanging up, she turned to Byron, saying, "That was River offering sympathy and wanting to help. I'll never forget what she did the day of the woods attack."

"Nor will I. River and Curt are two of the best, and I'm damned lucky to have them with me."

"And they're lucky to have you. Bye?" she began when the phone rang again.

"Mrs. Pinson," a deep bass voice said, "Quincy Tyler here. I thought you'd need to know that Sergeant Gus Dueñas was arrested this afternoon for the murder of his wife and your sister, Mallori Dueñas."

"I see," she said dully. "How can I help you?" She had known in her bones that Gus would be the prime suspect after the conversation that morning with Lieutenant Steele. Still, she felt a sense of sorrow.

The attorney cleared his throat. "He wants to see you— tomorrow morning if that's possible. Is it?"

"Yes. What time?"

"Would ten o'clock be convenient for you? I would pick you up, see that you get back to a place of your choosing." His voice was powerful, hypnotic. She recognized him as one of the best.

"Ten would be fine." She gave him Byron's address. She was going in to work late.

"Good. I'll see you tomorrow morning at ten."

Sherrie sat holding the phone after the lawyer had hung up. She listened to the steady dial tone and felt too drained to hang up. The valerian infusion had almost fully kicked in and she thought it wasn't wise to have drunk it so early.

"Who was it?" Byron asked. "You look on edge."

"That was Quincy Tyler," she said slowly. "Gus has been arrested." She repeated her conversation with the lawyer.

"I'm not surprised. A husband or wife is always a first suspect. Poor guy."

"Could he have done it, Bye? Oh, I know Gus is hotheaded, but could he have killed her?"

"Anything's possible, Shere. From what you tell me, it was an incendiary situation and she was tormenting him big time."

Sherrie bit her bottom lip. "Mallori was wild and could be unbelievably cruel. She hurt people, and when you do, you're going to be hurt, but she didn't deserve to die."

"No," he echoed her, "she didn't deserve to die."

He kissed her gently then, on her face and lips, then her brow. "I'd better get you to bed," he said. "You've got a hard day tomorrow. I could save Tyler the trip. Would you like me to take you to talk with Gus?"

"Thank you, but I think it will be easier if I just let Mr. Tyler pick me up. I want to know more about him. He wants to talk with me in his office afterward."

"Okay, my love, but pace yourself. You're very fond of Gus. Don't go overboard trying to help him. Danielle and her people are top-notch. The Minden Police Department is the best. They'll find out who did this."

They stood and he held her, kissed her again, and she loved the comfort of his arms. Would she ever be able to give him what he wanted, needed? And give herself the security of his deepest love?

Chapter 22

"Hello, Shere. Thank God you came and thank you for coming."

In his jail cell Gus looked incredibly drained. His voice was hoarse, raspy. Unshaven, bleary-eyed, he rose as she entered the room. Quincy Tyler had stayed in the outer part of the police station, letting her talk with Gus alone.

As the guard paced outside his cell, Gus and Sherrie were silent at first. For moments Gus sat with his elbows on his knees, his head in his hands. Then he looked up, and Sherrie felt the start of tears. He looked utterly defeated, in the depths of hell.

"I didn't—I could never kill Mallori. Do you believe me?"

She answered truthfully. "I don't know what to believe. You were furious with her, Gus. You were hurt—and with reason . . ."

"She gave me a dog's life and I should've gotten out. She was right. I know that now. We needed a divorce, but"—he groaned aloud—"I couldn't let her go. I loved her too much. No, not *loved*, past tense. I still love her. I always will."

"Do you have an alibi?"

"No," he answered after a while. "We quarreled on the waterfront. I got blind drunk, went back to the apartment and slept it off. I was very late to work and they called me, told me she was dead, had been killed. No, I have no alibi."

"You have the best of lawyers."

"Having him makes me look guilty as hell, I guess."

"You need him. What can I do to help you?"

"Mr. Tyler will tell you that. Just try to be there for me if you can find it in your heart. I'll need you to be a character witness, and how are you going to be? You heard us quarreling, heard me threaten to kill her. I never meant it, deep inside. I only wanted to hurt her the way she kept hurting me. Can you understand the way she treated me? I don't want to whine."

"You're not whining. The things Mallori did had to tear you apart. I'm so sorry, Gus. So sorry."

Fighting bitter tears, he asked her, "Why couldn't I have fallen in love with someone like you?"

With tears of her own, Sherrie told him, "We can't always determine who we love."

"In the beginning she was ardent, seemed caring, but that soon changed. No, I'm lying to myself, even when we courted, were engaged, she spun me around. There were always other men, other affairs. It was as if she couldn't be faithful, as if one man just wasn't enough. And she was sadistic, Sherrie. Mallori was so sadistic. The picnic thing with Lenny. I mean going to his picnic, but not mine. The August ball."

Sherrie nodded. "I don't know how much you two talked, but she felt deeply wounded by what happened when we were children. Mallori felt unloved, Gus, even though she was loved . . ."

"I should have talked more to you about her. I don't pretend to have ever understood her. I was so blinded by love and anger at what she put me through."

"You couldn't help that. Anybody would have been."

"She was mad with the world. It was as if she knew she wouldn't be around long, and she wanted to raise hell, settle old scores from what you tell me. I wasn't loved much either when I was a child. I came up the hard way, adopted by parents who just didn't care. Mallori and I never talked about that. We never talked about much of anything. We just fought and I, anyway, loved. I would have killed for her, died for her. I'd never kill her. Do you believe me?"

"I told you I don't know what to believe," she said slowly. "I can certainly understand if you did. I hope you didn't. You were drunk. Did you take her home?"

He laughed shortly. "I asked her out to a spot on the Chesapeake Bay to talk about where we were headed, to beg her again not to divorce me. That's when she told me she was taking Lenny to the August ball. I sure wanted to kill her. We both drove out, and she told me she was going on to Baltimore that night, that she was going to Lenny."

"Could you have blacked out?"

He shook his head. "Not before I got home and had the last drinks. I knew what I was doing up to then."

She was jumping the gun but it had to be said sometime. "It's early, and the police will hold the body for a while, but Mallori always wanted to be cremated. I want a beautiful memorial service for her."

"I'll say this for her. Mallori loved beautiful things."

"She told me she'd like her ashes strewn over the Chesapeake Bay."

Gus laughed shortly, mirthlessly. "She told you that, and that was the last place we quarreled. I don't want to hurt you, Sherrie, but she told me something different. Do you want to hear it?"

"Yes."

Looking down, he half mumbled. "She always told me she wanted her ashes strewn over Mike's grave. Like I said, I don't want to hurt you."

But it did hurt, quickly, sharply, then it was gone. She had Byron's love to insulate her, but this was old, remembered hurt.

"I'm not surprised. She didn't care who it hurt, but Mike was the love of her life."

"And she was the love of mine." He thought a moment. "As a suspected killer, do I have any right to say where her ashes will be scattered?"

She reached out and placed a hand on his arm, comforting him.

"You haven't been convicted."

Time was up then. When the guard announced that, Sherrie stood, moved close to Gus and hugged him for a long moment. His body sagged dejectedly, and he seemed unwilling to let her go.

"Can I bring you anything?" she asked.

"Thanks, but my lawyer is taking care of that kind of thing. But come back and talk to me. I value your friendship now more than anything in this world."

Quincy Tyler's Minden satellite office was sparsely furnished with luxurious touches of expensive African artifacts. Sherrie found him an imposing, barrel-chested man, urbane, sophisticated, sharply aware.

"What would you like to drink?" he asked. "How about a snack?"

"Thank you, but I managed breakfast before I left. I'm fine."

Seated side by side in deep chairs, he leaned forward, smiling. "Thank you for seeing my client, Mrs. Pinson, and for talking with me. You can give me immeasurable help."

"How can I do that?" she asked bluntly.

"You knew both Mr. Dueñas and your sister well. I run a complete background check, get psychological particulars on all my clients. In time, I will ask you—if you will—to tell me all about Mallori Dueñas, from her childhood and yours . . ."

"We were half sisters, but I feel we were whole."

"Gus told me that. Would you mind just talking freely— whatever comes to mind. And may I record our conversation? Do you mind?"

"No, I don't mind."

"Just say whatever comes to you," he said gently. "No matter how disjointed, even if it doesn't make sense. Snippets of information can be very helpful."

Tensely Sherrie talked about the past, growing up with Mallori as a headstrong, willful, angry child and teenager. Sherrie was two years older than Mallori. The battles with both their father and Sherrie's mother, Mallori's stepmother. And as she talked, she felt Mallori's spirit with her, laughing, sometimes angry, bitter, cruel. Driving her husband to the brink of madness. Selecting the perfect dress for her little niece.

When she had finished talking about the past, Quincy Tyler looked at her gravely and commented, "Very helpful. Thank you. I understand Mrs. Dueñas better now. And lately? What are your memories here?"

She monitored herself when she spoke of Mallori and Gus's life as she knew it. She spoke gingerly of the violent quarrels, the sadistic cheating. Had all the love been on Gus's side? When they were first married, they had seemed ardent, close. When had it changed? Ended?

"Would you say Gus loved his wife?"

"Devotedly. He worshiped her."

"But she gave him, as we say, a dog's life?"

"Yes. That about sums it up."

"How often would you say you heard him threaten her?"

"Often enough," Sherrie said tiredly. "It happened more frequently lately."

"Did you think he was serious? Could you see him killing her?"

Sherrie thought a long moment. "He was furious, that much was certain. He had gotten to be beside himself with rage. Yes, I thought he could hurt her, begin beating her if she let him."

"Would you say she was a masochist?"

Sherrie shrugged. "Don't they say that under the sadist there is always a masochist?"

Quincy Tyler smiled. "You're astute." He leaned back, said softly, "The police only have circumstantial evidence against my client."

"And that can be damning enough."

"You're right, of course. Mrs. Pinson, I will want to talk with you several times, and I do not wish to tire you. You've experienced an enormous emotional shock. Will you talk with me again? You can call and tell me when you wish to do it. And may I call you when I wish to talk?"

Sherrie nodded. "I'll be glad to talk with you again, and Mr. Tyler . . ."

"Quincy, please."

"Very well, and it's Sherrie here. I just met you, but I know you by reputation, and I'm very impressed by talking with you. If I was in trouble, you'd be my choice for a lawyer."

Quincy Tyler's eyes nearly closed as they crinkled in a wide smile. He loved beautiful women and loved dealing with them, and this one was something special. His investigation sheets told him she presently lived with the highly successful prominent and well-known Byron Tate. And he thought, *the lucky dog*.

It was late that afternoon when Sherrie talked with Lieutenant Steele at police headquarters.

As they sat in chairs in Lieutenant Steele's office, she asked, "How are you holding up?"

"As well as can be expected."

"Did you get at least some sleep?"

Remembering, Sherrie said, "I tossed and cried out so loudly that Byron came in. I keep seeing her, Danielle." Tears came to her eyes. "I tried to get them to talk with a marriage counselor. Gus wanted to. Mallori scorned my advice."

"Your sister was an unhappy woman. You talked with Gus this morning?"

"Yes. I hadn't clearly thought about it until now, but Gus could kill himself."

"I'd thought of that. He's under suicide watch."

"I'm glad. I want to help him. Danielle, do you think he killed Mallori?"

Lieutenant Steele pondered the question. "He could have. From what you tell me, he certainly had the provocation. We obviously think he could since we arrested him. I hate these domestic violence cases. I hate murder and murderers."

Sherrie sat thinking that Lieutenant Steele's mother, a police sergeant on Minden's police force, had been murdered, and the murder had been unsolved for thirteen years. Then her mother's charge, and later Lieutenant Steele's partner, had been found to be the perpetrator. He had been involved with Mafia hoods in smuggling aliens and Lieutenant Steele's mother had found out. He had killed her.

"You know, of course, about my mother," Lieutenant Steele said now. "It was the talk of Minden for many, many moons. You comforted me. You were so kind."

"You've always been one of my favorite people."

"Thank you. As you have been one of mine."

"Danielle, when will Mallori's body be released for cremation?"

"Within ten days or so. We have to run all kinds of tests, make numerous photographs. Get DNA. You're asking early. You're anxious."

"Yes," she said, sighing. "I talked with attorney Tyler this morning."

"I saw you with him when you came to talk with Gus. I thought he'd be talking with you."

"He wants to talk with me several times."

"He's a thorough man. Gus is lucky to have him."

"I think so. What if Gus killed Mallori?"

"Do you think he did?"

"Do you?"

Lieutenant Steele looked at her levelly. "I can only say he could have. You know I think the world of Gus Dueñas. I had high hopes for him, even if his wife didn't think he was climbing far enough or fast enough. Gus is bright. If he didn't do this terrible thing, he will eventually get where he's going. Family matters to him more than anything."

"He looked like a brutally beaten child. A hopeless child."

"I know. Seeing you helped. Please stand by him as best you can."

"And if he killed my sister?"

Lieutenant Steele drew a deep breath. "Let's cross that bridge when we get to it." She pyramided her fingers with her elbows on the desk.

"We've gotten a world of information on the diamond smuggling ring and the part of it that operated in Minden, but we still don't have enough. I think we will shortly. Mike was climbing rapidly and there are shadowy others we haven't gotten a bead on. Sherrie, we think they're behind the attacks on you. We're going on the assumption they feel Mike told you things they don't want you to know. Names. Plans for action. Keep Tucker in mind. Mike might have been killed because he knew too much. You *will* be careful?"

Sherrie nodded. "You know I will."

Nap Kendrick jogged in place in the middle of his small living room. He wore old, gray sweat clothes and dirty white tennis shoes. Smiling, he walked into his bedroom, opened the closet door and looked at the wall to the left of the shelf. It held precious cargo just like Mike Pinson's false wall. He flexed his knees and threw out his arms, looking grim. Mike had betrayed him, betrayed them all. And he had paid with his life.

He purely hated what had happened to Mallori Dueñas. That fabulous shape, the movie-star face. She had been too beautiful to die. Already he missed her vivacious laughter, the effervescent way she handled her body, which always left him slavering. She had been kind to him, had acted on his level. Not like the deeply reserved Sherrie, her sister. It wouldn't have mattered if Sherrie hadn't been reserved. She'd sealed her fate with him in looking like his reviled dead mother.

Chapter 23

The day that Mallori was to be memorialized and her ashes scattered was overcast, misty. It was as if she had taken the sun with her. Sherrie's small church welcomed the little group that drew together in Mallori's memory.

"For Mallori Dueñas was a child of God even as we are all children of God," the minister intoned. "She knew joy and sorrow, weakness and strength. Her life was a celebration of living, and her death is now a grieving of dying. . . ."

Sitting with Byron, Sherrie looked around her. Some of Mallori's coworkers were there. She had sometimes gone to church with Sherrie, and a few parishioners were there. But most of all, Gus was there, escorted by Lieutenant Steele and another officer from the Minden police force. He looked dazed, drawn, blind.

And Lenny Hyde was there. Lenny Hyde who may have inadvertently caused this terrible scene. Handsome, nattily attired, Sherrie wondered if he looked scornfully at the broken Gus. Or did she imagine it?

The minister's words were brief, succinct. The small group sang "Rock of Ages" and "Amazing Grace." And they sang the spiritual, led by the choir, "Goin' Home." Sherrie found her eyes filling with cold tears.

Yes, she thought, Mallori was going home. *Had* gone home to everlasting joy and no more pain and wrangling. There would be no morbid jealousy and no more bruises from a love gone mad. Sherrie wondered as she had wondered since the murder: Could Gus have done this thing?

The group was quiet when the minister called her name and Sherrie walked slowly to the podium.

At first her throat closed when she tried to speak, then it relaxed, permitting her to begin. "She was my sister and my friend, and I will miss her terribly." She did not try to stanch the flowing tears, but kept on.

"Mallori was not your perfect person, but she loved life. Loved life to a fault . . ."

Looking out on the group, she saw Gus's eyes focused on her, saw him lean forward. "To those of us she leaves behind, I say weep not, for she is at peace now. Her ofttimes hard struggles have ended. There is no more strife for her. She rests in the bosom of God, as we all will one day rest . . ."

She sounded like a minister giving a eulogy and knew the formality was to cover the truly awful rending grief.

After a brief time she finished, and her face was wet with tears. She walked back to Byron and sat down. He took her in his arms, cradling her, and she thanked God that he was there.

The pastor called Gus's name, and he shuffled up. He wore no handcuffs and Sherrie knew this was a measure of Lieutenant Steele's faith in him, that he would not try to escape. His eyes were reddened, his face haggard, and his jaw was tight. His voice was a hoarse croak.

"She was my wife," he said, "and I loved her. She will always be my wife." Did he pointedly look at Lenny Hyde when he said it? Sherrie wondered and felt fairly certain he did. Both she and Lieutenant Steele thought wryly that he had not helped his case with that statement.

Sherrie's glance segued to Lenny Hyde who looked at Gus with naked contempt as Gus came back to his seat, slipped in between Lieutenant Steele and the other police officer and heavily sat down.

It was a short service. Several more people spoke. A supervisor extolled Mallori's brilliance at work. "She had gone far," he said, "and was going farther. God be with us all in a world where this can happen. We will miss your sunny smile, Mallori Dueñas, your genius for getting things done. Oh, how we will miss you."

The group sang "Amazing Grace" again and the choir echoed it. The small organ played the old, old hymn as if it had no meaning other than grief. It was a hymn, Sherrie thought, for all times, for all seasons.

After the service, the pastor told them that they were free to select flowers to take with them, and Sherrie went to the altar and selected a single bloodred rose. She saw that Gus selected the same shade of rose and clutched it tightly. He looked at her long and anxiously. Seeking friendship? Begging forgiveness?

A short while later, in a cabin cruiser out on the Chesapeake Bay, an even smaller group was ready to witness the sprinkling of Mallori's ashes on the bay waters. At the railing, Sherrie held the plastic bag with the ashes. A gray mist hung over the waters. Everything was gray. She couldn't stop shaking, and Byron was like a rock beside her.

"Steady, my love," he told her, and she grew calmer.

Gus and the officers stood beside her. As she held the bag, she thought, was this really the end? Did you live life in all its glory—be warm, vibrant, feel so much and come to the end in a coffin or as a bag of ashes? And she thought, too, of what Gus had said: Mallori wanted her ashes sprinkled over Mike's grave. Sherrie shook her head. She couldn't do that. She had Byron, and Mike no longer mattered to her, but how to explain that action to a grown-up Tressa?

Sherrie sprinkled the ashes onto the waters as the boat moved steadily along. "You cover a long trail," she said to Mallori's spirit, "in death as you did in life."

When half the ashes had been strewn, she turned to Gus. "Would you like to sprinkle the rest?" she asked him.

He shook his head sadly. "No. You go ahead. I don't want to let her go."

The captain turned the boat around when the last ashes were strewn and soon they were ashore where Lenny Hyde stood on the pier as they pulled in.

"Mrs. Pinson," he said as he came up to her, "may I speak with you a moment?"

Sherrie could only look at him as Gus walked away with the two officers. This time there was no mistaking the hard, contemptuous look Lenny gave Gus. Excusing herself, Sherrie stepped aside with Lenny Hyde.

He wasted no time. "I never met you," he said, "but Mallori talked about you so much. I loved your sister. Maybe this will let you know how much." He pulled a small, black velvet box from his pants pocket and snapped it open. A lovely diamond ring winked up at her.

"In a week or less I would have given this to her. We would have been married later."

Outrage hit Sherrie then. "And what about her husband?" she demanded. "My sister was a married woman. Did either of you think of that?"

He was silent a long moment. "She wasn't in love with Gus . . ."

"Did she tell you about another love—the great love of her life?"

He smiled sadly. "You mean Mike? She told me. These things happen, and I'm very sorry it caused you pain. She was sorry too. Then I came along and she said I took his place."

He closed the ring box and put it back into his pocket. "Another woman will never wear this ring," he said. "Thank you for talking with me. I cannot tell you how much I appreciate it."

She stood in the woods at midnight. It had been a long day and now she waited. This was the woods out past the Henderson place where Mallori's life had been so ruthlessly snuffed out. She had sent a message, and the suspected murderer had responded. No, not Gus. The man with the bushy black hair and the mad eyes. The man who had pursued her in another woods near her house, had sent bullets singing past her.

She stood in the clearing, waiting. She had come seeking closure. Seeking justice. Would he come? She had waited a long time. Had she been a fool to come?

Then she saw him behind a tree, and he beckoned to her. She went forward to ask him to confess, to bring him in. He raised a gun as someone had raised a gun at Mallori, and Sherrie could *hear* the shots—no silencer this time—and she was hit. The pain was terrible, shattering bone, digging deep into her heart tissue as hellish pain tore through her. She screamed and screamed.

"Sherrie! Wake up!" Byron held her, rocked her. "You were having a nightmare. What was it?"

Chilled to the bone, trembling wildly she came awake. "Oh my God," she kept saying.

She told him the nightmare and he crushed her to him. "Sweetheart, it was a nightmare. Try to relax."

He stayed with her the rest of the night, and she did not sleep again. Lying on the bed, he held her, stroked her, thinking she was more precious to him than life itself, that he would always protect her, but he couldn't stop her dreams.

"I think you ought to talk with Dr. Jones," he said grimly. "These nightmares will probably come again. She could help."

"Yes," she said. "I'll make an appointment."

Ending in Ecstasy

Early August 2002

Chapter 24

"I'm not sure I approve of this dress, although it is magnificent and does you full justice. I have reservations," Byron said.

"Then it's a good thing I waited to let you see me in it." Sherrie smiled until her eyes crinkled. He was teasing her again. "Now why do you have reservations?"

He looked at the small brown mole on her right breast. "The dress displays my mole, and I don't think I want it exposed to the world."

Sherrie threw back her head, laughing. "It's yours. No one can take that away."

"Be sure it is."

It was August and they stood at the edge of the ballroom floor of the Lucerne Hotel in Crystal City, Virginia. High up and beautiful, the ballroom was part of Tate Supreme Manufacturing Company's annual August ball. It was the social event of the season, and everyone who could wangle an invitation was there.

Byron looked at Sherrie in her ball gown and sighed. Passion for her luscious, rounded figure with its narrow waistline and wide hips was going to be the death of him yet. He had only to see that form, and visions of her nakedness rose before him and he groaned. Would he ever get used to it? Her gown was superlative. Fashioned of midnight-blue silk chiffon, off-the-shoulder with fairly deep décolletage and long panels that flowed artlessly when she moved, it was a superb fashion statement. The sapphire pendant and the studs he had given her seemed made for it. Her silken brown skin glowed. Her earth-brown hair was shaped into a soigné French twist.

Byron's wide-shouldered, slim-hipped body in his specially tailored tuxedo made Sherrie's heart flip-flop and warmed her all over. His cummerbund and carnation were burgundy. He might have come from the cover of a high-fashioned men's magazine. She thought he was the most attractive man she had ever known. It didn't come from the physical—that too— but from his heart and soul.

The ballroom held the ample stage and was where the food would be served. Dancing was on the highly polished floors and on the roof. Angled, soft lights flattered the many dancers. Potted palms and evergreens were set about. Birds-of-paradise graced low tables. Roses and gardenias spread their sensual scent. Gaily colored balloons and rose and white crepe paper streamers graced the room. It made a splendid picture, and photographers with their strobe lights caught every angle.

The ball was well underway. Tate Cosmetics had the roof and the ballroom. Two bands played; a well-regarded and popular sophisticated D.C. orchestra and the growing-in-popularity Cass and the Cupids, featuring Rafe Sampson and his wild harmonica and Cass's wife, Ellen, as vocalists. Cass and the Cupids held sway, and they ran the gamut of popular songs.

Roland came and greeted them. "Girlfriend, you do look delectable in my creation," he told Sherrie.

"I'm glad you like it," Sherrie said impishly. "It took you long enough."

Roland laughed. "But look at the results. I had to be here tonight. Half the women in this room are in my gowns. Man, am I proud."

"You should be," Byron said. "You've outdone yourself, but especially with my wi—" He caught himself, blinking. He had been lost in thought and had started to say *wife*. He glanced at Sherrie quickly and thought she might not have caught his intended word, but Roland grinned broadly and winked at him.

Roland laughed a little and said, "One day soon, man." He moved away to mingle, a glass of champagne in hand.

Sherrie and Byron moved among the guests. Having the roof and the ballroom meant there was plenty of space and there were a great many people from all over the United States. The motif of the ball was River West's Black Magic Perfume and the theme was Tate Supreme: A Half Century of Black Magic. And the women at the ball proved it, in spades. The Black Magic crystal perfume bottle was a design triumph, and it was displayed all over the ballroom.

Mr. Sampson's harmonica played out the melody of "That Old Black Magic," as Sherrie and Byron danced. As he held her close and nestled against his shoulder, she knew a moment of sadness. Mallori would have loved this ball. And Sherrie would have permitted her to bring Lenny Hyde if it could have brought her back. And Gus? Gus was still in jail. A grand jury would be convened in late September.

"Yes, honey," she said, realizing she had missed something he said.

"You've gone away."

"I was thinking about Mallori—and Gus."

Byron drew a sharp breath. He had been thinking about them too. He drew her closer, and there were no words that could really comfort her, but after a long moment she brightened.

Mallori had described the dress she had been having made by Roland, and as a woman in a yellow gown danced by, Sherrie recalled the sketch Mallori had quickly drawn. It featured a bodice of hand-fashioned wildflowers and a clinging yellow silk jersey skirt. She would have been lovely, Sherrie thought.

"You're the most beautiful woman here tonight," Byron complimented her.

"But then you're prejudiced," she murmured.

"Damned right I'm prejudiced," he responded.

"You're blinded by love."

"I'd never deny it, but I have twenty-twenty vision where your beauty is concerned."

"You're so sweet. Do I deserve you?"

"That and more," he whispered. "You deserve the world, and I'm going to get it for you."

The dance ended and they walked over to Curt and Helena. The two women hugged. "That dress! Oh, that dress!" Helena exclaimed. "It's you. And the jewels . . . You look very—special."

"She, ah, cleans up nicely, doesn't she?" Byron teased her.

Curt laughed. "She's the best thing that ever happened to you."

"I'd never deny it."

Helena was lovely in aquamarine crepe and cream cultured pearls and Curt couldn't take his eyes off her. "Speaking of certain people being the best thing that ever happened to certain other people . . ." Byron raised his eyebrows at the couple.

"I could never deny it either," Curt admitted as Helena blushed deeply.

Katherine was there in vanilla cream and amethyst jewelry that set off her very dark skin and made her even more beautiful. She and Sherrie had done each other's hair and makeup. The two hugged and each congratulated the other.

"I just get the feeling," Katherine said, "that wonderful things are going to happen here tonight."

"Those things are already going on," Sherrie said.

Katherine's tall, handsome husband came up then. "You and my wife are the most beautiful women here tonight," he told Sherrie. "And I want you to save me a dance."

River and Tucker danced by, stopping at the two couples. "Congratulations," Sherrie said, hugging her. "Byron tells me you're the stellar award winner for Tate this year."

"Thank you," River said softly. "There are others who deserve it more than I do."

"Oh no, you don't," Byron said. "I know you're modest, but Black Magic sales have gone through the roof, and I'm going to see that its creator gets her full due. River, I salute you."

"Thank you, boss. You always were kind."

Tucker kept looking at Sherrie, his eyes narrowed. He needed her to be his woman, not Tate's. His love for her had gone unfulfilled since he had known her, but from the beginning he had had plans, wily dreams. Frustrated, he kept hoping, praying, but he wasn't getting any closer. When she had hated Byron, there had been a possibility of them becoming closer. Now? He shrugged. He intended to woo her tonight, right in Byron's face.

"You're quiet, Tucker," Sherrie said. "Cat got your tongue?"

"You look beautiful," he said gallantly. "I've never seen you looking so well."

"Thank you," Sherrie said as Byron's arm went around her protectively. He didn't like Tucker Weeks, didn't like what he saw in his eyes as he looked at Sherrie. "She's beautiful all right," Byron said and the words just slipped out, "Beautiful, and thank God, mine."

Tucker clenched his teeth a bit. So the battle lines were drawn early, with Sherrie as the worthy prize, he thought.

Nearly all of Tate Cosmetics' employees were there, ebulliently dancing, enjoying themselves, waiting for the many awards that would be given. The awards would be early so people could have time to savor and enjoy them. Byron and Curt walked onto a stage in a corner of the ballroom and under angled floodlights began the ceremony.

"We're reversing the order in which we usually give these awards," Byron said into the microphone. "We want to get the spirit of the awards underway as quickly as possible and so we announce our main award, Tate Supreme Cosmetics Stellar Excellence Award. Two superlatives for a superlative employee and woman: Ms. River Patricia West!"

The crowd roared. People had come down from the roof and

the ballroom was packed. "River! River! Speech! Speech!" they hailed her.

Flushed and breathless, clad in an off-white plain crepe designer dress, with her fair skin glowing, River looked her best as she took the golden plaque and a cardboard-thick envelope from Byron. The envelope contained a voucher for a very large sum of money. River spoke softly and evenly, briefly touching on her years at Tate and her happiness at working there.

"Thank you, Byron, for giving me every chance. I am grateful," she ended, and the crowd again roared its approval as Byron kissed her cheek.

An award went to Curt for excellence as well. Then a joint award went to Curt and River for holding the company together while Byron was away. Tate Cosmetics was a benevolent company, so many awards were given, most of them cash.

Finally, Byron said, "I can't say I've saved the best for last, since all the awards are 'best,' but this one is certainly outstanding in my mind. For long devotion, excellence and making us know that beauty never fades, I present this plaque and this envelope to my secretary and my friend, Mrs. Marcia Keely!"

Tate employees loved Marcia Keely; she always went to bat for them. And the people who used Tate products valued her expertise. The crowd clamored for her presence and she spoke to them briefly and ardently. "Byron Tate is a man for all seasons," she finally told them. "He has headed Tate Cosmetics with a vision that few can match, and I tell you what is in my heart tonight. May my love for you go with you always, Byron. Tate Cosmetics tonight! Tate Cosmetics forever!"

The crowd went wild and Marcia stood with happy tears in her eyes. Sherrie saw the woman she had done so much to create. Dressed in pearl-gray draped chiffon, with gray pearls set with a large emerald clip, she looked splendid.

Her brown skin was smooth now, the silver-gray hair still in its artful bangs and blunt cut. Sherrie nearly burst with pride at what she had helped accomplish.

Marcia said, "I want the love of my life, Hal Keely, to come up. And I want to thank Byron Tate and Sherrie Pinson for making me what I am this night."

A delighted Hal joined his wife and kissed her passionately as the crowd cheered. Sherrie thought, what a night this had become, and Byron stood with pride filling him for his company, his friends, and most of all the woman who shared his life.

Afterward, many of the crowd went back to the roof; others stayed to congratulate the award recipients. The wonderful scent of Black Magic permeated the air. Heady. Sensuous. Provocative. Pheromones harnessed in the name of romance. Sherrie went to River, hugging her again. "It's really your night," she told her. "Be happy."

River's face sparkled. Sherrie thought she had never seen her look so pretty. River turned to Byron. "Dance with me," she said. Then she looked at Sherrie and smiled. "Do you mind?"

"Oh good Lord, no," Sherrie told her. "Dance! No one deserves it more."

Tucker came up then with two glasses of champagne. "Well, I see the two golden ones have deserted us. Shall we gulp the champagne and dance?"

She didn't much feel like dancing with Tucker, but she drank up, put their glasses on a waiter's passing tray and danced. It was a waltz, so at least they weren't too close. Already, Tucker was a little drunk. Maybe not drunk, she amended, but definitely tipsy. She never stopped remembering what Lieutenant Steele had told her. Tucker, she thought, and the diamond smuggling ring. She held herself away from him.

In spite of the distance usually between waltzing partners, Tucker drew her closer than was necessary. "God, I can't get over you in that dress," he said. "Sherrie, you know how I love you . . ."

"Tucker, please."

"Please what? Hold you closer? Kiss you? Do you know I've seldom kissed you, and oh, how I want to kiss you now."

"Please don't," she said sharply.

"You've given me few chances. You don't know that you prefer Tate. Why in hell did you move in with him anyway? What possessed you? You know what he did to—" Tucker began but he didn't finish because a ripple of excitement swept the room. Jasmine and her escort had made an entrance, and *what* an entrance.

Jasmine's dress was black silk jersey, intricately draped and formfitting. Backless, décolleté, it was a work of art from a Paris designer, and she wore it like the model she had been. Her breasts spilled over the top and everyone held their breath, thinking of those gorgeous breasts bursting free. The music had stopped and Byron came back to Sherrie's side, giving her arm a heavy touch. Tucker moved away.

"Well, well," Sherrie said. "How stunning. Backless. And darned near frontless." She looked beautiful, Sherrie thought. Jasmine was ravishing and she headed straight for Byron.

"Don't let the green-eyed monster get to you," Byron said evenly. "She's glitz. You're pure class. And I love you."

"Hello, Sherrie," Jasmine bubbled. "You look very nice. Byron, you're even more handsome in a tux. I could eat you alive, and you owe me a dance for old time's sake." She turned to Sherrie. "Surely you don't mind."

Byron smiled. "Fact is, I just danced a lot of rounds and I've been pretty busy with awards. Give me a rain check? Your dress is a wonder."

"I did it all for you, darling." Jasmine pouted prettily. Her escort was nowhere in sight.

Jasmine began to move away and a grinning man stopped her, holding out his arms in an invitation to dance and she took it.

* * *

Food was served on long, white damask-covered tables, buffet style, and it was scrumptious. A table of meats—beef Wellington, prime rib roast, crispy fried chicken, pork roast and Cornish hen. A table of beautifully carved raw vegetables and salads. Fifteen varieties of breads. Drinks of every description and an absolutely huge fruit punch bowl.

Sherrie groaned when she saw the dessert table. An array of cakes and pies and puddings, containers of ice cream and sorbet on ice.

"We'll be paying for this for a long, long time weightwise," Sherrie said.

"Double workouts. We're going to need all the help we can get. What do you want? I'll do your plate if you wish," Byron said.

"Great. Let's be twins. You choose."

She knew his preferences and chose beef Wellington, fried chicken and shrimp salad. The heavy china plates were big and she filled them.

They sat near the stage, enjoying the delectable food.

When they had finished, he took their dishes, stacked them on the dirty plate table and asked her, "May I have this dance?"

"You just told Jasmine you had danced enough."

"I'm a terrible liar. I want to dance with you. What do you say we move up to the roof?"

In the elevator, Sherrie drew a quick, sharp breath when they reached the rooftop. It was so beautiful up there. Nature had given her fullest cooperation with millions of clustered twinkling stars and a nearly full moon. Thousands of tiny bright lights shone in the plants on the roof. The air was fresh, pleasantly warm and the fragrance of Black Magic was there as in the ballroom.

The band played a softly danceable tune. Romantic. Sensual. He held her close, and Sherrie felt herself wanting to meld into him. His body mesmerized her. He was in his element—a leader who enjoyed what he did. Oh, she loved him, she thought, but she had loved before, had felt scalding pain that seared and lasted, and she did not intend to go there again. Torn, she drew a little away.

"What's wrong?" he asked her.

"Nothing," she answered quietly. "I'm having a great time. You're quite a man, Bye."

"I'm a man in love—with you."

"And I'm glad. You've brought so much to my life, and I'm grateful."

"Don't be. I've wanted to do it all for you. There's more to come."

Curt cut in then. "May I interrupt something special, beast that I am?" he said, laughing.

Byron smiled. "Just this once and never again."

"That's good enough for me."

As Byron relinquished her, Sherrie looked at Curt who said, "Now it's not often a man usurps his boss, I know, but this night is different—"

She closed her eyes for a moment, enjoying the rhythm of the song. Curt danced well.

"How much do you love Byron?" he asked abruptly.

Surprised, she answered, "A lot. He's gotten to be a part of me."

"That's good because he's certainly gone on you."

Looking around, she didn't see Byron and wondered to where he had disappeared. Maybe, she thought, he was lost in the circle of so many dancers.

"Byron's going to tell you something tonight. Give him your best ear. He's a serious man, especially so about some things."

"I know."

Sherrie smiled as she saw Roland tap Curt's shoulder. "I saw you move Byron out, now I'm doing the same to you. Sherrie's the belle of the ball. I want my chance to dance with her."

"Hmmm," Curt said with mock sternness. "I guess I'll permit this."

Dancing with Roland was quite a spin, Sherrie thought; he was an excellent dancer. The set ended and another slow one commenced.

"You're my best model ever," Roland said. "Sherrie, you're beautiful tonight. I guess you've heard that often."

Sherrie smiled. "No woman hears it often enough."

He was exuberant. "If I didn't already have a reputation as a first-rate dress designer, I'd make it tonight. I've got nothing to be modest about."

"You're at the top of your form."

"Speaking of being at the top of forms, Byron is certainly at the top of his."

"Yes."

"He made a Freudian slip of the tongue tonight."

"Oh?"

"He started to say *wife* when he was talking about you. Did you notice?"

"I can't say I did," she hedged. But she had noticed, and it had started her heart to racing. He'd let her know he wanted to marry her, but he hadn't been so public about it.

"If he asks you," Roland told her, "say yes. You two were meant for each other." His eyes narrowed. "I've got fanciful and real dreams of your wedding gown in my head. I will be making it."

"Whoa!" she exclaimed. "If I ever get married again, you'll do the gown, but talk about going too far too fast."

"Not really. Life's not promised us. Mallori should have let you know that."

A shudder passed the length of Sherrie's body. The dance ended and the music stopped for a few minutes. Roland stopped a waiter and got two glasses of champagne. He eyed the huge fruit punch bowl.

"That's more my speed," he said, nodding toward it.

"Mine, too, although I love champagne. It makes me tipsy."

"My secret too."

As they stood talking, Curt came up. "I'm afraid I'm

going to have to take the lady away," he said, "but listen. This includes you."

There was a microphone near them and Curt took it over, announcing that they were all wanted in the ballroom for a few minutes for an important announcement. Then putting the microphone back in his holder, he offered his arm to Sherrie.

In the ballroom with Byron, Sherrie noted that they were the only ones onstage as the crowd pressed around them.

"Ladies and gentlemen," Byron began, "tonight promises to be one of the most important in my life. I'm in love and I want to ask the object of my affection to be my wife."

Sherrie stood transfixed. Her heart lurched with excitement and passion, but it also lurched with fear. She wasn't ready for this, but when would she be ready?

Byron continued. "Now it may take a while for the lady to come around, but that's all right. I've got the rest of my life to wait for her answer."

It was a hell of a gamble, he thought, but nothing ventured . . . He looked at Sherrie with his heart in his eyes and reached into his jacket pocket, took out a navy velvet ring box and snapped it open. She gasped with delight at the sight of a six-carat oval, brilliant white diamond throwing its light on her face. Taking her trembling hand, he slipped it on her ring finger.

"Wedding band to follow," he whispered.

She would not disappoint him, she thought. Engagements didn't always lead to weddings; they were short-circuited often enough. Love did not always lead to a lifetime commitment.

His kiss was long and deep amid the cheering and clapping. When they broke apart, the crowd demanded that he kiss her again and he obliged. Then he grinned. "Even passionate kisses have to stop sometime."

Friends rushed to the stage. Helena caught her in a bear hug, her eyes moist. Katherine hugged her, then River, whose face lit up in a huge smile. "Oh, I am so happy for you two," River said.

Roland lifted her off her feet. "Told ya!" he said again and again.

Marcia had tears in her eyes as she hugged Byron, then Sherrie. "I think I'm happier than you two are," she said.

Stella and Joe, Lieutenant Steele and her gospel-great husband, Whit, came up to them. "We came in together," Stella said. "Congratulations!" She hugged them both.

"You're what we want for him," Joe said. "You'll make each other happy."

Stella and Joe couldn't stop smiling. Stella said, "We're late because a strap broke, and I had to go back and change. I looked in on the little one and she was sleeping like an angel."

Sherrie smiled, hugging her again. "Your dress," she said, "is lovely." Stella blushed. "I made it," she said proudly, "from a *Vogue* couturier pattern."

And the dress was lovely. Fashioned of silk jersey in a red and yellow lilies print with green leaves on the white background, it was simply draped and very flattering.

"It's lovely," Byron said, grinning. They hugged again.

Lieutenant Steele and her husband stood quietly by. Then they hugged Byron and Sherrie. "I'm so happy for you," Lieutenant Steele said, tears in her eyes. "You both deserve the best."

Sherrie admired Lieutenant Steele's dress, a Roland design of lavender silk over blush-pink organza with hand-fashioned roses drifting from one shoulder.

A fan of Whit's came up and asked for an autograph, and as Whit obligingly signed, called out, "Here's to you, man! Whit Steele!" The gospel singer was soon surrounded. Smiling, he told them, "I'll move away. I don't want to take the spotlight away from you." He and Lieutenant Steele moved off, and Joe guided Stella to the dance floor.

Jasmine pushed her way through to them. "Now you've got to dance with me," she said to Byron. "I want to celebrate with you." Her voice was slurred. "This is for old time's sake. Remember how we danced back when?"

"I can't say I do," Byron said evenly.

"Then it's because you don't want to. I certainly remember."

Jasmine sulked. Was she going to make a scene? Sherrie turned to Byron. "Honey, dance with her," she told him.

Byron seemed reluctant, but when they got on the dance floor Sherrie thought it had been like pushing a cat toward cream. After congratulations, many of the crowd had moved back to the roof and she could clearly see Byron and Jasmine in a slow dance.

"May I have this dance?" Tucker asked at her elbow.

"Sorry. I'm sitting this one out." She wasn't too nice about it either.

"Then I'll stay here with you. Keep you company. Tate certainly seems to be enjoying himself dancing with my sister. Jasmine's a card—sees what she wants and doesn't quit until she gets it. She married and divorced one of the biggest wigs in New York. She and Byron were once quite tight. Did you know that?"

"She made sure I did." And speaking of tight, she thought, she was getting *up*tight. She'd had her chance and wasn't taking full advantage. Her fear wasn't Byron's problem.

"Oh yeah," Tucker said, "a belated congratulations. You're making a mistake, Sherrie."

"Let's not go there, Tucker," she said sharply.

On the dance floor Jasmine's backless gown left nothing but her bare flesh for Byron to put his hand on. She strained against him, her head against his chin, her lush body pressed hard against him. Aware of the display they made, she played it to the hilt. When he tried to draw a little away, she went closer.

Jasmine kept saying, "I've got rhythm," and, "With you I've got everything."

Byron suffered in silence. The woman felt good, but he wasn't interested. She looked wonderful, but he didn't care. Unfortunately, it was a double set and in the end Jasmine ground her hips against him. Then she grinned. "Better behave myself. Are you really getting married?"

"I hope so."

"With me, you wouldn't have to hope. You'd know." She suddenly sobered. "I will behave, Byron. I want your friendship more than anything."

He was touched by the longing on her face. He knew from gossip that her ex-husband had led her a dog's life full of humiliation and scorn, finally leaving her for a very young woman.

"Okay," he said, "as long as you behave yourself."

"Friends?" She stood a little away from him, and he breathed a sigh of relief.

He repeated it. "As long as you behave."

The set finally ended and Byron went back to Sherrie and Tucker.

"I kept your bed warm," Tucker said. It was a statement that made Byron hot under the collar, but he said nothing. Tucker did not congratulate him. Usually a suave, smooth man mindful of his business connections, he was affected by the champagne and the woman with whom he seemed to have lost all chances.

Tucker soon moved on and Sherrie asked Byron sweetly, "Did you enjoy your dance?"

"You were the one who encouraged me to dance with her."

"She was going to make a scene."

"Maybe. Maybe not. You could say she made a scene anyway. But she apologized, promised to behave."

"Behave," Sherrie said slowly. "I really don't think Jasmine knows the meaning of the word."

Rafe Sampson, one of the lead singers with the band, moved over to them, harmonica in hand. A handsome, silver-haired man with betel nut–colored skin, he was tall, limber, an ace musician. Dressed in tight black velvet, he announced that he would sing the tune written and made famous by Nick Redmond in the past season: "What I Want From You."

Grinning at Sherrie and Byron, he began in his gravelly, affecting, passionate voice.

The melody was gorgeous, and Rafe sang two more verses, then bowed low. "I know love when I see it," he said. "Be happy." He bowed again and moved back to the bandstand.

Sherrie and Byron stood smiling. He kissed her face. "This is a night I'll remember the rest of my life. I can't wait for the second part to begin."

Chapter 25

By early morning the August ball was winding down. Everyone agreed it had been the best ever. The main ballroom and the roof were nearly empty save for a few stragglers. A small group of perhaps fifteen to twenty people had moved into the empty dining room of the Lucerne Inn, a small building adjacent to the main hotel.

As a few sleepy people milled about and sat at tables, Sherrie looked down at her precious ring, touched it. It was so beautiful as its fire caught and reflected the light. In a very little while she and Byron would be in their large, luxurious suite in this inn—making planned-on love. She forced her fears to rest and thought instead that it had been a quiet time for her these past few weeks after Mallori's death. A quiet, sad time. The beast who stalked her had not surfaced again, but each time he had, the stakes had been higher, the danger more deadly. When would he strike again?

"I've been remiss." Jasmine's petulant voice cut into her thoughts. "I failed to introduce you to my escort. Mercer Tillman, say howdy to Sherrie Pinson."

Smiling, Sherrie shook hands with the attractive, chocolate-brown Mercer, who grinned delightedly and said, "I've been admiring your dress and you all night. I told Jasmine, and I think she's a little jealous."

Sherrie laughed. "She couldn't be. She's the night's knockout."

Mercer shook his head, laughing. "Boy, isn't my date

something else? I'm surprised she's still in one piece. The women want to tear her limb from limb, and the men just want to spirit her away."

Jasmine batted long, false eyelashes at him. "You flatter me, darling."

"Impossible!" he said.

"Where's Byron?" Jasmine asked. "He's pretty much stuck to you all evening."

"He's around somewhere."

Jasmine's countenance brightened. "Excuse me a sec," she said to them. "I've got a little business to take care of."

Mercer turned to talk to a couple of people, then moved off with them. Taking off her navy, silk, high-heeled sling backs, Sherrie put them in her tote bag and brought out a pair of navy, crocheted, leather-bottom socks. Slipping them on, she breathed, "Ah!"

"Well, engagement girl," River said, sitting down at the table. "How does it feel?"

"Wonderful." Sherrie said, laughing happily.

River pressed her friend's hand. "You both deserve it all."

"Are you and Tucker getting serious?"

River didn't hesitate. "I could be. I think Tucker's got a thing for you. His eyes follow your every move."

"Nothing going on there," Sherrie offered lamely. "I think he's yours if you want him."

"I'd like that. I could fall for him," River said, then, "Listen, love, I've got to be going. I'll just go over and collect Tucker and leave the rest to Curt and Byron—and you. Congratulations again."

River kissed Sherrie's cheek, then went over to Tucker and began talking with a small group. Tucker came to Sherrie.

"I'm going to say good night, and I think you're making a huge mistake."

"We all have our opinions," she said, "and as far as I'm concerned we're welcome to them."

"Sherrie," he began.

Sherrie threw up her hands. "This conversation has ended, Tucker," she said and turned her head. He shrugged and went back to River. In a few minutes they left.

Sherrie looked at her watch. She and Byron had planned to be in their suite by two o'clock. She prepared to slip away.

Around the corner of a long corridor, Jasmine found and waylaid Byron. "I had a really wonderful time," she purred to him, moving close as Byron moved back from her.

"Byron," she said silkily, "give me a little kiss to end it all. I'll never bother you again."

With a start of pure delight, she was positioned so that she could see Sherrie coming down the long corridor, walking on silent slippers. Byron couldn't see Sherrie, and a plan formed in Jasmine's mind too delicious to contemplate.

"A kiss for old time's sake," she said.

"I think not, Jasmine."

"Then please let me kiss you. What could it hurt?"

Not waiting, she flung her arms around him, kissing him full on the mouth and clung to him. He was so surprised he went a little off-balance as her arms wound tightly around his neck. It was a minute before he could disengage her—time enough for him to see Sherrie pass swiftly up the corridor.

"Sherrie!" he called twice.

Sherrie rushed past the two and ran to their suite, went in and slammed the door shut, locking it.

In a minute or two, she heard his soft knock as he tried the door.

"Shere, let me in!"

She didn't answer, but stood with narrowed eyes, hot tears damned behind her eyelids. The tomcat! How dare he?

"Sherrie!" This was a command. "Open the door. I can explain."

Oh, I'll bet you can explain, she thought. River's unkind comment had been right, but what about him? He hadn't seemed to exactly fight Jasmine off. What had happened between those two in the past? What was happening now?

"Sherrie," Byron said in a low lion's roar, "don't let me have to break this damned door down!"

She smiled grimly at the thought of even his massive frame overcoming that heavy oak door. Then, in spite of herself, she listened carefully and well and she heard his words, but she also heard the feeling in his voice and knew he sounded haunted, hungry, hurt.

Drawing a deep breath, she went to the door, opened it. "Impatient?" she asked him. "Feeling a little physical, are we?"

He stepped inside as she stood back and closed the door behind him, locking it. He came to her, gripping her shoulders. "Honey, don't walk away from me like that. I love you, and it kills me."

"But you were otherwise engaged," she said coolly.

"I know what you saw, but it wasn't what you think. She asked for a last kiss. Said she wouldn't bother me again."

"And I was nowhere around."

"I would have kissed her before you under those circumstances. Only I didn't kiss her, she kissed me. I never put my arms around her. Sherrie, come on. I've always respected women, and I respect you beyond all others. I love you. You've got to know that. I've always played fair and square with you. I always will."

"People change," she said stubbornly. "Mike—"

"Don't go there!" he said sharply. "I'm not Mike. The changes I make will always be in your favor. Stop comparing me with Mike. You're going to have to do that."

His sharp words cut through the fog that had enshrouded her—jealous and raging—from a past she wanted and needed to forget. This man loved her in ways she had never been loved before, and she didn't want to lose him. "I'm sorry," she said softly. "Will you let me show you I'm sorry?"

Humbled, she moved close to him and kissed him deeply,

opening completely. He caught her close and whispered huskily, "Try me."

She took his face in her hands, pulling his mouth hard against hers, and her tongue teased the corners of his mouth, then explored the depths avidly, gathering honey, making love. Flames of desire licked around them as he caught her hands in his.

"Baby, cool it a little," he told her. "Everything is taken care of, and we've got a long time for this. We won't be leaving until midday."

Dazed with passion, she looked at him. The room was filled with roses and gardenias; the heady scent permeated the room. He snapped on the music system and Lionel Richie's haunting "Lady" surrounded them. He took her hand and led her to the ornate bathroom with its big, oval, rose-colored sunken tub. A plastic container of four magnums sat nearby, as well as an ice bucket holding two bottles of champagne. The foil had been stripped from the champagne magnums.

"What on earth?" she began, laughing.

"I'm going to make this a night we both remember all our lives," he said.

"Oh," she responded, "we have so many nights to remember. Our first night is one I could never forget."

"And I certainly will never forget it. Just wanted you to see the layout," he said.

They went back into the bedroom, where he told her, "Now for the first part. Turn around." He unzipped her dress, which fell to the floor and pooled around her feet, then unhooked her navy bra, setting her firm breasts free. He stopped to kiss them.

"My mole," he said gently, and his tongue flicked across it. "I'm going to put your dress on a hanger."

"No. There's no time." She wanted him so.

Stepping out of her matching satin bikini panties, she quickly lifted the dress and the bra and threw them on a chair, then turned to him. Her fingers trembled as she helped him out of his clothes; deftly, swiftly she moved as he stood still, letting her undress him. She threw his clothes on top of hers. She needed him *now*. She was so tense with wanting him.

When they were both naked, he kissed her lightly, took her hand and led her back into the bathroom. Soft rose lights threw shadows around the room.

"We're going to have to wait a few minutes," he told her. "Get into the tub and sit down. He stood beside the tub.

"What about you?"

"Just follow my lead."

She laughed a little, teasing him. "We're not dancing. Follow your lead?"

"All right, Ms. Women's Libber. Yes, follow my lead. I'd follow your lead anywhere."

She sat down in the tub and he knelt and kissed her lips, which were like warm honey. Getting up, he took a magnum of champagne, uncorked it, stoppered the tub and poured the champagne over her shoulders. She shivered with pleasure as the warm liquid streamed over her body.

"Oh Lord. This is decadent—and *wonderful*," she said, laughing throatily.

"The best is yet to come," he promised. "It's going to be a long ride."

Repeating the procedure for the second bottle, he then uncorked the last two and set them on the floor beside the tub. Uncorking one of the bottles in the ice bucket, he set it and two glasses beside the tub. By then, she was half fainting with desire.

"I asked for plastic glasses because we're going to be at least a little off-balance, and I didn't want glass flying around."

"You think of everything."

"I think of you. I know that much."

He got into the tub, and she followed his lead, pouring the magnum of champagne over his body. Then, impishly, she saved some from the last bottle and dumped it over his head as he laughed. Sputtering, he said, "You little devil. I'll get you for that."

The champagne covered the bottom of the big tub and they lay in it as he clutched her to him feverishly. She stroked his swollen, throbbing erection that was larger than he had ever been. "Is all this you?" she asked.

Grinning wickedly, he told her, "Why don't you see for youself?"

"You'll have to help me see."

He grabbed a condom from beside the tub and put it on quickly.

Spreading her legs, he came between them and slipped slowly, easily into her tight nectared sheath that was like sun-heated fruit syrup, hot and yielding. His mouth found her breasts and his tongue went wild on them, very, very softly suckling, then hard and harder. Soft again, gently licking the tender brown flesh.

"This is such a thrill," she said, gasping. "And you're a fantastic lover."

"Champagne in tubs don't make a lover."

"I'm not talking about that, although this is exciting enough. It's you inside me, the expert, loving way you move . . ."

"Love drives me, spurs me on. Like what you're getting?"

"Sweetheart, if I go any higher, I'll be flying."

"Then join me in the sky."

They were silent, moving in rhythmic unison. His big shaft throbbed and swelled even more, and her fingers encircled its base in wonder. "You're so good," she told him. "This is so good."

"I promised you the best of everything."

"And I'm getting it. Oh Lord, how I'm getting it!"

Their kisses grew even more fevered, drugged, and he moved over her champagne-wet body with tormentingly soft sensuality, his tongue patterning dark, rich touches of magic over her.

She kissed his face, which tasted of champagne and his

own healthy, desire-flavored skin. Then he entered her again and she gripped him tightly, held him, making him tremble with delight, making him hold himself against explosions in his loins and hold her against his chest. His wet body with its well-developed muscles and hairy chest enthralled her, even as her beautifully wide hips and narrow waist filled him with desire he could not seem to quench.

"Maybe in a hundred years I'll get enough of you," he said.

"And in a hundred and fifty, maybe I'll get enough of you," she responded.

Slowing then, he withdrew and poured champagne into the glasses. Sipping the fruity liquid, they lay back in the wide tub and her toes traced up and down his hairy legs.

"Happy?" he asked her.

"I'm always happy with you."

"We go to the mountaintop, sexually and otherwise."

"Sex—lovemaking—with us is so special. It's so much more."

"Don't tell me. Show me." He took the glass from her and set both glasses down beside the tub, then took her in his arms.

"This saga continues," he said as he spread her legs and entered her again. There was only this narrow space, she thought, this limited action, yet it was unlimited in its glory. He barely moved, letting his sheathed loving instrument speak for itself. He slipped into a deeper place and it inflamed him, set his heart racing as he drew her closer to him.

They changed positions then and she was on top of him. He reached up and undid the pins that held her hair, sent it tumbling over her wet shoulders. "Do you mind?" he asked.

"No," she answered breathlessly. "Do anything. Do everything to me."

They had caught fire from each other, and gasping for breath she pressed herself down onto his shaft, savoring every delicious moment.

"We're going to run out of condoms!" she exclaimed.

"Nope." He reached over and opened a small door, displaying dozens of condoms in neat rows. "You like to do this."

"It gives me a thrill."

Inside her, he worked even more feverishly this time, clutching her wet buns, his strength flooding her. Squeezing her buns, kissing her face, her shoulders, sucking her breasts, he felt a sense of wonder he could not get over.

"You're so beautiful," he said huskily. "I love you more than I can ever tell you."

He said it often, and every time he did her heart expanded, went on high. She bit him lightly on his corded neck and as he flinched, bit him again.

"You're asking for trouble, woman," he told her. "Keep it up and you'll find yourself flat on your back and me so far in you'll never get me out."

"Oh promises," she teased him. "Think I'll take another bite."

She took another small bite, and he pressed her down on him and worked her slowly, carefully until his loins were bursting with pleasure. Holding her buns firmly, he felt her start to tremble and knew she hovered on the edge. He held himself in check until he felt her rhythmically gripping and relaxing again and again and knew she was reaching a climax. Wildfire swept his loins then and Fourth of July explosions of pure delight shook his body as they came together.

Lying on top of him, breathing deeply, Sherrie felt the wild tremors of her body, then the blessed shaking of another heavy orgasm. She felt awe and wonder that each time could be so engrossing, so wonderful. Passion for him still held her even as passion for her held him.

He lay under her with her delicious weight astride him and thought that loving desire was their bedrock and passion was the name of their game.

After resting a few minutes, she whispered, "What a turn-on."

"You're the turn-on, honey."

"I'm glad you think so, because I sure think you are."

He blotted them both dry with huge bath towels as he said, "I've got something else going on I think you'll like." He lifted her and carried her out of the bathroom and into the bedroom.

She noticed the two big rose satin cases near the head of the bed.

"What's in those?" she asked.

He placed her on a chaise longue, walked over and unzippered the bags, scooped up a handful of petals and brought them to her. She held the petals in her palms and sniffed them. "Roses and gardenias," she murmured. "How romantic. What are you going to do with so many of them?"

He spread his arms. "They go over the waterbed." The king-sized waterbed sat in all its splendor, covered in rose satin sheets. She drew a quick, excited breath. This was incredible!

Getting up, she said, "I'll help you."

He laughed. "No. Sit back down. You're going to need all your strength for what I'm going to put you through."

"You're merciless."

"I'm going to make you beg for mercy. You said I'm a fantastic lover. I've got a lot to live up to."

He emptied and spread the first case of petals, smoothing them as they released new scent into the room, then unzippered and spread the second case. He stood looking down at the bed, feeling what they would know there. A thrill of pure excitement shot through him. He came back to her, bent and kissed the top of her head and went into the bathroom, got the champagne bucket with the last bottle of champagne and set it beside the bed. Coming back to her, he held out his arms.

"Come on, lover," he said gently. "It's time to begin a new set of memories."

Chapter 26

"Do we have to talk about Jasmine?"

"Yes, honey, it will help ease your jealousy."

Sherrie and Byron lay on the water bed, reveling in the sensual feel of the gardenia and rose petals beneath their bodies. Raising to her elbows, Sherrie drew a deep breath, leaned over and softly blew a stream of air onto his face. "You keep asking for it," he said.

She smiled and, picking up a couple of petals, placed them on his head.

He stroked her as he said, "Jasmine was very kind to me when we were in grad school. She dated a friend of mine and when we thought my mother was dying—she didn't die then—I was going under. I felt that the love I'd never gotten from my mother, I'd never get, and I began drinking too much. Mike was away with family troubles, so I really had no one I cared to talk with. Bob —that was the friend Jasmine was dating—and Jasmine picked me up from bars many nights, took me home, took care of me. Jasmine was especially kind. I was—I *am* grateful."

She stroked his back. "I can understand now. I wish you'd told me sooner."

"Yeah. I wish I had too."

"You had so much on your shoulders, so much to bear. So much hurt. How did you turn out to be the golden person you are? I know you said Stella and Joe helped."

He kissed her lips briefly. "Stella and Joe never let me

down. They were always there for me. Honey, we don't need too much sadness here. Time for fun and frolic."

"Sex is serious with us, sweetheart, not all fun and frolic. Serious sex. Dedicated lovemaking."

"The only thing we're lacking," he said thoughtfully, "is commitment on your part, then we'd have it all. We need to get married. I know you shy away, and I'll just wait for you. How did you feel about my surprising you with an engagement ring—in full public view yet?"

Words rushed to her lips. "I'm going to be honest about this. I surprised myself. I loved it. You were so sweet. I like being engaged to you. It's getting married again that terrifies me."

He lifted her hand, kissed the ring on her finger. "You can select your own ring, you know."

"No. I adore this one. Bye, it's so beautiful." She held out her hand, admiring the ring.

"You're so beautiful."

"I'm not. You're prejudiced."

"I never said you were perfect, but to me you're gorgeous, the whole enchilada. I look at you and rapture climbs all over me." Reaching out, he switched on the music system and Luther Vandross's magnificent, haunting voice began to caress them with a love song. Byron took a few petals and crushed them on her breasts.

"Notice I'm not crushing any petals on you," she told him.

"Why?"

"Because I have something to do to you, something you'll like."

"Bring it on," he said lazily.

"Now follow my lead. Lie back and relax. Relax, my love."

She stroked him lightly, kneaded him, glorying in his rippling muscles, in his smooth, leathery olive skin. "I'm going to make you pass out with rapture."

"Stop talking and bring on what you keep promising."

She blew on his chest lightly, then lifted her head to his forehead and began to pattern kisses over him with the tip of her tongue, going to his face, his neck and down to his fairly hairy chest. She circled her tongue over his flat nipples, loving them as he breathed hard and groaned. This was a huge turn-on for him. She stroked as she kissed and he groaned again, sucking in his breath. "I'm going to need this all the time," he told her.

The muscles of his wide chest rippled and his abdomen muscles were tautly wonderful.

She went the length of his body, gasping with the pleasure that he created in her. She stroked his shaft, held it against her cheek, kissed it. He lay beneath her ministrations and felt wild with suddenly wanting to penetrate her again, but there was something else he wanted to do first.

The tip of her tongue patterned kisses over his back and shoulders and into the valleys of the gorgeous muscles. Her womb thrummed with wanting him.

When she had finished kissing him all over, she propped herself on her elbows again and looked at him, smiling. "Like what I just did?"

"Baby, I love what you just did. Now, I've got something of my own to do to you."

On her back, she bent her legs and breathed deeply as he began kissing her the way she had him. His kisses were rougher, harder and she gasped with ecstasy. He suckled her breasts avidly, licking the nipples, making them crinkle and contract. He made circles on the little brown mole with his tongue and gently squeezed her breasts. His tongue was wild on her stomach, into her navel indentation. Then he began the slow, slow, torturous journey below her navel, French-kissing every inch until he had reached her female core. His tongue moved with ardent precision, making her cry out his name and entangle her fingers in his hair, bringing him closer, closer until she thought she would faint with rapture. As his tongue worked the soft tender bud of her, loved her, she bucked wildly, and he placed a big hand on either side of her hips, steadying her.

He heard her heartfelt cries, and it spurred him on, but this was only a lovely beginning. Early morning sunshine before the hotness of a long midsummer day.

"I told you what you taste like," he said. "Peaches from my tree. Ripe and soft—and as sweet as nature makes them."

"You're sweet. I know that." She was dizzy with passion and excitement.

Together they slipped a condom on him and lay with him horizontal and her vertical, a tangle of arms and legs. She was hot and wet and yielding—holding him like a snug sun-heated glove. He focused on her face, her breasts, the narrow waist and closed his eyes against the onslaught of passion. He was going crazy with what he wanted to do to her.

Lionel Richie's "Lady" came on and Sherrie smiled. "You *do* like that song."

"Love it. You're my lady." He was slightly hoarse with passion, and his loins were tense with continuing need. Inside her, he felt that he had come home.

Her heated womb clamored for him, could not get enough of him, and her breasts sought his mouth, his touch.

Changing positions then, he lay back and she sat astride him. The satiny petals shifted under them and the waterbed undulated slowly, sensuously. "This is so heavenly," she said.

"You're heavenly. Being inside you is life itself."

"And having you inside me is one of the best things I've ever known."

She rode him easily, her eyes half closed, and he watched her lovely face, loving her so much it hurt. She had come to him one stormy night, let him inside her beautiful body, and it had never stopped thrilling him. He had set this night in motion, and it had come full circle.

His big erection throbbed wildly inside her, bringing joy and excitement, an intensity he could not remember ever having felt before.

"Am I being good to you tonight?" he asked her.

She shuddered with delight. "You're being so good I almost can't stand it."

"Well, you're surely good to me. I'd like to put you in my pocket and keep you there forever. Don't ever leave me, baby. I certainly won't ever leave you."

"I won't leave you."

"Promise?"

"I promise." But where was it going to end? she wondered. Would she ever be able to get over the devastation of Mike? Byron deserved what he wanted to give her, the best of everything.

Slipping on a condom, he turned her over on her back and entered her, sliding in deeply, and she tightened her muscles then relaxed them around him repeatedly as he laughed delightedly.

Wanting to go in more deeply, he pulled her legs over his shoulders, and she cried out with ecstasy as he brushed her womb. With expert strokes, he worked her avidly, kissing her breasts and her shoulders, then her mouth, his tongue going deep inside as their tongues danced in desire and seduction.

She held him tight against her, half gasping for breath so deep was her feeling for this man. Then one long thrust and she was falling into a fevered place of soft wonder as waves and waves of passion took her and she shook wildly with a sudden siege of bliss and rapture. A raging tide crashing against a shore was what she felt as wave after wave crashed over her, and she was breathless and limp.

He knew moments then of pure pleasure, wonder and powerful satisfaction. A volcano of passion erupted in his loins as he held her to him, melding bodies and souls. Then she began to quiet as she felt him throb hard and release his seed.

"I love you, baby," he panted. "Love you so much."

"And I love you," she whispered.

Spent, they lay side by side, giving each other a few light kisses.

"This has been a glorious night," he said.

"And we'll live happy, my love. I'm sure of it," he told her.

Sherrie wished she could be so sure, but she knew how much she loved this man, how much she wanted to marry him. She felt so good, it was like a blessing. She yawned and stretched, and her eyelids were heavy with sated desire.

They slept and he kept waking to guard her against her nightmares. But she slept quietly, blissfully, with joy, peace and contentment mirrored on her face.

Nap lay back on his bed. He'd seen the beautiful people go into the hotel. He'd bet she'd had a good time. And he thought: *Enjoy your life, Sherrie. It isn't going to last much longer*.

Chapter 27

Byron's wide shoulders sagged with dejection, and his big body tensed with deep anger as he talked with his board of directors president, Ron Evans, in the corridor near his office.

"We're with you all the way," Ron said. "This is a rotten, dirty shame."

"Yeah. Thanks for sticking with me."

"You're very welcome. We can do no less. What're your plans for getting to the bottom of this?"

"We're linked to Jordan Clymer's security firm, and they've got the best investigators going. I've got a few ideas I'll share with you a little later."

"I'd like to hear them. That letter being circulated about you is one of the worst possible. As I said, we're behind you all the way, but you need to move fast. In so many ways, you are Tate Cosmetics, and public relations in the African-American community are so important."

"Yes, I know. Believe me, I will be moving fast."

Ron clapped Byron's shoulder. "Good luck, and my prayers are with you."

"Thank you more than I can say."

Byron and Ron separated at the corridor just outside his office. The scurrilous letter had etched itself on Byron's mind. Who? And why? And why now? he wondered. His company was riding high on the sales charts and everything was in order. They hadn't fired anyone in ages, and when they did, it was a gentle, caring undertaking. Personnel people found the person another job, if they could, gave them generous severance pay, counseled them. He sighed, brushing a hand across his brow.

"Byron?"

He hadn't seen River come to him. She touched his shoulder, and there were tears in her eyes.

"I'm so sorry," she said. "You don't deserve this."

He smiled mirthlessly. "Sometimes we get more than we deserve; sometimes less," he said gently.

"Both Curt and I wish this wasn't happening to you," she said sadly.

"Don't get too disturbed. We'll find out who's behind it."

Her fair skin reddened with anger. She hugged him, kissed his cheek lightly. His friendship with River went deep.

River said, "Things have been so hectic, I haven't had a chance to talk with you. Have you any idea what's causing this?"

He nodded. "I've taken time to think about it, and I do have an idea or two. I just can't talk about it now. Don't worry, River. We'll find out what's going on here."

She touched his arm again, and her eyes were misty. "You get some rest tonight, you hear. We're a solid block on your side, Byron, Curt and I, all your employees love you."

He smiled then. "And I love you all."

She walked away, and he went into his office to retrieve his briefcase to go home to Sherrie. This was going to upset her, and he hated that.

"Here's my hero," Sherrie greeted him when he found her in the sitting room by her bedroom. "How are you, baby? You look a bit down."

She came to him, gave him a long, lingering kiss and pressed her soft body against his. He breathed in her light patchouli essential oil and tried to relax. Putting his arms around her, he held her close for very long moments, gaining solace from her love for him.

"Sit down," he said. "I've got something to show you. Don't get unduly upset. We're on top of it." His mouth set in a grim, straight line.

Opening his briefcase, he took out the libelous letter, took it from the envelope and handed it to her. The words on the page seemed to her to have a virulent life of their own.

TO WHOM IT MAY CONCERN:

Extra! Extra! Extra! Read all about it!

Here in Minden we harbor a rattlesnake in our bosom in the presence of Byron Tate. This man who masquerades as a pillar of this community is almost surely a major diamond smuggler and worse.

Byron Tate was a very close friend and associate of the late Michael Pinson who was murdered more than a year ago. This crime has gone unsolved.

I believe Byron Tate knows all about this murder. I believe he had it done, and I will say more about this in subsequent letters. Wasn't it a falling out of thieves?

Today, Byron Tate rides high, heading a multimillion-dollar cosmetics manufacturing firm. But he is no role model for our children, no leader for our community.

I call on you to renounce him, put him where he ought to be. See that his company's books are examined. Ask him what he knows about his former buddy's murder.

Destroy this rattlesnake in our midst before his bite proves as poisonous to us as it was to Michael Pinson.

A caring citizen

Reading the letter as she sat beside Byron, Sherrie felt a rising sense of alarm.

"This is terrible," she commiserated. "When did you get this?"

"It came in the mail late this morning. I got Jordan Clymer on the case immediately. All board members got a copy, of course, and Minden has been blanketed with them in the mail. The letters were sent from different points across the northeastern region, which makes tracing more difficult. Someone had to have some money or access to money to finance this and the moxie to make it happen."

She leaned forward and kissed the corner of his mouth, stroked his tense back.

"What are you doing about it?"

He told her his plans, and she listened carefully, nodding frequently. Mike, she thought. The trouble with Mike was reaching from beyond the grave. When would it end?

"We were going to have an early dinner," she finally said, "but I don't think you feel much like eating. Lie down and let me bring you some green-pea soup and oyster crackers. It will soothe you. Then you can eat later. Tonight I'll give you a Melissa oil bath to massage you, relax you." She broke off then, saying soothingly, "Byron, sweetheart, I love you so."

He drew her close, putting his face in her soft hair, kissing the line of her throat. What would he do without her?

"I've got a couple of things in my briefcase I have to attend to and fax," he said. "I'll be in my study."

He left, and she watched his retreating back and hurt for him. As he closed the door, she picked up the intercom and asked Stella to hold dinner until eight-thirty or later. Then she sat down heavily. It was plain to her that the trouble with Mike was never going to be over.

She went to the walk-in closet in their bedroom and looked at a suitcase that sat on a shelf. It was Mike's perfidy that was causing all the trouble and she was a part of Mike's former world. She wasn't going to let this ruin Byron's life. She thought her presence had to hurt him even if the hateful letter said nothing about it. As Mike's widow, she had to hurt Byron.

She decided she was going home. Mrs. Hall checked on her house every few days and she checked on it once a week, so moving back in would be no trouble. She waited for Byron to return.

"Well, that's taken care of," she said a little more than a half hour later, as she paced her bedroom. "Byron?"

"Yes, baby."

"I'm going to move back home."

He stood stock still for a long while, then shook his head. "No, Sherrie. You're not going back home. I'm not going to let you."

"Nothing's happened lately. I'll be very careful."

"Nothing had happened lately when Mallori was killed," he told her, his eyes flashing. "Nothing had happened lately when that devil kept shooting at you. No, love, it's far too dangerous. I'm keeping you here where I can protect you. Can't you understand that?"

Sighing, she said, "I know what you're trying to do, but you're hurting yourself protecting me. Being here, being Mike's widow, only adds fuel to the gossip fire. That letter is deadly to your reputation, Bye. You've got to know that, and my being here doesn't help."

"You stay here with me," he said adamantly, "where I can keep you safe."

Her voice trembled. "And who will keep you safe? You've spent a lifetime building a good reputation, being the best possible person. Who will keep you safe from scurrilous slander? Byron, let me go, for your sake."

He caught her to him. "Let's sit down." And close to her, he told her, "Do you think I care about that where you're

244 Francine Craft

concerned? We should be married now. That would solve a lot of this. I want to take care of you."

"You do take care of me."

"Not the way I want to. I want to know you've got the best if something happens to me."

A shudder went through her as he continued. "And it's the simple things too. I want Tressa to be able to come into our room and get into bed between us—open and natural. I want to introduce you to the world as my wife. I've told you before, I want the best of everything for you, Shere. And I can only do that if we're married."

She didn't know where the tears came from, but she wept brokenly then with fear and longing and despair. She wanted him so much it hurt, but should they marry?

He gathered her in his arms, held her. "Honey," he said gently, "please don't cry. I can't take it when you cry."

Through sobs, she told him, "I don't want my past with Mike to slop over and ruin you. I just couldn't stand that."

"Mike was a big, big part of my life," he said slowly. "Sherrie, look at me."

Looking at him through tear-wet eyes, she listened with her heart as he told her, "I would have had no life if it hadn't been for Mike. When we were teenagers, we went swimming one day, too soon after eating, and I went under, was drowning. He pulled me out of that secluded creek and dragged me to a sandy strip, worked on me until I threw up the water I had swallowed. He knew all the right moves to make. If he hadn't, I wouldn't be here. So, I forgive him anything, even when what he did hurt me. Can you understand that?"

"Yes."

"Sherrie, if our roles were reversed, if someone were slandering you, I'd want to marry you more than ever, to protect you, to comfort you. Please, sweetheart, marry me."

As she sat with him holding her, a curtain opened in her mind, and she felt the strength to come to him, be with him. For a long time she was silent as the sunlight of stark reality cut through the nebulous clouds of doubt that had stopped her. Finally she told him, "All right. You win and I win bigger. I'll marry you, Bye."

He crushed her to him, his heart thudding against her heart, which raced and somersaulted. "In a few days? We can go to Elkins," he said. "No hassles. No waiting. I want a quick resolution to this. I want you for my own."

"Tomorrow if you wish." She laughed then. "No, not tomorrow. I need a little time."

"We've got time," he said, "and I've got you. You're what I want most in this world."

"And you're what I want most too."

His tongue in her mouth was hot and seeking as she responded vividly. His big hand began to reach beneath her blouse as a knock sounded and Tressa came bounding in.

"You two look so happy," Tressa said. "What're you up to?"

Sherrie half closed her eyes. "How would you like Uncle Bye to be your new daddy?"

An ecstatic look spread across Tressa's face as she ran to them, hugged them both. "I would love that," she said.

Chapter 28

At My Beautiful Self on Tuesday morning, Sherrie arrived early and found Katherine already hard at work. "Why, you're positively on top of it this morning, and I'm happy to see that," Katherine greeted her.

"I'm going to marry Bye," Sherrie told her. "Think that's enough reason?"

Katherine whooped and hugged her. "Oh, Sherrie, this warms my heart. You've been through so much. When?"

"Thursday in Elkins."

"Whoa! Couldn't wait, huh?" Katherine grinned slyly.

Sherrie laughed. "Something like that. Oh Lord, Katherine, I'm floating. Look, we're only inviting a few people, but there'll be a big reception. I want you and Helena to have a big hand in it."

"I'll be needed here in your absence. It's a busy day today, but I've got to go to work on you. Tomorrow you'll need all the rest you can to reflect, plan, dream. Today, I go over you with a fine-tooth comb. Massage, facial, manicure, pedicure, aromatherapy—the works."

"You're too good to me."

"You really love him, don't you?"

"Oh Lord, yes."

"And he adores you. I'm not your manager today, just a happy-for-you friend."

Not as many people were in the salon and by eleven-thirty Katherine had largely done with Sherrie most of what she wanted to achieve. The last thing was aromatherapy. In the beautifully appointed room, Sherrie chose a raspberry-colored cubicle, slipped into a rose-colored terry-cloth robe and settled in to the soothing strains of Brahms' "Third Symphony." She chose niaouli oil for protection and healing. She added patchouli oil for sex, money, appeasing and anxiety. There was rose oil for peace, beauty, stimulation, emotional shock and grief, among other things. Then ylang-ylang for euphoria, stress and nervous tension. It was both a sedative and a stimulant. Lying back on the chenille-covered lounge chair, she basked in the marvelous essential oils.

As the music washed over her and the wonderfully soothing aromas filled her nostrils and lifted her spirits, she leaned back and dreamed of Byron. Her mind flew to the night of the ball and their splendid lovemaking that was so much a part of their relationship, then to their first time in the storm that had matched their passion and his first kiss—deep and impassioned—that had stirred her so. That memory was still fresh.

She thought of their life together and how they loved each other and touched her stomach. She wanted a baby for him. Tressa would love that, she thought. The child had blossomed incredibly with Byron's love.

Byron called around one as she finished her aromatherapy session. "Hello, my wife," he said, and she thrilled to his words. "Already I'm neglecting you. I've got a hell of a day ahead of me or I'd take you to lunch."

"It's just as well. Katherine is giving me a makeover one day early. She insists that I stay home and rest tomorrow—and dream."

"Your life is going to be full of dreams if I have anything to say about it. Sherrie, if I can swing it, how about if I take off a bit early, go home and make my Texas chili to remind us of when you first came back to my house—*our* house? Like the idea of that?"

"Oh yes. You don't make it often enough. Oh, I love you."

"And I worship you. I've got to run. See you tonight. Friday morning you wake up belonging to me."

She laughed. "Women don't want to belong to men anymore. The old chattel thing, but I think I want to belong to you."

"And I surely belong to you, body and soul."

They gave soft, smacking kisses then and Sherrie held the phone for a few moments after Byron hung up.

It was two o'clock when she remembered a framed pressed-flower arrangement she had for Katherine and she went to the small parking lot to retrieve it from her car. She breathed in deeply. It was such a glorious day—clear azure skies with thin streamer clouds drifting. The parking lot was nearly surrounded by the backs of apartment buildings. She was so engrossed in her thoughts she didn't notice the sheet of paper and the brown bag suspended from the driver's side door. Frowning, she lifted the paper off; the string it hung from had been attached by Scotch tape. Turning it over she read the large typed words: *Don't grieve Mallori too deeply. You'll be joining her soon.* Chills seized her body. Fear nearly blinded her.

Willing herself to some degree of calmness, she lifted the bag and opened it, removing a hard rubber toy dagger with its blade smeared with blood. She dropped it as if she held fire, then stooped to lift it, putting it back into the bag.

She heard it then, laughter from hell. It didn't last long but it froze her blood, and the evil pervaded her brain, nearly conquering her, but she fought back. Looking wildly around her, she expected to see the shaggy head, the brown face, but she saw no one except a lone homeless man crouched in the shadow of one building. She walked slowly toward him on unsteady legs, clutching the sheet of paper with its few deadly words.

Going to the man she asked him, "Did you see anyone go up to my car?"

"Can't say I noticed," he answered, not unkindly. Taking up

a brown bag from beside him, he opened it, held it to his mouth and drank deeply.

He had to have seen someone and she persisted. "Did you hear laughter a minute ago?"

"Sure did. Like some crazy fool."

Again she asked, "Have you seen anyone around the cars?"

The man scratched his head. "Well now, I saw a dude with right rough, wild black hair, brown-skinned, evil looking." He grinned slyly. "Frienda yours, lady?"

"No," she said quickly. "I'm going to call the police. Would you be willing to talk to them?"

The man shook his head vehemently. "I was jus' leavin', lady. Sorry I cain' help you. This has come to be a' evil world. Maybe he be watchin', lookin' at me talkin' to you now. What's to keep him from comin' afta me?" He shook his head. "No, I'm really sorry. I cain' help you."

Sighing, the man rose and began to shuffle away. As he left, he muttered loudly, "Sure was a crazy laugh. He still be somewheres close by mos' likely."

Somehow she hadn't thought of the man still being close by. What if he still watched her? A new spasm of fear shook her as she turned and fled the parking lot, with the sheet of paper in her hand. At the back door of her salon she suddenly turned. She was going to need the bag with the dagger in it that hung on the door to show to police. Retracing her steps, she forced herself to walk over, remove it and go back.

As she came in the door, she leaned against it, legs shaking the way she hadn't let them in the parking lot. Katherine came to her.

"Sherrie, what's wrong?" Katherine asked.

Gasping for breath, Sherrie told her what had happened.

"I'm going to call the police," Katherine said indignantly.

"No, let me. I can. I'm going to call Lieutenant Steele and I've got to call Byron too."

Katherine got her cell phone and Sherrie sat down in her

office and made the calls. Byron swore when she reached him. "You hang tight. I'll be right there."

She stood, shaking, as she dialed 911.

The police got there swiftly.

The crime team photographed and fingerprinted the car. A police sergeant read the note and looked at the bloody dagger. "It may be animal blood," he said. "We'll have it tested, and it won't take long."

Byron came and caught her in a bear hug; his eyes were full of tears as he swore softly. "River is arranging to get you a bodyguard from Jordan Clymer's security firm, beginning this afternoon. I thought you'd be safe here. There's a cop stationed just down the street."

"Byron, when does it end?" she asked tiredly.

"Baby," he said sadly, "I wish I knew the answer to that."

But she was thinking: *How does it end?*

Chapter 29

They were married by a simple justice of the peace, but Sherrie and Byron had made additional arrangements. At high noon, dressed in a cream silk faille suit with a cream silk closely fitted rose hat and carrying a bouquet of white cattleya orchids with purple throats, Sherrie stood proudly beside Byron who wore a flawlessly tailored black Italian silk suit. They smiled at each other, and Sherrie closed her eyes, savoring the moment. Small thrills ran through her as she looked at her beloved. He was so handsome. Somehow, the parking lot trauma of Tuesday before seemed light years away.

Byron drew a deep breath. In a few minutes Sherrie would be his and he had the culmination of his dream. Her beautiful face was alight with anticipation as her eyes met his, blazed with passion and she dropped her glance.

Helena, dressed in aquamarine crepe, was the maid of honor and Curt, in charcoal gray, was best man. Tressa was their flower girl. Clad in ruffled pink organdy, she was a little excited doll who kept looking from Byron to Sherrie as if she couldn't believe what was happening. Joe and Stella stood by, proudly beaming. The new bodyguard, Clem Patton, stood at the door, and to the right of the couple, Husky sat on his haunches, surveying the room.

The justice of the peace, a slight, friendly man, looked at Husky. "What a beautiful animal," he said. "His expression is almost human."

Sherrie laughed. "Shhh," she said. "He doesn't know he's not."

The justice of the peace smiled and began the ceremony. As he read the words that would formally give them to each other, Sherrie and Byron listened carefully. This was it, Byron thought, the beginning of a long, new and glorious road.

It seemed only a few minutes before the justice of the peace said, "I now pronounce you man and wife. You may kiss the bride."

Byron only meant to give her a light kiss, but as his lips met hers, a thrill surged through him, and he pressed her closer. His tongue lightly flicked hers, and her arms tightened around his neck. The justice of the peace smiled broadly. He liked marrying couples who were so obviously in love.

The couple was congratulated then. Husky came to full attention, his tail wagging as if he knew very well what was going on. He came to Sherrie and she bent and patted him, ruffled his fur. He leaned against her leg, then stood away. Joe shook Byron's hand, kissed Sherrie's cheek and Stella kissed them both. Curt grinned as he shook Byron's hand and kissed Sherrie.

"You've both got the best there is," Curt said gravely, smiling at Helena who blushed vividly as she looked at him. He caught her hand, lifted and kissed it.

Clem, the bodyguard, came up. "Congratulations," he said earnestly. A big, bluff, hearty man, he felt he was going to like his new job.

Sherrie gave her bouquet to Helena who took it, smiling, dreaming of her turn.

They left the building on happy feet and began the trek back home. Both Sherrie and Byron reflected that this had been one of the happiest days of their lives.

They spent the afternoon with Tressa and her dolls.
Stella prepared a lavish four-course dinner with all their

favorite dishes. Delicious prime beef rib roast was the centerpiece with ham and turkey and beautiful vegetables. Stella made her delectable Parker House hot rolls. There were colorful garden salads with her homemade dressing. Desserts were vanilla and late summer peach ice cream, praline cake and rum-raisin pudding.

"The praline cake is your advance wedding cake," Stella told them. "Now for the reception, I will bake a wedding cake to end all wedding cakes." She rolled her eyes. "I didn't have much notice."

Dinner was served early so Tressa could take full advantage, and she was in child's heaven.

"When I get big and get married," she asked Stella, "will you fix me a dinner like this?"

Stella laughed. "I promise to pull out all the stops."

That night Byron got a call from Germany. He came to her in their bedroom, told her ruefully, "Heintz Shulman needs a few comments on the book we're working on and, of course, he needs them immediately. I'll only be a couple of hours or less. Why don't you get undressed, take a nap and get ready for me to take you to heaven?"

She blushed when he said it, imagining the things they did to each other.

"What if I take you to heaven?"

"We always take each other."

She went down the hall and checked on Tressa who slept peacefully. Then back in their bedroom, she selected a trousseau gown of deep rose shadow lace with sheer inserts at strategic places and a flowing, matching sheer peignoir. Going into the bathroom, she drew warm water into the big rose tub and sprinkled in rose essential oil. Ahhh, it smelled wonderful. Roses were the flowers of love. Rose-colored lingerie, rose essential oil all portended a rosy future.

Earlier she had purchased and set out fat candles that hid in opaque rose globes. She touched one globe and fantasized the magic glow it would cast. She smiled as the water ran in the tub and she moved about the room, putting a few drops of the essential oil on their pillows. It smelled so sensual, so inviting.

Stripping off her clothes, she eased into the tub and smiled. It was going to be a long and glorious night. She lazed, scrubbing lightly with a loofah sponge and finally emerged, blotting herself dry with a bath sheet and smoothing on Tate Cosmetics super-moisturing lotion. Byron loved her smooth, soft skin.

In her nightgown and peignoir she glanced at herself in the mirror. She looked the way she felt, floating with happiness. She really should take a brief nap, but she wanted to give her new husband a quick, light, tantalizing kiss.

Opening his study door as he sat in a deep plush chair, she paused on the threshold, came in and locked the door as he looked up and whistled long and low.

"Oh my," she said, laughing, "there's a wolf in here. He must be one of Husky's ancestors."

"There's a wolf in here all right and I'm howling. It began when you came in."

She walked over slowly and straddled his lap as his breath caught.

"Woman, this is so unfair. I'm only flesh and blood, and where you're concerned, I don't have much control."

"I just want a quick kiss," she told him, laughing, "then I'll let you work."

He put his papers on the small table beside the chair. Shaking his head, he raised her up and spread his hands across her buttocks, cradling them. "No, baby, you don't want a quick kiss. You want some long, hard, deep loving and you want it now."

Her mouth opened. "How on earth can you tell?"

"Because," he said with narrowed eyes, "your buns are hugging my thighs like crazy. I can feel your heat on my thighs and your eyes are smoldering." Then he chuckled. "Your eyes aren't the only thing smoldering."

Sherrie leaned into him, nuzzling his face. "Okay, I'll go quietly, but I'll be waiting."

She got up then and began to move away. "Come here," he said suddenly. She turned and went back. "Sit down the way you sat before."

"You've got to work. I'm going to let you work."

"No, honey, you made that impossible when you came in. I can give you a prelude, finish this and come to you later for the full symphony. Ready?"

"I'm always ready for you. But when do we sleep tonight?"

"Who needs sleep when we've got paradise? I can sleep for a couple of hours. We'll make it. First things first."

He pushed aside her peignoir and pulled her gown up over her thighs, stroking the brown, burnished flesh. Then he slid a big forefinger into her nectar-laden secret place and felt her tighten around his finger.

"You're so ready," he said, "and I'm ready for you."

He unfastened her sheer peignoir and threw it over a nearby chair, pulled her nightgown over her head and she sat naked on his lap. "You're so beautiful," he told her, "and I'll love you forever."

"That's the way I feel about you."

His mouth went to one breast, gently suckling at first, then more avidly. His tongue flicked back and forth, and she moaned as his mouth found the other breast.

"I want to be fair," he murmured, raising his lips. "Equal time. Equal treatment." No condom was needed now. They both wanted a child as soon as possible. She thrilled endlessly at the thought.

She raised her hips a little from his lap and he entered her as she lowered her body onto his shaft—slowly, voluptuously. He was swollen, throbbing, his heart hammering against hers, which beat too fast. She kissed his face, her tongue tracing patterns. Nibbling his ear, she nipped it lightly, and he jumped a bit.

"What sharp teeth you've got, lady."

"The better to bite you with. I could eat you alive, you know."

"If it would stop this terrible craving I constantly have for you, I'd let you. I don't think I'll ever get enough of you."

"That makes two of us."

He stroked her back, her buttocks, her arms, shuddering with delight. "Just what is it you've got that drives me crazy?" he finally asked.

"My love for you," she answered without hesitation. "Our love for each other. When you touch me, I go out of control. It's a unique feeling, sweetheart. I've never felt anything like it before."

"And I surely never have."

They were silent then, feeling the rapture of their joining. He was so engorged, and she responded to him with delight. She moved lazily up and down on him, riding expertly the way he had taught her. His massive strength came up to her, and she gloried in it. Then she felt the mild trance beginning and waves of pure ecstasy gripped her body as she trembled deeply and after a moment felt him thrust long and deep, shudder hard and release his seed into her womb.

They held each other a very long time before he murmured, "We're making a baby now. We've always been too good to believe. Is that why it's even better now?"

"I expect so," she said softly. "I expect that's the reason."

She sat on his lap. "I don't want to leave you."

"Then don't. You can catch a quick snooze in here. Lie on that sofa. I won't be too long."

She chose a chair near him and settled down as he worked. He got up, switched on Beethoven's "Symphony No. 6" and went back to work, glancing at her from time to time.

With the sharp edge off her desire, she fell into a light sleep, and the dream came quickly. She walked in the woods and a man with shaggy black hair darted in and out of the trees. He held a gun and he meant to kill her. She opened her mouth to scream and no sound came. She jerked awake quickly, sat up.

"Sherrie?"

"Yes."

"Were you having a nightmare?"

She didn't intend to let this precious night be ruined by nightmares. "This time it was an old dream of being chased by a bear," she fabricated to protect him. "Just an old nightmare."

He looked at her closely. She looked shaken, and he hoped she was telling him the truth, that it wasn't the new nightmares she experienced.

She stayed awake until he finished and faxed his comments. He came to her, took her hard.

"Now for a quick shower and a light snack—and the ecstasy begins."

"I've just had a nice, long bath."

"Take a quick one with me, or stand in the tub with me. I don't want you out of my sight."

"Obsessive."

He smiled. "If you had heaven and an angel, wouldn't you be obsessive?"

"I do and I am."

Later, sitting at the breakfast nook table, they sampled the delicious food Stella had spread for them. Turkey and ham and Swiss cheese club sandwiches, cut in quarters. Thin sliced roast beef sandwiches with Dijon mustard. Chicken and shrimp salad sandwiches. The praline cake sat under glass, and there was a tray of fat strawberries dipped in dark chocolate. Sherrie picked one up, bit into it.

"That's the way I'm going to bite into you," Byron said.

"Promises." She looked at his beautiful, naked biceps and abs, his wide chest and felt desire flame in her belly.

The food was delicious, but Sherrie ate little. "I've got other hungers," she told him.

"Didn't I give you a great appetizer?"

She laughed. "Oh that," she said, "was shrimp with Tabasco sauce. I'm now ready for pheasant under glass."

Eyes narrowed on her, he reached over and squeezed her hand. "And you'll get that and more." His breath intake was sharp as he grinned at her with a mock leer, asking, "Care to play hardball?"

"What kind of hardball?"

"Just answer the question."

She put her head to one side. "Tonight I'm game for anything."

He took her bare foot and placed it against his heavy, pulsing shaft, and a thrill shot through her.

"Let's take this upstairs," he told her.

"Think we can make it?"

"If we can't, the stairs are carpeted."

They took the tray of chocolate-dipped strawberries and a few sandwiches with them. He picked up the ice bucket with the magnum of champagne and they headed toward the bedroom.

Food and champagne put on a table, she lit the candles with a taper and turned out the lights.

"It's our wedding night," she said softly.

"All night and into morning," he responded. "Be careful I don't consume you."

"What if we consume each other?"

When she came back to him, he took her in his arms, unfastened and slid the peignoir from her shoulders, throwing it on a chair. He feasted on her voluptuous body and his rock-hard tumescence pressed through the sheer rose lace. He kissed the top of her breasts and his tongue darted to the mole. "My very own brown mole," he murmured.

"All of me is your very own," she whispered.

And he knew that she spoke the truth. She was the quintessential individual, and she would go back to being that, but for now they belonged wholly to each other. He slid her nightgown off her shoulders and watched as it pooled at her feet.

He knelt then and hugged her hips, his arms around her waist. His tongue laved her navel and patterned fiery kisses across her belly, going down and ever down. She leaned across him, gasping with desire.

He stood then and lifted her, took her to the king-size bed, which had the covers thrown back to reveal rose satin sheets. "Rose and rose and rose," he said. "This is going to be one rosy night. And morning. I don't plan to let you go anytime soon."

"The champagne," she murmured. "We've got a lot of champagne to drink."

"Let it wait. We've got love and passion bubbling in our blood. Besides, I don't want you to get too dizzy. I want it all, Shere, everything you've got to give me."

"You greedy, wonderful man."

"Yeah, your man."

He knelt by the bed and pulled her to the edge, spread her legs, and his tongue found her secret place and gently laved it as she bucked wildly above him. She pressed his crisp, curly head into her body and moved her fingers in his scalp, moaning like a woman possessed. She cried out his name, and hearing her cries spurred him on.

"I can't stop telling you how sweet you taste." His big hands held her buns, squeezed them, kneaded them. There was magic in his hands. "You're loving this, but I don't want you to come. We're in baby city, and I want to save it all to pour into you."

She quieted then and waited as he rose. Moving farther up into the bed, she drew him to her side and they lay there for a moment before he caught her to him and kissed her so savagely it startled her. Her mouth opened completely to him as she was already completely open to him. Their tongues did a dance of fire and enchantment and his big forefinger explored her wet orifice.

"I'm more than ready," she told him. "Give it all to me."

He entered her rocking body, and her muscles clutched him, held him like a hot, tight satin glove. He moved slowly, easily, pulling out to the edge, then thrusting deeply, and thrills shot through her again and again. Dizzy with passion, he knew he belonged to her—body and heart and soul.

Reaching over, he switched on the music system and Billy Daniels's "That Old Black Magic" filled the room. That deep, husky voice intoning the words, that low moan of surrender to love resonated with her, and her nails dug into Byron's back. The singer's moans of love were hitting her where she lived. She wrapped her legs around Byron's back and held him her prisoner, her tongue laving his flat nipples.

It always surprised him that he felt such sharp ecstasy when she tongued his nipples. His shaft was bursting with desire and need.

"We made love the first time in this room," she told him. "It was heaven then, now it's gone beyond. Bye, I want your baby so bad."

"And we'll have a baby. We're either making one already or practicing. And we'll keep practicing if we haven't made one."

She was torpid beneath him and she seemed to him beautiful beyond the telling. Her eyes on him were full of love, rife with passion, hot with desire, and he held her to him with his heart drumming and hers fluttering wildly. They lay still then, resting a bit, prolonging the incredible feelings. Then he flipped her over and she sat astride him.

"Haven't we made this trip before?" she teased him. "Just a little while ago in your study."

"You can't have too much of a good thing. And this is really a good thing."

Suddenly overcome with passion, she leaned down and kissed him, then tongued the corners of his mouth. "I love you," she said. "How can I tell you how much I love you?"

"Honey, you're showing me, and that's better. We're showing each other. I adore you."

He had taught her the ropes of riding him. How to lift up slightly, then slide down easily again and again. Her secret muscles squeezed him and he shuddered. "Keep doing that and you haven't got a prayer of my lasting. I want to give it to you a very long time. Records, that kind of thing."

"And I don't want records now. I want to feel you fill me again. A baby, Bye—that's going to be the zenith for us."

"Yes," he told her, working steadily, stroking her back and her buns. He caught one of her lush breasts in his mouth, suckled it hungrily, then suckled the other one.

"These are our halcyon days," he murmured, "and may they last forever."

The wings of her hair fanned out as she leaned in on him and kissed him again.

"I can't get enough of you," he said. "I never expect to get enough of you."

"That makes two of us."

Their strokes were languid, ebbing and rising, when he set her aside. "I want to do something," he said.

Reluctantly she let him go from her body and watched as he went to the music system and put on a record. He came back, stroked her stomach, lay down and entered her again. Wagner's gorgeous liebestod from *Tristan und Isolde* came on the air and its passionate beauty swept over them, moving them both greatly.

He felt her with wonder as she went out of control, wildly giving herself to him. This was unique. With him, there was no need. They were both out of control and they gloried in it. This was a time based on love and trust and passion as old as the earth.

Inside her he moved faster, his big shaft turgid and throbbing with desire. Again she wrapped her legs around his back and drew him in tighter. She came three times in quick succession as he hit a deep place and his seed came spilling into her eager womb.

Spent, tired, yet exhilarated, they lay locked in each other's arms. "That music is so beautiful," she said.

"You're so beautiful."

"I'm not, you know."

"You're not perfect. I never said you were, but you're beautiful. Even if I couldn't see you, my heart and soul would tell me that."

"Thank you." Then after a long while when the music had stopped she said, "Wagner was reputed to have been quite a racist, yet his music is splendid. So moving."

"It happens. People are gifted, yet they destroy and cause damage to the bone."

"Yes." And she knew he was thinking about Mike.

They slept then and she dreamed of meadows and babies and she held a tender, fat baby in her arms as Byron's arms encircled them both.

They came happily awake at first dawn and neither felt very sleepy.

A little later, she said, "Well, we're something. We never touched the champagne."

"We didn't need it, but there's no time like the present."

He got up. "The ice is mostly melted. We're going to have to settle for cool champagne."

"That's fine."

He stripped the foil from the bottle and uncorked it, poured them both a flute and handed one to her. He sat on the edge of the bed.

She sipped hers slowly with the fizz going up her nose. It tasted fruity, sweet, the best.

"It tastes like you," he said and bent over to kiss her.

His mouth on hers brought up new, sharp longings, and she asked him, "We've had so much of each other tonight. How much is too much?"

"How much is never enough?"

He drank his champagne down to half a flute, poured some into his hand and spread it across her breasts, stomach and thighs. Then he put both their flutes on the table and set out to slowly, tantalizingly lick the liquid from her body. When he had finished, she pushed him back, reached for the champagne she had left in her flute, poured some into her hand and spread it over his chest and down his body. And she finished what he had started, kissing the rippling wide chest and belly muscles and lower.

Finally he could take no more of the exquisite torture, and his fingers threaded into the mass of her hair and pulled her up and entered her. This time she put her legs over his shoulders and locked her ankles around his neck. He groaned and thrust hard, filled her womb with his seed again and sent her over the edge into a sea of surging hot waves that engulfed and shook her body for a very long time. She cried his name and the muscles of her secret place gripped him and relaxed again and again until they both lay spent on a sandy shore as ancient as time itself.

It was still early and they talked quietly, sipping more champagne and eating chocolate-dipped strawberries when the small knock sounded. That would be Tressa, Sherrie thought.

"Just a minute," Sherrie called, getting up and slipping into her gown as Byron slipped into his pajamas. She grabbed an opaque robe from her closet before she opened the door and scooped Tressa up, kissing her.

"You look so happy and so pretty," Tressa said.

"And so do you." Tressa wore a blue-and-yellow gingham dress with white eyelet ruffles. "Are you ready for school?"

"Uh-hum." Running to Byron who sat on the edge of the bed, Tressa hugged him. "Uncle . . ." she began, then, "Can I call you Daddy now?"

He hugged her tightly. "You bet you can, pumpkin. I'm your daddy all the way."

"Thank you. I'm gonna like that. I've got to go now. Mrs. Hall is waiting to take me to school."

Back in bed, Sherrie and Byron cuddled. "It's what I've dreamed of," he said. "You, me, the munchkin and at least one other munchkin. Baby, we've got the world in our hands."

"And we'll keep it," she told him, "I think, forever."

Chapter 30

Around nine the next morning Helena walked down the second-floor hallway of Helping Hands toward Nap's small office. She wanted him to build her a small bookcase. A young female social worker stopped her to ask for advice about a youngster who wasn't shaping up. They stood in earnest conversation for fifteen minutes or so.

Helena couldn't stop smiling as she talked and remembered the marriage ceremony the day before. She was so happy for Sherrie and Byron. Her turn would come when she and Curt were married in November. She envisioned him and hugged herself.

"My, you're happy today," the social worker said.

"Yes. I have a lot to be happy about."

Nap sat at his battered desk, drawing feverishly, putting embellishing touches on the sketch he'd done the night before.

That bloody dagger now was something, he thought. Clean lines, sharp rendering. He had real talent and maybe one day he would use it for all the world to admire. His middle shallow drawer just in front of him was open and he hunched over it as he drew on the desk.

He felt groggy. He moved in his own orbit as he studied his drawing, smiling a narrow smile.

"Nap."

He jumped, sliding the sheet of paper into the drawer and closing it in swift movements. "Jeez, Helena, you scared the crap outta me."

"I tapped on the door; it was open a bit. You didn't answer. Hey, that's a good drawing. Of Sherrie?"

He was trembling a little. "No," he quickly lied, "it's my mother."

"I didn't know you had artistic talent. We could use it."

"Well, I—ah—a friend did the drawing from a photo of my mother. I was just fiddling with it."

Helena nodded, wondering why he lied. She had stood behind him long enough to see him finish the dagger. And it flashed into mind—the first tape that had been sent to Sherrie. The drawings and the bloody dagger.

"I see," she said. "Compliment your friend for me. He's really good."

"Yeah. I will."

"You look a little tired," she told him.

"Yeah, I guess I am. I was up late."

"I worry about you. Is your social life extensive enough?"

He leaned back in his chair, on safe ground. "Yeah. I've got a couple of really good friends." And he had the master.

"I'm glad." She patted his shoulder and left.

Two hours later Helena sat in Lieutenant Steele's office across from her. She shuddered as she told the officer her suspicions and Lieutenant Steele nodded.

"Nap's a strange one," Lieutenant Steele said. "He helped me in my yard a couple of times a while back. I felt spooked and didn't ask him again. How has he worked out at Helping Hands?"

"He's been wonderful. He can do just about anything. He's moody and keeps to himself, but he manages to get along. He's really good with the kids and the puppets." She frowned. "Now, why would he lie about being a good artist?"

THE BEST OF EVERYTHING 269

"He's hiding something would be my guess."

"If he had anything to do with what's been happening to Sherrie . . ." Helena began and broke off. Then, "What are you going to do about what I've told you?"

"Plenty. I can't talk about it now because that would tip my hand, but I'll set wheels in motion immediately and we'll find out the truth. Helena, I can't thank you enough for realizing this so quickly and coming to me. You may have provided us with a missing link we badly needed."

A couple of hours later, Sherrie sat in the same chair Helena had occupied. Lieutenant Steele drew a deep breath.

"How well do you know Nap Kendrick?"

Sherrie looked surprised. "I hardly know him at all."

"Has he ever helped you?"

"Once or twice a couple of years back; he ran errands for us at my salon."

"But not lately?"

"No. He didn't seem to like me very much. At first I thought he was just bashful. He avoids me when I visit Helena. But at the salon, I caught him looking at me with dislike— distaste, something I couldn't define. I figured I didn't need that grief. We hired a young woman who loves doing errands, and I didn't ask Nap again. When I run into him at Helping Hands, he's civil, nothing more."

"Then you're hardly aware you resemble his dead mother who Helena says he hated."

"No. I certainly didn't know that."

Elbows on the desk, Lieutenant Steele made pyramids of her hands.

"Why are you talking about Nap Kendrick?" Sherrie asked, her voice suddenly hoarse.

"Because he may be implicated in your troubles, or he may know who is. You've told me you have no enemies you know of. No run-ins with anyone. We were at a dead end on this, but maybe we no longer are. . . .

"We got quick and lucky information on Nap Kendrick," Lieutenant Steele continued. "Philadelphia police want him for questioning in the choking of a woman there. He lived there for a few years. By some stroke of fate, she didn't die. They e-mailed us a photo." She hesitated a moment. "She looks a lot like you. You called to tell me you have a bodyguard now. I'm glad."

"Byron insisted on it. I don't mind telling you that incident on the parking lot nearly unnerved me. That laughter, Danielle. He's crazy, isn't he?"

"It's likely. Or drug-ridden. Sometimes they're the same." Sherrie drew a deep breath. "Will this never be over?"

"A bodyguard helps and yes, I think it will be over. You'll still need to be careful. You know that, don't you?"

"Yes. I'll do my best."

"Another thing, our investigators have found a deeper link between Tucker Weeks and the diamond smugglers than we'd thought. It seems he's their main link in this area now."

Lieutenant Steele expelled a harsh breath. "He's got enough money to hire the best lawyers to keep him out of jail. We don't have the evidence yet to confront him." She shrugged, sighing.

"Sherrie, there's something else I want to run by you. Byron and I have talked a bit lately about the slander trouble he's having."

"Yes. My heart really hurts for him. Byron is such a straight shooter."

"We're working on it with his investigators. Whoever's doing this is clever. It doesn't seem to be an amateur job. When we get in Byron's position, we have enemies, even when we don't know it. Envy, after all, is one of the seven deadly sins.

"They mean to do damage," said Lieutenant Steele. "I'm thinking this, too, may be tied in to the diamond smuggling gang. This is the kind of smooth, underhanded operation they do so well."

"But why?"

"Well, even if by some dumb luck and/or good police work they are caught, his reputation would still be compromised. He wouldn't be nearly as effective as a witness. They're nothing if not smart, and they cover all bases. But Byron's investigators are smart and savvy too. Jordan Clymer's group always amazes me. We've got some hot leads and we may prove to be smarter any day now. I've got a meeting shortly. You'll keep in the closest touch?"

"I will. Danielle, how is Gus doing?"

Lieutenant Steele thought a moment, said slowly. "He isn't doing well. We had him under a suicide watch for two or three days. He's a little better now."

"I'm sorry to hear that. You were very close to him, weren't you?"

"I was and I still am close to him. It doesn't just stop. I've learned a lot about human nature on this job. Everybody has a breaking point. Most of us are lucky that we never reach it. Maybe Gus reached his. I don't know."

"May I see him?"

"Yes, of course. He's changed a lot. We're guarding him against himself."

"I brought him the chocolates he loves and a few sundries."

"That's thoughtful." Lieutenant Steele picked up her intercom and told the jailer she was bringing a visitor back. The two women hugged and went out.

"Hello, Gus. I won't ask how you are, but I'd like to know."

Gus's face was grim, but he tried to smile and it fell flat. He got up, came to her, hugged her. "I'd prayed you'd come." He was so thin she felt his ribs as they hugged. His face was haggard, bereft, his eyes bloodshot.

"I brought you a few things. I'll bring more later. I would

have come before, but you sent word by Lieutenant Steele that you didn't want to see me."

"I was wrong, too busy trying to die. Then I began to read a Bible Lieutenant Steele brought me. I would have laughed six months ago if someone had told me they found God, but I'm not laughing anymore. I didn't kill her, Sherrie; I never would, but if I'm found guilty, I can take it now. If by some miracle I'm acquitted, I'm moving to Alaska, and whatever the outcome, I'm going to work to end domestic violence."

His voice sounded wistful. "I always wanted to get marriage counseling. Mallori refused."

"I know. I'm sorry."

"It could have been so different. I still love her. I always will." His voice was full of tears.

Sherrie stepped close, held him again. "Let's sit down," he said.

They sat on his cot, and he cleared his throat. "I wonder if you kept any of her ashes. I wanted to ask you at the service, but I couldn't. I didn't feel I had the right. Maybe I haven't, but I'm going to ask."

"Yes, I did keep a small box of Mallori's ashes."

His eyes beseeched her. "Then could I have a very small amount? You see, I want to have two very small silver cases made up. One case I would keep with me always. The other I'd keep at home—or in prison. That's so if the case I carried somehow got lost, I'd have the other one. Would you do that?"

"Of course I will. Do you want me to get the cases made up?"

"Thank you, but my lawyer says he'll do it. Thank you again." He seemed to brighten then and asked, "And you, Sherrie, how are you?"

She told him about her marriage.

"That's wonderful. Congratulations." He pressed her hand. "I always liked Byron, even when you hated him." He was silent a moment before he asked, "How's Tressa? And tell me about the wedding."

"Tressa's fine. I'll bring her to see you."

"Would you?" His eyes lit up. "I'd love that, if it's not bad for her."

"No. My daughter's a savvy little girl. And she loves you. She asks about you."

"I wanted children," he said wistfully.

She told him about the marriage ceremony then and he listened attentively, living through her life, enjoying her happiness. She was a close link to Mallori, and he wanted to know everything. He had been married once; his glory days at the beginning of that marriage and scenes swept into mind of love and kisses and steamy nights and days and he alternately rejoiced and wept inside with remembering.

Lieutenant Steele walked back to Adrienne, her crime analyst's, cubicle. "I think we may have a live one," she told her. "Put a tight tail on Nap Kendrick twenty-four-seven. Get a search warrant order from Judge Lanier and try to get it for this afternoon. He plays golf often, so you'll need to get to him as soon as possible. We may be getting the break we need, Adrienne."

Later that afternoon, search warrant in hand, Lieutenant Steele, Adrienne and a rookie policeman stood in front of Nap Kendrick's dingy redbrick high-rise.

"He's not likely to be home yet," Lieutenant Steele said, "but I wish we were earlier. I want to do a careful search. We may be able to find out a lot."

Adrienne shrugged. "Even if he comes in, the search warrant gives us license to go ahead."

"I'm never really at ease with a suspect at home," Lieutenant Steele said.

They rang a doorbell surrounded by cracked white paint and after a few moments of waiting, a gray-haired man in his

sixties let them in. He seemed friendly, a bit bleary-eyed.
They introduced themselves.

"Are you the super? We're looking for apartment four sixty-six," Lieutenant Steele said. "We have a search warrant."

"Yeah, I'm the super. Been on the job thirty years. Seen it turn from a nice family building to just about a flophouse. You got something on Kendrick?"

"We're trying to find out if we have anything on him," Lieutenant Steele told him.

"He's a strange one, I can tell you that. Him and his friends. Got a temper too. I teased him about his dead white skin and his red hair when he first moved in. He told me to knock it off, looked at me like he wanted to kill me. My blood gets cold when I think about it and that was a long time ago."

"What time does he usually come home?" Lieutenant Steele asked.

"Late, usually. He's got a friend I heard him call Poke. Strange as he is. I'm telling you he's a weirdo. You be careful if Kendrick comes in. I'll try to stay around and see you when you leave. I need to know if you find drugs, something like that . . ." He cackled. "Now who I'm kidding? The way things go now, I reckon half the people in this building got a stash."

The super walked them to the creaky elevator and they rode up to the fourth floor. "Right down the hall," he said, leading them. Nap's apartment was near the elevators.

"Sure, I could let you in, but I wanta see how you people get in. I always wondered. You mind?"

"It's okay," Lieutenant Steele answered. "We have our ways."

"Yeah, I know," the super responded. "It ain't like I'm no stranger to cops. You all are here nearly ev'ry day."

The super waited until the policeman jimmied the flimsy top lock and took a slim jim and popped the bottom lock. The door swung open.

"I reckon I'll leave you now to do your job," the super said, "while I do mine. You don't see me when you leave, it's because I'm busy doing somethin' around. Please try to find me."

They thanked him and went in. Lieutenant Steele drew a deep breath, looking around the cluttered apartment. It was clean, she noted, but there were papers everywhere. The living room was nondescript. In the bedroom, a big, sagging, double bed covered with a snow-white chenille bedspread was pushed into a corner and a half-empty glass of brown liquid sat on the table beside it. Lieutenant Steele picked it up, sniffed it. Good brandy and an open package of cigarettes lay on the night table.

There were stacks of magazines and newspapers, a long rack of cassettes sat atop a bookcase. Nap had a lot of detective novels and magazines.

"Lieutenant," Adrienne said as she stood by the fairly new wooden desk, "look at this."

Lieutenant Steele walked over. Several sheets of white paper lay spread out on the desk and under one of the sheets was a colored drawing of a woman's torso—Sherrie Pinson, now Tate. Helena had been right. Nap was a very good artist, good at sketching, anyway. There was a dagger dripping blood and pointed at her heart. Lieutenant Steele felt a chill go through her.

There were other sketches started, all of Sherrie from what she could determine. He would hardly have had time to bring the sketch Helena had seen this morning back home, so this was another one. It seemed like an obsession, and she knew from experience that obsessed people could be deadly to deal with. She picked up the finished drawing, walked over and put it in her briefcase.

They searched dresser drawers, desk drawers, under the bed and under furniture and found nothing else of note.

At the closet door Lieutenant Steele paused, her psychic antenna going off. What was there about this space? She summoned Adrienne and the other policeman and they stood on chairs and made quick work of the cluttered closet. Pushing old stacks of clothes aside, at first they found nothing unusual. Then, in the corner on a shelf Lieutenant Steele shone her flashlight on a woman's red pocketbook.

"What have we here?" Lieutenant Steele asked.

Dragging the purse down, she brought it out into the room. "This is a Coach bag, and they don't come cheap," Lieutenant Steele said. Opening it, delving into its center, she found three business cards with the scripted letters spelling out Mallori Dueñas's name.

Adrienne and the rookie cop whistled at once and all three looked at one another. Lieutenant Steele's mouth went dry and her adrenaline started pumping. "We'll need to question this man," she said, "and right away." She nodded to herself. It looked like she was dead right to put a tight tail on Nap Kendrick.

Puzzled, Lieutenant Steele's mind kept segueing back to the closet and she went there again, stood there with waves of anxiety sweeping through her. Had her psychic powers led her to the red Coach bag? Alarm bells were still going off in her brain. What else was in that closet?

Getting a chair again, she searched a stack of books more carefully and found a hollowed-out one. Drawing a quick breath, she opened it to reveal a .357 magnum gun. Climbing down, she took it out into the room where the three policemen examined it.

"This could be the gun used to shoot at Sherrie Tate," Lieutenant Steele said.

Adrienne nodded. "Mallori was killed with a twenty-two-caliber. Do you think that gun could be around somewhere?"

"We can certainly do a more careful search and see," Lieutenant Steele said, as she turned back to the closet.

A key sounded in the lock and Nap came in.

"What're you doing in my apartment?" he asked calmly, masking fury and fear.

"We have a search warrant," Lieutenant Steele answered, fixing him with her level gaze.

"Let me see it." She saw his hands shook badly. She got the search warrant from her pocket and showed it to him. He read it and handed it back.

"Yeah," he said. He felt sick when he saw the male cop holding the red Coach bag and the gun. Cops could make a case on nothing, and they had plenty.

"We need to ask you a few questions, Mr. Kendrick," Lieutenant Steele said gently.

"I can't stop you."

"Please sit down." Lieutenant Steele's voice was a soft command as she pointed to the chair at the desk. Nap's eyes fell on the drawing of Sherrie, and he quailed. He slumped into the chair and looked up at the three police officers.

Lieutenant Steele fixed him again with her glance. "The cards inside say this purse belonged to Mallori Dueñas. Why is it in your possession?"

He didn't hesitate. "I helped her the way I help a lot of people. I admired it one day. She said she didn't like it. Her husband gave it to her for her birthday. I—ah—like pretty women's things. So make a federal case outta it."

Lieutenant Steele was silent a very long time as Nap stewed, sweat running down his back. Finally she cleared her throat. "And the drawing, the finished drawing of Sherrie Tate and the several unfinished sketches? Do you help her too?"

He shook his head. "I did once or twice. She let me go. I'm not crazy about her."

"Then why have you been drawing her?"

He shrugged. "I'm an artist," he said defiantly. "I draw everything. I'll probably draw you when you're gone. You're a good-looking woman."

The compliment was lost on Lieutenant Steele. "Are you perhaps obsessed with Sherrie Tate?"

"You mean Sherrie Pinson?"

"She's Mrs. Tate now."

"I didn't know." But he had known. He had taken yet another

day off, had driven by Byron Tate's house and seen the group coming out of the house, and the bouquet Sherrie Tate carried told him. He prided himself on being an excellent liar.

"Why draw a dagger, Mr. Kendrick?" Lieutenant Steele asked evenly. "A dagger pointed at Mrs. Tate's head?"

He thought about that one. "I—ah—like guns, knives, that kind of thing."

"*Bloody* daggers?" Lieutenant Steele asked scathingly, thinking Mike had been killed with a dagger that resembled the drawing. The dagger in the tape mailed to Sherrie had been different. She felt a start of recognition.

"We're taking the bag and the drawings and the gun with us, Mr. Kendrick, for evidence."

She was deliberately failing to ask him about the gun, letting him swing in the wind. Then she struck. "Is this your gun?"

"Yeah. I use it for target practice."

"In the woods perhaps?" she asked sarcastically. "On women?"

"At a target range. You can check it out."

"Oh, we will. Do you own other guns?'

"No. That's the only one."

"Did you kill Mallori Dueñas?"

The sudden question unnerved him. "Hell no!" he exploded as Lieutenant Steele calmly thought that the steel nerves, the frequent aplomb of violent murderers had often astounded her.

"But you do know something about her murder?" Lieutenant Steele's probing was deft, even, expert.

"Just what I read in the paper. You're the cops. You ought to know."

"And maybe we do—now."

She was whistling in the dark, she thought. If he said Mallori Dueñas had given him the purse, maybe she had. Mallori had been carrying a purse when they found her, a tan Coach bag. And the drawings—well, they held more promise. She hadn't mentioned it to him, not wanting to tip her hand, but Sherrie had been stalked, pursued and shot at. A gruesome videotape had been made and sent to her. There was what Sherrie described as the laughter from hell. But the man in question had shaggy black hair and brown skin.

"So you're an artist," she said. "Are you proud of it? You're certainly talented."

"I'm damned good."

She thought she knew why he had lied about being an artist. This way, no one could ever trace him to Sherrie's stalking.

"As I said, we're taking these items for evidence."

"I can't stop you. You're the police," he mocked her.

He was defiant, feeling they had nothing definite on him, but he still sweated. This female lieutenant seemed smarter than he needed her to be.

Nap sat alone on his bed after the police officers left, bent over, his head hung, his hands between his knees. He felt emptier than he had ever felt, hungry for his dead father's presence. He was going to have to talk to the master—tonight.

Chapter 31

At My Beautiful Self the next day, customers began coming in early. Katherine was late due to a sick husband and Sherrie settled in for a long, hard day. She had just fixed herself a cup of strong coffee bolstered with dry milk and natural sugar when River came in.

"I just need a quick trim. I'm getting a little shaggy. Can you do it instead of an operator? I need to talk with you."

"Sure," Sherrie answered. "What are you drinking this morning?"

"Tell you what, I'd love a cup of the tea you offered me a while back that I told you tasted so good. I forget the name. An herbal tea."

"That would be nettle, as I remember. It's good."

"That's it. And thank you."

Sherrie asked Dora to prepare the tea and slipped a cape over River's shoulders. As she sectioned off River's hair and cut, Sherrie smiled. "You've got hair to kill for, a really healthy scalp."

"So have you."

"Yours is natural. Mine is due to sheer hard work. When I think of women who complain about their hair and do nothing . . ."

"What can they do?"

"There are herbs that work magic and I never get tired of talking about them."

Dora brought the tea and River thanked her as Sherrie continued.

"The herb for the tea you're drinking—nettle, sage, rosemary. A mix of all three in a decoction works wonders."

"What is this decoction?"

"Simply put, a rounded soup spoon of each herb in a little over a pint of boiling water. Let it boil a minute or two. Let it steep, then strain. If you use oil, simply add to boiling oil and let it steep—both for an hour."

"I think I'll try it."

"Indian hemp roots are excellent too. The leaves are magic, but they're illegal. Too many people smoked the leaves and they're a drug."

"Interesting," River said. "You know so much cosmetic magic."

"You look great today," Sherrie complimented her.

"Thank you. I'll bet you're happy with getting married and all."

"I'm very happy. River, I'm sorry we couldn't include you in the marriage ceremony plans, but Bye and I have talked about it. You and Helena and Katherine will handle the reception. We're leaving it all up to you. Do with it what you will."

"I understand how few people you could have there and it's perfectly all right. I'll enjoy working on your reception. Byron's already mentioned it to me."

The two friends happily talked of community affairs before River said, "You know I've got a cocker spaniel, Susie, and she's gone to Bottomless Canyon behind the big oak to have her puppies. Can you imagine? I walk her there all the time. I saw them yesterday and I want to go back Sunday morning and get them. I put a beach umbrella over her and the puppies, fixed a bed. I want you to go with me to see them. Will you? I know Byron is away Sunday morning for a meeting with Russ Winslow in D.C. and their meetings go on forever."

"I'd like that," Sherrie told her. "Tressa wants a puppy. Bless her heart. She's spending Saturday with Helena."

River smiled. "She's a lucky little girl."

Sherrie laughed. "Byron and I are so lucky to have her."

"We won't be long," River said. "Afterward, we'll take the dogs home and ride into Minden for a long, leisurely brunch, my treat."

"It all sounds good to me."

Sherrie finished cutting, brushed a few clumps of hair off River's shoulders and removed the cape, shaking it. She handed River a mirror and River studied her sleeker hairdo.

"Your expertise never stops amazing me," River said.

"Thank you."

River stood. "Now don't forget. Around nine-thirty. I'll call you. I know Byron's meeting with Russ is very early. Those two go way back. Russ is a lawyer."

"Byron's mentioned him. I know about the Sunday meeting."

"Then we're on, and I'll pick you up around nine-thirty."

"See you then," Sherric said.

An angry Byron strode into Sherrie's office a little after she had finished eating lunch. He paced in front of her desk, glaring at the world at large.

She got up, came from around the desk and hugged him, kissing the corners of his mouth before she told him, "Simmer down. What has you so upset?"

He expelled a harsh breath and didn't answer.

"Sit down, love," she told him.

He shook his head. "I've got somewhere to go. A certain rat to see."

"Who?"

His mouth set in a grim line. "Tucker Weeks."

"What about Tucker?" she asked, alarmed.

"It didn't take long to get to the bottom of this, with help from the police. Tucker and God knows who else is behind the slander campaign against me. They were caught with another batch of lies they were getting ready to mail. I can't believe he was dumb enough to be with the guys doing the mailing, but his stupidity paid off for me."

"Tucker," she said. "But why?"

"He may be part of the diamond smuggling gang. As you know, he and Mike became the best of friends after I pushed Mike out of Tate. They were inseparable. I'm going to his office."

"Byron, should you? Let the police and your investigators handle it."

"I will, but first I've got to do this. Maybe the most important thing is he was very likely trying to smear me to gain points with you. Tucker is in love with you, Sherrie. You can't help but be aware of that."

"I give him no encouragement."

"I know. You're in love with me. You wouldn't."

"I'm glad you realize that."

He hugged her then. "I know it, baby, know it with every breath I draw." Kissing her, his tongue moved across hers hungrily before he said, "You're my woman, and I share your deepest love with no man."

He had been announced by Tucker's secretary, but when Byron strode into Tucker Weeks's office, Tucker was surprised at the rage on Byron's face. He stood behind his desk.

"Have a seat, Tate, and tell me what's your business with me."

"I think you know why I'm here," Byron grated.

"No, I don't know. Why don't you tell me?"

"Then let me refresh your memory. Those poisonous letters linking me to diamond smuggling, saying Mike Pinson and I were partners in crime and my role continues. Saying I ought to be kicked out of Tate . . ."

Tucker looked alarmed and had trouble getting his breath. His man in the mailing caper had called his lawyer and his lawyer had called him, but he hadn't expected Tate to come to his office. Tucker had been crushed, disappointed. He had planned it so well and thought it was succeeding. Sherrie would see that the man she loved wasn't who she thought he was. For a moment he was speechless, gathering his thoughts.

"You had it coming," Tucker finally said. "Always the black knight in shining armor. Damn you, Tate, for taking Sherrie away from me."

"Grow up, Weeks," Byron spat. "She was never yours to take."

"She hated you for what you did to Mike."

"And you know all about that. You and Mike became running buddies, so you have to know about the money he embezzled, the diamond smuggling. The extra women. He nearly destroyed Sherrie."

Tucker sat down heavily. "What do you plan to do?"

"You've got a good lawyer, so you'll probably spend no jail time for what you've done, but keep away from Sherrie, do you understand?"

"Yeah—if I can. I love her."

"Keep away from her," Byron roared, "or I won't be responsible!" His voice calmed a bit then. "You won't be working with Sherrie anymore."

"Did she say that?"

"She will. Keep your distance; maybe you'd like another location in another city."

"No way. I've got it made here in Minden."

"I can and I will file a massive lawsuit against you for defaming me, Weeks. You've got a good lawyer. I've got better ones. Much better. I believe we can make the charges stick. I can ruin you, and you know it. Think it over and decide like a man with common sense instead of being a fool."

Byron went out then, feeling a little better. He and Sherrie had so much, he thought, as he strode down the hallway of Tucker's building, and he intended to see that they kept what they had.

* * *

By midafternoon, dark clouds had begun to gather. Clem, Sherrie's bodyguard, came to her. "Mrs. Tate, I have an appointment to get my transmission tended to at a garage on the edge of town. I should be back before time to escort you home. A buddy of mine, a cop who used to work for Clymer Security, is on duty outside. He'll pop in from time to time, check the parking lot. You'll be safe with him. Now, you wait for me. Will you?"

"Of course I will. I hope nothing much is wrong with your car."

He shrugged. "I'm going to have to have a new transmission put in, and soon."

He left and in a few minutes the city policeman came in and introduced himself.

"How about a cup of coffee?" she asked him. "Danish? Doughnut?"

He accepted coffee and selected a chocolate doughnut, walked around, went out to the parking lot and in a few minutes came back through.

"All clear," he said, smiling.

The parking lot still spooked her, even with other people around. She thought about the threatening note and the rubber dagger with the blood smeared on it. It was animal blood, police said. Also, she would never forget the threatening face in the woods that day.

She had slumped into a chair in the salon when her cell phone rang. Reaching into her smock pocket she answered to hear the frantic voice of Mrs. Hall.

"It's Tressa," her housekeeper told her. "She's running a high fever and she keeps asking for you. What should I do?"

There was no question. "Sit tight," Sherrie said, "and I'll be right there. Call Byron and tell him."

"I will."

Hurriedly, half falling over herself, Sherrie quickly pulled her things together. There wasn't time to call Clem. He would have to come from the edge of the city, and by that time she could be home. For the moment, gone was her fear of the parking lot. She told Dora what had happened and set out.

Driving through the city she chafed at traffic and the darkened sky. At least it wasn't raining yet. Then after what seemed an eternity, she was on the open highway that led home. "Hang on, baby," she said out loud. "Mommy's coming."

The clouds had steadily darkened until they were black. She cut on her headlights. She drove too fast, but she couldn't help it. She would scoop Tressa up, take her to the emergency room. Bye would be home if he wasn't in Minden or D.C. for an unexpected meeting.

As the car hugged the road, speeding, the motor slowed and began to cough. She pulled over to the right, then far over onto the wide shoulder and the motor died, sputtering. Frantically, she tried to restart the engine, pumping the pedal in a useless frenzy. She was two miles from home and she needed to call AAA for assistance.

Digging into her tote bag, she sought for her cell phone and tears of frustration sprang to her eyes when she remembered leaving it in her smock pocket. She prepared to get out; she would thumb a ride home. Her heart quailed. She had neared that stretch of woods where the man had shot at her, but she steadied herself. She had to get to Tressa.

A scream rose in her throat and her body went cold when she saw him. Where had he come from? On the other side of her window, inches from her stood the shaggy, black-haired man, grinning. "Get out!" he ordered.

She stared at him as if her malevolent gaze could frighten him away. Cringing against the seat, she waited as she saw him take out an object with a cutting edge. Dear God, he was going to cut the windowpane. He began to cut with a sharp sound, and with his left hand drew a small gun from his pocket and pointed it at her.

"Get out, or I'm cutting in," he growled and he laughed fiendishly.

Her mind worked furiously as she looked around for something with which to hit him and found nothing.

It was over almost as soon as it had begun. Cars came from behind, from in front. Police sirens screamed. An ambulance was there. She heard someone yell, "Stop him! He's getting away!"

Almost calmly she unlocked the door and fell into a policeman's arms.

Clem, the ambulance crew and two policemen who had been investigating an accident were there.

"Are you all right, ma'am?" an ambulance attendant asked. "We were nearby when we saw the commotion."

"I'm all right," she said. "I've got to get to my little girl."

Borrowing a cell phone from an ambulance attendant, she called home and Mrs. Hall told her Bye had taken Tressa to the hospital. Shortly after, in a summoned police car she sped to Minden Hospital and her ailing child.

Clem and city policemen took off across the clearing and into the woods in hot pursuit of the shaggy-haired perpetrator. He was getting away when one of the policemen drew his gun and shot him in the leg. Still he ran, going deeper into the woods. Then in a clearing, they tackled him, felled him as his leg gushed blood.

"Let's get him back," one policeman said. "I think he's going into shock." The skies had cleared somewhat and they had good vision.

Three policemen carried the shaggy-haired man back to the ambulance where the attendants took him from them, stretched him out in the ambulance and began to cut off his pants.

"He's in shock all right," one attendant said. "Let's hurry up and get him in. I've known guys to die from shock trauma no worse than this."

Another attendant nodded and kept cutting cloth until his mouth fell open with surprise.

Chapter 32

"What the hell?"

The ambulance attendant stared with his mouth open at the expanse of white flesh on the man's lower body contrasting starkly with his brown head, shoulders, hands, wrists and lower arms. The three men looked at one another and the one they called Jimmy laughed shortly.

"You guys are lucky I'm in training to be a prosthetist. I've seen this kind of thing often in burn and accident victims."

"We'll need to cut it off him," one man said.

"No," Jimmy cautioned him. "These outfits cost a small fortune. I'll take it off."

As the other two men worked on the wounded leg, Jimmy unzipped the artfully concealed zippers and slid the gloves off the man's hands. Jimmy sighed deeply, wondering what this guy's story was. He didn't seem deformed or injured in any way. Other zippers were opened and the stretch knitted fabric that underlaid the prosthetic mask slid off, revealing Nap Kendrick.

"Hey," one of the men said, "I've seen this guy around. Yeah, he works at Helping Hands."

"Well, if we don't get a move on, maybe he used to work there," another commented.

At the hospital in a small office, a frantic Sherrie talked with Tressa's pediatrician, who patted her hand as a worried Byron sat with them.

"I must say I'm relieved," the doctor said, brushing errant strands of hair back from her tan face. "Tressa's got tonsillitis, and the fever that would be dangerous in an adult simply happens sometimes with children. Her tonsils are puffy and swollen, but she'll probably be running strong tomorrow or the next day. I do want to keep her overnight in case there are complications. A mere precaution."

"I'll need to stay with her," Sherrie said.

"That's fine," the doctor agreed.

Clem stood near the door and looked in from time to time. He was still rattled by what had gone down that afternoon, and he wanted to keep a weather eye out for the wounded thug the police had brought to the hospital.

"We were lucky you hadn't left for the day," Sherrie told the doctor.

"I'd have come back on the double. Tressa's one of my favorite patients. I've got her mildly sedated. Why don't you two get something to drink from the cafeteria?"

Much later Lieutenant Steele sat in Nap Kendrick's room, waiting. He was out of shock. Doctors had removed the bullet and sedated him. He tossed fitfully on the hospital bed, guarded by rails. His leg was swathed in bandages. She was there instead of another police officer on the off chance that Nap would talk in his sleep, perhaps tell her some of the things she needed to know.

A nurse came in, checked him as he murmured incoherently at first. "He's delirious," the nurse said.

Lieutenant Steele pulled her chair close by Nap's bed, reached into her tote and turned on her recorder. Recording without his permission would never hold up in court, but she thought it might help her fit some of the pieces together. She had quickly learned about the prosthetic false shaggy head and the gloves. Nothing surprised her anymore.

"Love the master," he said clearly. "Come to get me. Save me." He rose a bit, said loudly, "Dad! Help me! Save me!"

She couldn't understand what he said next, but suddenly his face contorted, the white skin flamed scarlet, and his every word was unmistakable. "Mother," he said gutturally and launched into a bitter tirade of invectives and foul names. Then he said, "You wanted me to die. One day I'll kill you."

He was silent then for a long while, seeming to have burned out, but she jumped to attention and leaned closer when he said clearly, "Sherric. Sherrie Pinson's like mother. Looks like her, so much like her." Then much louder, "Sherrie's going to die, like the others." And he laughed the fiendish laughter Sherrie had described to Lieutenant Steele, and her blood chilled.

Lieutenant Steele sat bolt upright. It was all coming together. The evidence. The laughter. Guns. Drawings. A red Coach bag that had belonged to Mallori Dueñas. Oh, this was coming together beautifully.

The rookie cop who had gone with them when they searched Nap's apartment came in to relieve her. Nap slept hard, snoring.

"Listen to him well," she told the rookie, "and tell me anything unusual he says. If you need me, just call."

"Sure thing, lieutenant," he responded. "You try to take it easy."

She shook her head. "It's going to be a little while before any of us can take it easy."

As she neared the pediatric corridor, Sherrie came out of Tressa's room into the hall.

"Sherrie," Lieutenant Steele greeted her. "I've been wondering about Tressa. I heard you tell Byron you had to get to her. Is she hurt?"

"No. She was running a high fever. It's tonsillitis, and the doctor says she'll be fine, but she kept her overnight. Thanks for asking."

Lieutenant Steele patted Sherrie's back. "You're my friend. Can you spare a moment?"

"Yes, all the moments you need. Tressa's sleeping, and

we're right by the nurses' station so I can take a little while. I was going to the cafeteria to get a cup of coffee. Join me? We won't be long."

In the cafeteria, they stood at the coffee machine, drinking the bracing brew. The place was nearly empty.

"Your troubles may be nearing an end, if they're not over," Lieutenant Steele said.

Sherrie's heart jumped with hope. "What do you mean?"

"The man under that shaggy mask you saw is Nap Kendrick, Sherrie, complete with his prosthesis."

"Nap Kendrick? And why the mask?"

"One and the same. Masks are for disguise. Have there ever been harsh words between you, any kind of misunderstanding that lasted? Can you think of anything?"

Sherrie stood thinking and nothing came to mind. She hardly knew the man existed. Sure, he acted strange, but he was a strange man. Even Helena said so.

"No," she responded. "Nap and I had few words at all, harsh or otherwise. I'm sure of that. I'd remember."

Sherrie looked at Lieutenant Steele and grew alarmed at the sadness in her eyes.

"Why do you ask?"

Lieutenant Steele told her then about Nap's ramblings that she had just heard and his death threat against Sherrie, who felt her heart squeeze and her whole body constrict with anxiety.

"I think he's the one who killed Mike and Mallori. All the evidence points to him. He certainly had the opportunity. We just don't know a motive yet. A few minutes ago, he said you were like his mother, that that's why he hated you. I thought he might be just rambling and had other reasons to hurt you.

"But you've still got to be careful. Nap spoke of a master, someone he loves. So there may be others involved in this. Diamond smuggling rings are powerful, Sherrie, with long, long arms. God only knows what they were trying to get or find out from Mike and Mallori, and what they want from you."

Clem came in, smiled at them, looked around and left, going a little distance down the hall.

Sherrie turned to Lieutenant Steele. "Danielle, I don't worry about myself. Whatever will be, will be."

"That doesn't always have to be true. We can prevent a lot of things."

"I worry about Tressa and Byron. After Mike's death, I wanted to move away. I should have moved away."

"I don't think that would have helped you. You've got something somebody wants badly, and that person intends to get it. We don't know who or what Nap Kendrick is. Background checks are turning up information. He's into marijuana—buys and sells. He holds a more or less steady job and, in spite of some misgivings, Helena thinks well of him.

"He had a hellish home life and left when his father died, and, shortly after, his mother remarried. I'd know now if I hadn't already found out that he and his mother hated each other. She's destroyed him."

"Do you have enough evidence to arrest him and make it stick?"

"I think so. I can't be positive, but tests show that the gun we found in his apartment is a match for the bullets we dug out of trees the day you were shot at. You told me he jammed a gun against your car window and we found a twenty-two-caliber gun he dropped a short distance from your car as he was running. That same caliber weapon was used to kill Mallori.

"Evidence piles up, but if he gets a topflight lawyer, he can rip apart the best evidence. I'm pretty sure he doesn't have the money for a really good lawyer, but he's into diamond smuggling and it often brings big money with it. Where did he get the money for the prosthetic suit? Jimmy, in the ambulance crew, told me such outfits would cost upward of a hundred thousand dollars. This person he calls his master may have unlimited funds."

She paused, sighing, then went on slowly. "I've got a few

tricks up my sleeve. Nap's a vulnerable man; I'm certain of that. I'm going to work on him relentlessly. I'm going to try to crack him like an egg and hope he'll be like Humpty Dumpty, never to go back together again."

Apparently Nap had said nothing the rookie policeman deemed of particular interest, so he hadn't called. But Lieutenant Steele was back at nine the next morning just as an attendant was removing Nap's breakfast tray. She went to the bed; he didn't acknowledge her presence.

"How are you doing this morning?" she asked with a pleasantness she didn't feel.

"How would you be doing with a bullet hole in your leg? I'm in pain."

"You were sleeping well when I left last night."

"You were here last night?" He sounded anxious.

"You were out like a light. You talked a lot. You were delirious."

He licked dry lips. "What'd I say?"

She drew a deep breath and sat down in a chair by his bed. "You said a lot, Mr. Kendrick, most of it very revealing."

"Would you tell me?" he wheedled.

She had listened to the tape again and again and she almost had it by memory.

"I'll get to that later."

Bug-eyed, he stared at her as his breath came faster. "What do you plan to do? What do you think you've got on me?"

She gave him a lineup of the evidence they had against him as he seemed to gasp for breath. When she mentioned the .22 caliber gun, he snorted, "You can't prove it was mine. Anybody can drop a gun."

"Your fingerprints will be—" she began and thought, no, his prosthetic gloves would mean no fingerprints.

"Why do you need to cover yourself?" she asked abruptly. "You're an attractive man. What are you hiding?"

His voice sounded choked then. "My mother used to say I was too white and ugly as sin, and she hated sin. My dad was great. He loved me and I loved him."

"Parents can be cruel. I'm glad you had your father's love." She sounded warm, sympathetic, and he liked her in spite of himself.

"You have wonderful artistic talent. You could have been so much."

"Hey, you sound like my life is over."

"You might have caused it to be. Mr. Kendrick, why do you hate Sherrie Tate so much?"

He didn't hesitate. His voice went raw with anger. "She's like my mother. She looks like her. She is her." He was mocking then. "They own the world, Sherrie Pinson and my mother. Proud. Independent. Cold. Hostile."

"No, she isn't like that. She's my friend, and I know her well. She may look like your mother, but it ends there. You said last night she had to die. Did you intend to kill her? Were you trying to kill her?"

"Li'l Al may have been going to," he muttered.

"Who is Li'l Al?"

He was silent a while then. "He's the one in the prosthetic getup. Li'l Al is my alter ego. I couldn't have made it without him. What'll become of my mask?"

"We're holding it for evidence. You even laughed last night the way you've laughed when you stalked Mrs. Tate."

"Do I get a lawyer?"

"Who is the master?"

"Somebody I know."

"And love?"

"Yes. God, yes. The master will get me out of this."

He sounded confident, and it angered her because he could be right.

"Who is this master?" she asked again, changing tactics.

"Your mother let you down all your life, hated you . . ." She had an inspiration. "Are you close to the master the way you were to your dad?"

Eyes narrowed, he didn't answer. Then he said, "Yeah, the master's like my dad, kind and good. But *she* wanted me dead." His eyes actually sparkled. "She wanted to kill me, but I won." He seemed exultant. "She's dead and I'm still alive."

"And two other people are dead, and you may have planned to kill another one."

"You've still got to prove all that. Good luck."

She was angrier then than she had been in a very long time—at his arrogance, his lack of human compassion. His own life had been blighted, but he had no right to blight the lives of others—and kill. She remembered then the pain on his face when he'd said his mother wanted him dead, and she thought she knew his Achilles' heel.

"Be prepared, Mr. Kendrick. Although you love him, the master may fail to come to your aid and leave you to die for what he may have set in motion. These are horrific crimes, and you're going to get the death penalty if you're found guilty."

A deep shadow crossed his face, and he seemed less certain. His voice was the croak of a frightened child when he told her, "The master will never let me down.'

"I think you're wrong."

"If I die," he said tiredly, "I'll be with my dad."

"You may not be with him."

"If I'm not, I won't know."

"But you may know."

His eyes opened wide with fear, and his face was shadowed. Then his eyes closed and his expression was angry as she watched him carefully.

He was silent then. She had a quick flash of intuition. She had worked 24/7 and her new intelligence report said Nap Kendrick was possibly a courier for the diamond smuggling ring. A deep hunch told her the master he worshiped was high up in this ring.

She moved in closer, and her voice was softly lethal. "Make your dad proud of you. He would have helped you. No one else has come forward to help you. Your mother's spirit is winning, Mr. Kendrick. You'll die for your crimes. Talk to me. Tell me who your master is. You may be able to go up for life instead of dying. Otherwise, your mother wins."

His face contorted with fear and his breathing was ragged. She had struck a deep nerve and she intended to work it all the way through.

Chapter 33

By Sunday, Tressa fully lived up to the doctor's expectations. Her tonsillitis was quickly healing. After a very early breakfast, she, Byron and Sherrie sat on a section of lawn near the house and frolicked with Husky. Sherrie threw the dog a stick, he retrieved it and raced across the lawn. She came back and plopped down beside Byron.

"So Lieutenant Steele thinks our troubles may be ending," he said. "I certainly hope so. How do you feel, honey, after that scare Friday? At least it got results this time. We know who the perpetrator is."

Sherrie sighed. "I feel so much better. Danielle said there may be others, but I feel hopeful now. Just one downer. Lieutenant Steele says the twenty-two-caliber gun Nap dropped near my car hadn't been fired in many months. A twenty-two was used to kill Mallori, but that wasn't the gun."

"However, he was caught dead to rights."

"Yes."

Tressa came dancing up. "A puppy," she sang. "I'm getting a puppy from Miss River. Isn't that neat?"

"It certainly is," Byron told her. "Just be prepared to take care of it."

"Oh I will." She began to tell them what she would do.

The Sunday paper was full of the story on Nap Kendrick and the prosthesis. The city was buzzing with the news. Minden didn't often have this kind of intrigue.

"How're you feeling?" Sherrie asked Tressa.

"Super."

Byron stretched. "I've got to go in a few minutes and get ready to go into D.C. for my meeting with Russ. We can be long-winded, so I probably won't get back until midafternoon."

Sherrie kissed his neck. "I'm missing you already."

"You'll be out with River, puppy collecting. You two are good for each other, and I'm glad you're friends."

"So am I. I owe her big time for her help when Nap was shooting at me."

Husky came to where they sat and got down on his haunches. He nuzzled in her lap and whined, looking at her with sad eyes. She stroked his electric fur and felt his body heave.

"Hey, boy, what's wrong?" Byron asked. He and Sherrie looked at each other. Husky growled, deep in his throat, finally got up and trotted away.

"Well, he's certainly acting weird," Sherrie commented.

"He's got something on his mind," Byron said thoughtfully. "I'm going inside now, honey. You and Tressa take it easy." He bent and kissed her and, laughing, flicked a corner of her mouth with his tongue.

Clem came around the house, walked across the yard, greeted them and strode on. Byron kissed Tressa, and Sherrie glanced at her watch. She looked forward to her time with River.

After Byron went into the house, Husky came back and sat on his haunches by her side. She patted him, marveling as she often did at his intelligent golden eyes.

Helena came to pick up Tressa. "Hey," she said to the child, "it's like you were never sick. Ready to go, lovey?"

"Yes," Tressa said.

"Sherrie, you look pensive," Helena said.

"Thinking, I guess."

"About Nap Kendrick?"

"Yes. Helena, have you ever heard of anything so weird?"

"No, I can't say I have."

"One thing. Lieutenant Steele says they have a noose around his neck. She feels they'll soon catch this master he talked about and whoever it is will be lying low and have to be careful. You know the police think the master is one of the diamond smuggling gang, and Danielle says they can play rough. They've killed—probably Mike—and won't hesitate to kill anyone they think is in their way. In the meantime, I've got the police—and Clem."

"He seems like a nice man."

"He's tops."

After Helena and Tressa left and Byron drove off, Husky came back and lay at Sherrie's side as she stroked him.

Tucker and Mike had been friends, she thought, and Mallori and Mike had been lovers. Mike was a proven diamond smuggler. Had Mallori stumbled on something she wasn't supposed to know?

Her thoughts made her head hurt. She got up and went into the house to find aspirin.

At nine-thirty Sherrie and River sat in the front seat of River's white Lincoln Continental on the back road near Bottomless Canyon. It was almost eerily quiet, Sherrie thought. "Clem will be following us," she said.

River shook her head. "No. I have the authority. I told him he could stay back at the house, that I have male friends who will be with us. They'll be on later. Remember I want to talk to you."

"Oh." Sherrie felt a bit uncomfortable. She liked having Clem around. Her door was locked from River's side. "Unlock me," she said gaily, "and let's get started. Tressa's climbing the walls waiting for her puppy."

When River was silent for so long, Sherrie looked at her, found her friend staring at her with suddenly cold eyes. Frowning, she wondered what was going on.

Finally River expelled a harsh breath. "Damn Tressa," she said softly, "and damn you, Sherrie."

"River, what's wrong with you?" She felt the start of sharp alarm.

"You're what's wrong with me, but I'm going to fix that."

Reaching into the tote bag on the floor beside her, River took out a small, silver .22 caliber gun and pointed it at Sherrie, whose eyes went wide with shock and fear.

Sherrie's voice sounded strange to her ears. "You can't mean this. Why would you want to hurt me?"

River laughed nastily. "Not hurt, Sherrie, *kill*. You signed your death warrant the day you married Byron. He would have been mine if you hadn't changed. You've slung your cheap-slut body at him, thrown it in his face. Men are weak. . . . You shouldn't have changed, Sherrie. You should have kept on hating him." Her voice was raw with rage.

Cold rivulets of sweat ran down Sherrie's body, but she had to speak.

"No, I didn't lead him on. We fell in love."

"Shut up!" River half screamed, holding the gun steady, then her voice quieted. Sherrie forced herself to look at River and panic squeezed her heart dry. River's face was mad, her fair skin blotched and red, contorted with deadly fury. Sherrie felt her body icing over.

"Byron and I are close," River said. "We were close years before you set your snare for him. Your families were close, so you know how much I mean to him.

"You've read the papers," River went on, "so you read all about Nap Kendrick and the master he talked about while he was delirious. I'm his master, Sherrie. There is one more man, Poke. Nap was himself and Li'l Al, his prosthetic alter ego. They would kill for me, but they don't have to. I kill for myself."

Oh my God, Sherrie sat thinking, trying to clear her befuddled mind. *She's killed before. Who?*

"I killed Mike and I killed Mallori."

Sherrie wanted to ask why, but she couldn't speak. She sat, mute, with cold tears trickling down her face. She had to think.

River spoke in a monotone. "I turned Mike on to diamond smuggling. I'm one of the best.

"Mike and I became lovers. We kept it secret at first and always met in New York. Then he rented an apartment here, and I visited him in disguise. I know now I was infatuated. I thought I loved him, but he loved you." Her voice was scornful and Sherrie found her own voice.

"He was my husband. He was supposed to love me."

"He loved your sister, Mallori, too."

River slumped, then, went on. "I gave Mike so much of myself—helped him through the rough spots of working with us in diamond smuggling. He was accustomed to doing things his way, and I saved his hide more than once. I was investing a lot of money in a cosmetics firm he intended to set up."

Sherrie heard the bitterness and misery in River's voice. "I gave him everything I had to give—my money, my help, my love. I sacrificed for him. And he gave me so little in return. . . ."

No vehicles passed. No one walked by. Sherrie was alone with this madwoman she had thought was her friend.

River's face reflected deep grief. "One night I wanted to talk with Mike. We had made love the night before. He said he was tired, didn't feel well. I got angry and went to his apartment anyway, the apartment he had rented for our trysts, let myself in . . ." Her eyes went flat, cold, and her voice shook with hurt and anger.

"I found Mallori and him making love on the bed I'd left the night before. I'll never know how I kept it together."

River licked dry lips. "Mike told me to get out, that we were through. He said he loved you but he needed Mallori more. He said nothing about him and me, just that it would be him and Mallori from then on. My heart broke, but I was so calm. I knew then what I would do. I asked him to meet me that next night. He picked me up and we drove near here to talk.

"I begged him to keep on seeing me, at least until I healed. He wouldn't. I killed him, stabbed him with a dagger I carried in my tote—this tote—through his heart as he had stabbed me through my heart. He was drunk, so it was easy. He offered almost no resistance, and if he had, I felt superhuman strength. I wanted revenge for his dumping me."

River sighed deeply then, her thoughts shifting. "Mallori guessed what I had done and began to blackmail me. She constantly threatened to go to the police. I paid her large sums of money. Then, just before I killed her she said she would go to the police the next day unless I came up with an amount I didn't have and couldn't possibly get. Mike and I both handled large sums. Diamond smuggling pays enormously well, but I didn't have the amount she wanted. I knew then I had to kill Mallori, and I did."

She stopped talking. Hypnotized with fear, Sherrie couldn't take her eyes from River's face.

Finally she went on. "Byron was turning to me after Alicia and Ronnie's deaths. As I said, we've always been fast friends. He's always depended on me. He didn't know about Mike and me, but he knew something was wrong and he comforted me. Byron was so kind. He would have understood and we would have been together. I comforted him while you hated his guts. Then you came with your whoring body and took it all away. You fell in love. He was in simple lust the way men have fallen for evil women since the world began."

Sherrie had to speak, had to try to reach this plainly mad woman. "No. It wasn't like that." Her voice broke then and she trembled. Even River's eyes were cold.

"We trashed your house, Nap, Poke and I. I was looking for a quarter of a million dollars and uncut diamonds worth a fortune I knew Mike had. Where are they, Sherrie?"

"The police have it all."

"Damn it! I need that money and those diamonds. I slashed

Mike's portrait, and it thrilled me almost as much as killing him." She gloated then, her eyes glittering.

"The tape, the note and the toy dagger on your car door in the parking lot. I set that all up to frighten you, break you down to make it easy for me to kill you.

"I pretended to help you when Nap shot at you. You were so pathetically grateful. I cultivated you, made fast friends. I was clever, wasn't I? My friendship with Tucker was always a lie, a cover-up for my plans to kill you. I hate Tucker now for slandering Bye."

Sherrie felt her mind clear a little and her heartbeat slowed. Did River intend to kill her in the car? Could she throw herself on River, wrestle her? She wished then she had signed up for the karate class Byron wanted her to take.

River laughed scornfully. "With you gone, Byron will turn to me again. We were meant for each other, and I will not let you stand in our way. You and I will walk to Bottomless Canyon, go to the edge where I will kill you and push you in. Poke cut the fence behind the big tree."

Her laughter was harsh. "I will say you looked too deeply and fell in. That's possible. You had complained of feeling dizzy. I told you to be careful. You weren't and you died. They will never find your body. It is believed the canyon goes farther down than anyone can reach."

Frozen with fear, Sherrie managed to say, with her mouth trembling, "You don't want to do this. You can't live with yourself if you do."

River drew a deep breath, and her eyes narrowed with triumph. "I can, you know, because I will be living with Byron. I've always loved him. Mike was only a diversion. After Alicia and Ronnie's deaths, I waited for Byron to heal. I didn't want to rush him. I always knew that one day he would be mine, that we belonged together.

"Then you came," she spat the words, "with your tricks and your wiles like the evil, despicable thing you are. You're history,

Sherrie, and Byron is mine at last. I'm going to unlock the door. Get out."

Sherrie opened the door with cold, stiff fingers and got out of the car on legs that trembled so badly she could hardly stand.

"Walk in front of the car and don't try to pull anything," River barked. "Cooperate with me, and your death will be easy. Try to get away, and I promise you you'll suffer horribly. I'll put a single bullet in you every few minutes."

Moving along, with River to one side of her, Sherrie sought an advantage as she forced her mind to function. Her vision had dimmed, but she thought the earth had never looked more beautiful, and she wanted badly to stay alive as best she could. She focused on the larger picture and minutiae. The high fence along Bottomless Canyon loomed. Ahead of them the large beach umbrella stand and the dog's bed—a big basket—holding puppies she couldn't see. Frantically she sought an advantage, an escape, and found none. Fear sprung from the ground itself up through her feet and legs. She was smothering in fear, and waves of nausea spread like poison through her body. "I love you," she whispered to Byron and Tressa. Her words gave her strength.

It was only twenty yards from the road to the place that had been cut in the fence, a place just large enough for her to walk through. The master, she thought bitterly, had laid careful, deadly plans.

"Walk over to the edge of the canyon," River ordered.

It welled up from somewhere deep inside her that she was not aware of. "No," she said defiantly, adamant.

"What?" River screamed. "Play games with me, and I'll make you wish you hadn't. Move!"

But Sherrie held steady and a blessed calmness came to rest in her bosom.

"No," she said again, more gently this time, and shook her head. She wasn't going to be a slave to this woman. She was going to rush her. She had to take the chance.

But River raised the gun and took aim as Sherrie felt an indefinable presence nearby. Sherrie thought of Byron in his meeting. How long before he and Tressa would know she was dead?

Then the heavens blessed her.

"River, put the gun down!" Byron shouted. "Put the gun down!"

At almost the same time, Husky's massive body flashed between Sherrie and River, bound for River's throat. It was too late. River had pulled the trigger and Sherrie saw the flash of fire, felt hellish pain tear into her chest. She heard other shots. She moaned and cold tears trickled down her face as she crumpled to her knees. Trying to get away from the devastating pain, she turned around and over and lay on her back as others came running to her. Byron knelt by her side, and she heard the whine of an ambulance siren. Husky crouched beside her, watching her with mournful eyes.

Kneeling, with his tears falling on her, Byron felt for a pulse and found only a weak one. Sherrie stared at his beloved face as she murmured, "Can't take it . . . when . . . you . . . cry." Her voice was so faint he could hardly hear her.

Scalding tears of rage dimmed Byron's eyes as he placed a hand on her bloody chest, seeking a heartbeat and finding none. His bloody fingers sought a pulse again, and this time there was no pulse. She had slipped away, had left his arms, the circle of his love. The ambulance crew and the others surrounded them. They moved quickly to get Sherrie's still form on the stretcher.

"Dear God, no-o-o-o," was Byron's anguished cry to God and His heaven.

Chapter 34

"Bye?"

"Yes, baby. I'm right here," Byron said fiercely. "I'll be here."

"I love you—so much." Sherrie looked so fragile, but she was wide awake and her voice was steady. Bandages swathed her torso.

"And I love you so much. All the love that can ever be," he told her.

Sherrie was silent a moment before she asked, "Am I going to make it?"

"You bet you're going to make it."

With wonder and horror permeating her voice she said slowly, "She would have killed me. I thought she was my friend. She loved you. Wanted you. Did you know that?"

"Not really. I should have guessed."

"Did you ever love her?" Her voice seemed stronger then.

"Only as a friend. Not the way I love you. River's dead. A police sharpshooter killed her. Husky saved you by throwing her off-balance. The doctor thinks that made the bullet miss your heart when it would have struck home. River was an expert markswoman."

She bit her lip, wanting to forget. "When will I see Tressa?"

"This afternoon."

"Good. How long have I been unconscious?"

"Two days. Today is Tuesday." He touched her face. "I don't want you to talk too much. You need rest."

"I want to talk. I never thought I'd be here talking with you like this."

She seemed to rally further. Her eyes looked brighter, and Byron felt new joy flood him.

The doctor came in, strode to the bed. "And how is my favorite patient doing?"

Sherrie smiled weakly. "That's for you to say, isn't it?"

"Well, my say is you're doing fine. You lost a good bit of blood, but not as much as you might have. The bullet missed your heart by more than an inch, and that's a wonder. I'd say you're going to be up and about in record time, lady. I'll be back a little later to check on you."

Sherrie had rallied greatly by that afternoon when Lieutenant Steele came to see her.

"I checked on you while you were unconscious," Lieutenant Steele said. "I'm so glad you're awake and doing better." She hugged Sherrie, patted her cheek. The police officer and Byron sat on the same side of the bed.

"How did you manage to get to me in time?" Sherrie asked immediately. She had been too groggy to ask Byron the question earlier.

"You can thank Nap for that," Lieutenant Steele said. "He broke down Sunday morning after I had questioned him intensely. He told me that River was the master. He was hurt, bitter that she hadn't been in contact. I worked on him, convinced him that she would never come, that she had abandoned him. After Nap told me, I called Byron to find out how to reach River and take her in. He told me you were with her, that you and she were on the back road on the way to pick up a puppy from River's dog. I told him about River's being the master and asked him to meet me at Bottomless Canyon in a hurry. I quickly called a crew, and we headed there. Binoculars helped us see what was going n. We asked for an ambulance as we rode."

"Nap is in this hospital," Sherrie said. "He scared me half to death, but his telling you about River helped save me."

"Yes," Lieutenant Steele said. "He's under tight police guard, so you have nothing to be afraid of."

"Husky saved you too," Byron said again.

Sherrie looked thoughtful. "No. You saved me. I heard you shout, and I looked at River. She started shaking when she heard your voice. Only then did Husky spring for her throat."

Overcome with emotion, Byron got up and kissed her as Lieutenant Steele smiled her approval.

"You brought Husky to Bottomless Canyon with you," Sherrie said to Byron.

Byron shook his head. "As I was racing away from the house, I saw him jump that tall fence and streak through the woods. He sensed something was wrong, and he loves you. Remember how he growled that morning?"

"I remember. But you had gone into D.C. for a meeting with Russ."

"I'm forgetting to tell you everything. Halfway there, Russ called and said he had a family emergency and our meeting would have to be canceled. I turned back and found you and River gone. Then I got the call from Lieutenant Steele."

Sherrie shuddered with recent memory. That horror would haunt her for a very long time, but it was over, and she was free. That was then, she thought, and this was now.

"Clem went with me," Byron said. "He was a rock."

Tressa came in with Mrs. Hall, Helena, Curt, Joe and Stella. Sherrie was surrounded by friends and loved ones. Tressa ran to her, crying, "Mommy. Mommy, I've missed you so much. How do you feel?" She fell on Sherrie's neck and hugged her tightly.

"Oh, I'm much better now that I've seen my precious baby."

"I'm a big girl now."

"And so you are."

Curt came to her, took her hand. "I'm sorry," he said simply

as tears stood in his eyes. The others hugged her. She love
them all, but it was her husband she sought at that moment.

She and Byron looked at each other, and their glance
caught fire. He squeezed her hand, lifted and kissed it. "I lov
you," he said gently.

"And I love you. I'll always love you. You're my best o
everything."

"And you're surely my best of everything," he told her with
heartfelt passion, as Tressa and the others beamed their happy
blessings.

Epilogue

A little over a year had passed, but it seemed much longer to Sherrie as she, Byron and her month-old son sat in the music room. She and Byron smiled at each other and she kissed the top of the baby's silken brown head. Byron Frank Tate, Jr.

"He's like a little peach," Byron said, "like his mother. And he comes from all that splendor that goes on between us."

Sherrie blushed, remembering.

Byron got up. "Honey, I'm going to send off several faxes to Germany and South Africa. The second cosmetics formulae book we're working on is shaping up nicely. It's about finished."

He left, and Sherrie blushed even more deeply as she thought of the passionate night more than a year ago in which she had unintentionally interrupted his work on the first book. There were so many passionate nights between them.

The baby stirred in her arms, gurgled and reached fat fingers toward her face.

"Yes," she said softly, "already you're reaching out to me, to your world. You've got it made, little one."

The baby yawned widely, and his brown eyes closed as he snuggled against her breasts. As he slept and the pastoral sweetness of Beethoven's "Symphony No. 6" filled the air, she thought of those who had inhabited her life in the past year for better or for worse.

Tressa was growing like the proverbial weed. Her little brother was "her baby," and she tended him devotedly. The love between her little girl and Byron always gladdened her heart.

Helena and Curt were married and couldn't be happier.

Lieutenant Steele and her team had largely tied up the loose ends of Sherrie's case. Sherrie didn't get the money, but if she had, it would have been donated to Helping Hands.

Poke, the man who had accepted River as his master, had fled the city. "We never quit," Lieutenant Steele had said gravely. "We'll find him."

Stella and Joe were still with them, but Stella worked at times with Roland who had found she had a gift for dress design. Joe complained jovially, "After all these years of having my wife to myself, I'm going to have a superstar mate. Don't know how I'm going to stand it."

And Stella always laughed. "You love my success as much as I do, and you'll always be my first priority. You know that." The couple adored Byron Jr. and brought him many gifts.

Gus was back on the police sergeant job he loved and Lieutenant Steele was as happy as he was. He worked with a group against domestic violence, had found his spirituality and was working with violent youth as well. He came to visit often and was doing really well. Gus seemed to be getting over his intense, painful love for Mallori and was dating again. "I have hope now," he'd said a day or two before, "where I never seemed to have hope before."

At their invitation, Clem, the security guard she and Byron liked so much, came back from time to time with his wife and two children. He planned one day to set up his own security firm.

She sighed then and drew her baby closer as she thought of Tucker, who was in state prison for his role in the diamond smuggling ring. He had faced her with tears in his eyes. "You can't kill a guy for trying," he'd told her. "I love you, Sherrie. I wanted to destroy Tate in your eyes. I was wrong. I know that now. I've lost everything, as well as losing you. Maybe one day I'll get out, get over you, find someone else. God knows you never gave me any encouragement." He had been grave as he'd kissed her forehead. "Be happy the way you deserve to be."

The baby whimpered, and his little fingers clutched Sherrie's breast. "You're the sweetest," she murmured. "Are you really mine?" He gurgled in his sleep as if to assure her that he really was.

Jasmine had gone back to her ex-husband, and according to Tucker, they were making it this time. She had not come on to Byron again.

Sherrie drew a deep breath as she thought of Nap and his master, River. Oh Lord, the pain, the torment she had gone through with those two. She shuddered as she remembered the anxiety and the fear that had lasted so many months and ended in River's death.

Nap was in state prison. He had gotten ten years for assault, stalking, vandalism, carrying a weapon without a permit and making threats. Also, for aiding and abetting River's criminal behavior. Several years had been taken off his sentence because he had cooperated fully with the state in wrapping up the case. He would be out in four to five years, with time off for good behavior.

Lieutenant Steele had seen something worth saving in him and had arranged for meetings with her sister-in-law, Dr. Annice Jones, a noted psychologist. Lieutenant Steele visited him in prison and had told Sherrie that he was making remarkable progress. He had forgiven his mother and was slowly getting over his hatred of her and of Sherrie. He was deeply sorry for his deeds. He was recovering from his deep depression over his father's death and he was painting. Lieutenant Steele had smiled broadly as she told Sherrie, "He doesn't hate his white skin anymore. He understands how that hatred came to be. Oh, Sherrie, it's at times like this that I know being a detective is what I was put on this earth for." And the love between Lieutenant Steele and her noted gospel-singer husband, Whit Steele, seemed to flourish by the day.

Yes, she thought, it had all come together wonderfully well, and happiness was where she lived.

She thought of River then and River's hatred of her and her obsession to have Byron for herself. An edge of coldness settled in her body. She too talked weekly with Dr. Jones, and she was healing slowly. The nightmares and the flashbacks were greatly diminished.

She often wondered how deep Byron's sorrow was at the betrayal of a woman who for so long had been his friend.

"Hey," Byron said as he came back in with Tressa in tow. "Mother and baby are both dreaming. Mother with her eyes wide open."

"Just reflecting," Sherrie told him. "Did you get your faxes sent?"

"All done, and the rest of the night is for my wife and my kids." He touched his son's head. "He's a secure little rascal. Sleeps all the time."

Sherrie laughed. "No. Often he wakes and gives me the most beatific smile. Or is it gas?"

They sat on the sofa, and Tressa bent over the baby. "I prayed for a little brother," she said, "and I got him. Now I'm going to pray for a little sister."

"Whoa!" Sherrie balled up her fist and touched Tressa's cheek. "Give me a rest, will you?"

Byron grinned at Tressa. "I think that can be arranged. We can make you a dozen babies if that's your heart's desire."

Sherrie drew a deep breath and shook her head. "Not unless you're willing to bear half of them."

Byron grinned. "I'm always more than willing—yeah, I'm even an eager beaver—to do my part in making them and taking care of them." He laughed deeply then and his eyes almost closed. "Making them is so satisfying, so much fun." He leaned forward and kissed Sherrie as Tressa's head went to one side.

"You guys are always kissing," Tressa said. "I'm seven.

When I get grown up, will my husband and I always be kissing on each other?"

Sherrie smiled. "Only if you're very lucky, little one."

"I'm not the little one now. *He* is." Tressa pointed to the baby. Then she said, "Listen, I'm making a new paper city with cardboard boxes and paper dolls cut from catalogs. It's a big-girl thing and Joe and Stella and Mrs. Hall are helping me. Come and visit."

"We will," Byron told her. "In fact we'll come tonight."

"Oh splendid!" Tressa cried, echoing her mother's phrasing.

Byron drew them all into the circle of his arms and held them. "You're smiling," Sherrie said, "like the cat who swallowed the canary. What's on your mind?"

"Just thinking," Byron said as he breathed deeply, "that it just doesn't get any better than this."

Dear Readers,

I really appreciate your support and comments through all this time. Your kind and useful letters have sustained me. Your comments have been priceless in letting me know what you do and do not like to read.

Most women use cosmetics, and we need to know more about them. Visit the Internet and your library and study how the products you use are made up. You can save a bundle making some of your own. There are books on the market telling you how to do this. Masks made with cucumber, buttermilk, oatmeal, papaya and other products give excellent results. Egg yolk, beaten and used for ten minutes a day for thirty days, is a most effective tool for alleviating eczema. In Chapter 15, you will find an herbal recipe for thinning hair and general hair growth that works well for anyone not suffering from physical or emotional difficulties. Do learn about the cosmetics world.

Within the last year *Haunted Heart* has gone on Amazon. com's best-selling multicultural romance novel list, along with several other titles. Black Expressions Book Club picked up *What Matters Most* for hardcover publication. I am delighted, and I think you will be too.

Hearing from you is always a joy and I will answer. I write a lot, so my response may not always be the promptest, but you will hear from me. Please enclose an SASE. I can be reached at Francine Craft, P.O. Box 44204, Washington, D.C. 20026. My website address is www.francinecraft.com and you may e-mail me at francinecraft@yahoo.com.

My next book is *Wild Heart* and comes out in October 2004.

ABOUT THE AUTHOR

Francine Craft is the pen name of a Washington, D.C.–based writer who has enjoyed writing for many years. A native Mississippian, she has lived in New Orleans and found it one of the most fascinating places imaginable.

She has been a research assistant for a large psychological organization, an elementary school teacher, a business school instructor and a federal government legal secretary. Her books have often received rave reviews.

Francine's hobbies are prodigious reading, photography and songwriting. She deeply enjoys time spent with her soul mate.

Enter the Arabesque 10th Anniversary Contest!

GRAND PRIZE: 1 Winner will receive:
- $10,000 Prize Package_

FIRST PRIZE: 5 Winners will receive:
- Special 10th Anniversary limited edition gift
- 1 Year Arabesque Bookclub subscription

SECOND PRIZE: 10 Winners will receive:
- Special 10th Anniversary prize packs

ARABESQUE 10TH ANNIVERSARY CONTEST RULES:

- <u>Contest open January 1–April 30, 2004</u>.
- Mail-In Entries Only (postmarked by 4/30/04 and received by 5/7/04).
- On letter-size paper: Name your favorite Arabesque novel or author and why in 50 words or less.
- Include proof of purchase of an Arabesque novel (send ISBN).
- Include photograph/head shot (4x6 photo preferred, no larger than 5x7).
- Name, address, city, state, zip, daytime phone number and e-mail address.
- Contest entrants must be 18 years of age or older and live in the U.S.
- Only one entry allowed per person.
- Must be able to travel on dates specified: July 30-Aug 1, 2004.
- Send your entry to:

BET Books—10th Anniversary Contest
One BET Plaza
1235 W Street, NE
Washington, DC   20018